Seduce
Me

Jenni Bradley

ISBN:099668381X
ISBN-13: 978-0-9966838-1-4

DEDICATION

For my wonderful mother and father who always cheer me on, no matter how crazy my ideas are!

CONTENTS

ACKNOWLEDGMENTS

Thank you to all of my family and friends who continuously encourage me to do what I love. A huge thank-you to all of my beta readers: my mom, Kelly W., Jenn M., Erin F., Liz L., Chad W., Kaleena A., Iris S., Bill S., and Norma S. Thank you Pat A., for helping me with the darker parts. A special thank you to Kim H., for encouraging me to keep writing. This book wouldn't be as entertaining without all of your input. Thank you to my editor, Faith Williams, for making this book a smoother read. Thank you to the Killion Group for formatting, designing the cover, and helping to publish it properly.

1 CANDICE

I sat in the large open area. The other dancers liked to call it the pussy palace. I just preferred to see it as a dressing room. I was older than most of the dancers here and seemingly more reserved.

Each dancer was given their own small vanity. The lights surrounding the oval mirror were bright enough to see all of my pores. It's a good thing I was a proficient makeup artist. I could easily conceal any flaw I had. In this business, flaws didn't pay well.

I lined my full lips with red lip liner. I opened the middle drawer of the vanity and pulled my cherry bomb lipstick out. I pulled off the top, twisted the bottom of the tube, and pushed up the fiery stick. I swiped the bright color along my lips, blending the pencil liner in seamlessly. My natural pink lips were now painted fuck-me fire engine red.

I grabbed my black mascara and eyeliner. It was crucial that I lined and shaded my eyes perfectly. I made thick lines across the tips of my upper and lower eyelids to create a cat-like appearance. This completely changed the inherent almond shape of my eyes. My look needed to exude raw sexuality with a sensual appearance. I was a professional, not a slut. I finished my upper lids with a smoky look that made my glacier-blue eyes seem electric.

I adorned thigh-high black stockings with white delicate flowers wrapped around the top. I snapped the matching garter belt to the stockings. I slipped a skintight black dress over my head and down my body. The hem of the dress reached about two inches below my ass, leaving my lingerie exposed. If I bent over, you would be able to see my barely there black thong. I slipped my dainty feet into tuxedo-black suede stilettos. Red leather wove around the mile-high heel.

I stood up and prepared myself for my current role. There are many roles that I fill. I am an actress of sorts. I am anything that my client of the night desires me to be. It's all an illusion and nothing is for free. This wasn't my dream job and I didn't start my life out in this profession. However, we all know that dreams can be crushed to the point of ceasing to exist. All that is left is pure survival.

I walked out of our palace and into the hallway that led me to my awaiting client. The lounge was dimly lit and pulsed with loud bass thumping music. Men and women of all ages and economic status filled the room, watching and drinking. Kitty, one of the other dancers, was giving an average-looking middle-aged man a lap dance. He was getting a little too touchy, so she slapped his hands away as she smiled coquettishly at him. I smiled and continued to walk to my destination. She could handle herself. Cinnamon was up on stage, currently hanging upside down on the pole. It made me giddy knowing that I didn't have to work the stage or lounge area all that often. I worked the VIP room most nights.

I still worked the other areas but not as much anymore. I had regular clientele who consistently reserved the VIP room for more privacy. Which, in turn, was more costly, and my wages drastically increased. I didn't have to hustle as much to sell dances or drinks to make decent money at the end of the night. Three to four clients five nights a week in the private room more than covered my expenses and then some.

I stepped in front of the door and turned the knob. We never used real names in the club. The club was all about fantasy and illusion. Tonight, Johnny——one of my regulars——lounged comfortably in the love seat strategically placed in the corner of the spacious room. Each room had the same type of furniture; a couch, a roomy chair, a pole, a wet bar, and some kind of coffee table. The rooms were arranged in the same fashion. Clients could move certain pieces of furniture around but most of it stayed where it was originally placed. A trunk in each room was filled with the clients' particular desires. Johnny liked to be blindfolded and teased. He was one of my easier clients. He never put his hands anywhere that was off-limits.

I remained quiet as I entered the room. I took my time sashaying to the wet bar in the opposite corner of the room. I exaggerated my reach for the glass and whiskey. This made my short dress ride higher up the back of my thighs. Johnny had a full view of the bottom of my ass cheeks. The room was so quiet I could hear his sharp intake of air. I slowly stood back up and placed two ice cubes in the glass. I poured the whiskey. Then I grabbed another ice cube as I turned toward Johnny.

I set the glass and the lone ice cube on the small round table next to the chair. I pushed his legs apart and straddled his lap. His chest heaved and his fingers dug into the arms of the chair. I circled my hips leisurely against his hardness as I sunk lower onto his fully clothed lap. I reached up to the top white button of his crisp dress shirt and slid it through the small opening. I watched his face as I worked my way down his chest. His brown eyes clouded and shifted to a deeper and richer chocolate color. His nostrils flared as he drew in a jagged breath. His thin lips separated fractionally as he breathed out.

I pushed my full breasts into his face as I reached over to the table where the blindfold had been placed earlier. I pulled the elastic away from the front of the small material. I gently stretched the blindfold over his head and covered his eyes. I leaned over to pick up the already melting ice cube. I spread open his shirt and gently skimmed the ice cube along his collarbone, down his heated chest. He shivered as I circled the ice cube over each one of his nipples. As the remainder of the ice melted beneath my fingertips, I traced my tongue along the same route. A feral moan rumbled through my fingers where they were splayed upon his chest.

"Take off my dress," I commanded seductively.

He unlatched his vise-like grip from the chair. He glided his large hands down my body in search of the hem of my dress. He pulled it up and over my head. He tossed it on the floor carelessly. He gently skimmed his callused hands up my sides and along my rib cage. The rough texture erotically tickled my silky skin. He caressed underneath my breasts and over my hardened nipples. He reached around my back and with practiced hands unclasped my bra.

He slipped my straps down my arms to expose my taut breasts. We have done this dance many times. He knew my body very well. Even in the pitch of darkness, he had no trouble navigating his mouth to my hardened nipples. He pulled one of the peaks into his mouth. He suckled and grazed my nipple with his teeth. I let out a soft moan and arched my back, pushing my breast farther into his mouth. I swiveled my hips in teasing circles. As his breaths became more frantic, I increased my gyrating movements along his hard cock.

His cock twitched beneath me as he drew closer to his release. I moved my hips forward and backward, faster and harder, as he growled with his climax. I placed a kiss on his neck and lifted myself off his lap. I retrieved my dress and pulled it back on. I picked up my bra and folded it into my hands as I walked out the door.

A sigh escaped my perfectly lined lips as I pushed through the doors of our dressing room. I sunk onto the vanity stool, taking a moment to erase the last room from my mind. I only had twenty minutes to change my wardrobe, reapply my makeup, and take a long overdue pee break. This night was going tortuously slow. I couldn't wait to whisk away my masks of working characters. For the most part, I loved my job. Tonight just wasn't one of those times. Thoughts of clocking out were making it difficult to fully concentrate on my client's desires. I only had to make it through three more rooms and I was free.

***

I pulled on my skinny jeans, boots, and picked up my purse. Safely tucked inside were my tips for the night. My smile lit up my whole face as I thought about the money I made. That right there renewed my love for this job. I strode up next to Ben, one of our bouncers. He nodded his head to signal for us to start across the parking lot to my car. Every dancer was escorted to their vehicle at the end of their shift for safety reasons. The club never took chances on some crazy customer trying to hurt one of us. For that, I was grateful.

***

I unlocked the front door and stepped into the sleeping house. Silently, I lumbered upstairs to the comforts of my bedroom. I shed my clothes as I walked into the bathroom. I let the water run in the shower as I brushed the men from tonight out of my mouth. Granted, I never kissed my clients on the mouth or had sex with them, but it was necessary to further separate myself from work. It was merely all in my head but when I was home, I wanted to just be Candice. Candy was left at the Brass Ass, along with her clients.

I relished in the silence of my house. It wasn't every day that I got to enjoy it. I went downstairs and made some tea. I retraced my steps and settled back into bed. I reached over to the nightstand and snatched my book. It was time to get lost in someone else's life. My eyes started to flutter the longer I read. I marked my place before I set the book down and then shut off the light. I curled onto my side and brought the down comforter over my body all the way up to my chin. Sleep would not be long now.

I awoke as the sun peeked through the blinds as if it were a silent voyeur. I stretched my body and threw the comforter off. I tossed my nightgown onto the dirty pile of clothes in my closet. I pulled on some oh-so-comfy yoga pants and a worn-out sweatshirt. I slid my tiny feet into a pair of wool-lined loafer slippers. After I snagged my purse and car keys, I headed out the door to Clyde's Bistro.

I parked my car next to Lucy's, grabbed our coffee's, and headed up the decorative stone-lined walkway. I rang the doorbell and waited for the door to open. I tapped my foot in time with the "Wheels on the Bus" song that ran through my mind. Don't ask. I don't even know why it popped into my head. Finally, Lucy opened up the large oak door. She flashed me a large white-toothed smile as she wrapped her arms around me.

"Like I haven't just seen you a couple of days ago. Let go or we are going to be wearing our coffee instead of enjoying its wonderful goodness," I stated sarcastically.

"Come on in, grumpy pants. You'll get your caffeine jolt and be the cheery friend you normally are." Lucy laughed.

I grumbled something incoherently as I walked in behind my chipper friend. I would probably be glowing too, if I were getting married to the love of my life. However, I was just the maid of honor and Lucy was the lovely bride.

I wasn't jealous of her, really. Envious was more like it. I had hopes of a wonderful first marriage too. Well, that didn't happen. Nope. Instead, I married the biggest loser in the whole state of Indiana. Thank goodness I realized my mistake before it was really too late to be fixed. I shook my head to clear my mind before I sunk into a hellish pit of depression. There was no way I wanted to rehash that part of my life, especially with Lucy so happy. I would tell her someday. Well, maybe I would. Probably not.

I plastered on the biggest, most sincere smile on my face. It was mostly believable as I walked to the living room. I said a quick hello to Phoenix as I passed the kitchen. I didn't even chance a look at the fine specimen that he was. He really was every girl's fantasy.

Phoenix was charming, passionate, loyal, and according to Lucy, a freak in the bed. *Hell, who wouldn't want all those qualities?* What made him tough to beat was the way he always adoringly looked at my best friend. His eyes reminded me of an early morning mist. They darkened with intensity every time they landed on Lucy. Being in the same room with them could get crowded at times. The inferno that they produced just being together made me want to run home, grab Rico (my vibrating dildo), and put the flames out. Hey, he was hidden in a secret drawer but used regularly. I wasn't a prude; I just didn't date much.

Before sex on a stick came into the living room and charged up the place, we needed to get a move on dress shopping. This was the only day that I could carve out the necessary time. She deserved my undivided attention. Her wedding was coming up quick and we hadn't even started to look yet.

2 CANDICE

I stepped into the house; my shoulders sagged as a pent-up breath shuddered out. I felt bone-tired. The house was still utterly silent, making me restless. My days were often spent jumping from one end of the house to the other. The quiet gave me too much time to reflect about my life and where it was not going. *Damn it. I was not this depressing woman.*

After a day with Lucy, I realized I was lonely. I wanted a sexy night with a hot, no-strings man. I didn't want to ever get married again. One night with a real man wasn't too much to ask for. *Shit, at this point, anything that didn't require a battery would suffice.* Hopefully there would be a gorgeous man at the wedding who would cherish me for an evening or two.

I soaked in the steaming bath until my fingers pruned and the water ran cold. Another shift at the Brass Ass would begin shortly. *Who would I be entertaining tonight?* I pulled my long blonde hair into a messy bun and peered at my reflection in the mirror. *How much longer will my looks keep me employed?*

The almond shape of my eyes made my piercing blue irises seem larger than they were. My skin was as pale as fresh snow and held a healthy glow. My pallor sharpened the midnight ring around the edge of my eye. The dark lining outlined the aqua pools coloring in the rest. My cheekbones protruded slightly and arched high. They created a slight hollow in the skin to elongate my face. My small, straight aristocratic nose accentuated my overly plump pink lips.

I know I am every man's wet dream. I am not vain, just stating the facts. I use my face and curvy body to make money. Outside of said job, I try to hide it from view. I don't like to attract unnecessary attention unless I'm in the mood to do so.

This face is what had attracted my sleaze of an ex-husband. Granted, I fell for the bastard but I blame that mostly on hormones. Merely a blonde moment that lasted three years too long. Irregardless——wait, fuck, regardless——that's water under the bridge. What's important right now was my job and to continuously move forward. I was ready for the wedding; I needed a weekend off. I might just be hitting burnout status.

***

I pulled into the smoothly paved parking lot of the Brass Ass. The lights strategically placed around the lot generated enough artificial light to ward off any shadows or shady characters. The building itself seemed to deflect the light, choosing to maintain the illusion of darkness and sin. The sign above the double doors was simple and tasteful. There were no neon red lights flashing for advertisement. Just the name of the club in thick black ink on a white sign hung above the entrance of the club.

It was more exclusive than the other strip clubs in the

neighboring towns. It had a pretty prestigious reputation. The owner, Logan, was a middle-aged woman who ran a pretty tight ship.

She kept the place clean and safe. She was also fair in her cut. Being an ex-dancer gave her the understanding that emptying too much of our pockets meant quality as well as quantity quickly diminished. Which would result in the closing of her doors. It was good to work for her: she knew our job was difficult because she knew the job. She expected a hundred percent every night, no excuses. If you didn't, then be prepared for the pink slip.

Logan was tall and thin with sharp facial features. Her acute mind fueled her intense personality. Years within the business had left her penetrating gaze bitterly cold. This didn't make her a ruthless owner. The result was more of a sharp businesswoman who didn't take anyone's shit. I liked her for it. To say we were friends would be inaccurate. We did understand each other and got along fairly well.

I nodded to her as I passed by and slipped into the pussy palace. I looked at the list of clients for the night. I had three regulars and one new client. The regulars were easy. I knew what they liked. For all new clients, there was a standard sheet for them to fill out. A particular dancer was matched according to the fantasy and likes the client wanted fulfilled. That is, unless they requested a specific dancer. I studied the sheet as if I were preparing for an exam.

In many ways, that's exactly what it was. Except my grade was either pass or fail. If I passed, they came back and I got another regular. If I failed, then I lost a potential regular. Then another dancer gained a client or we lost the business of the gentleman altogether. Talk about the pressure of a good performance.

His likes and dislikes were not out of the ordinary. His fantasy, however, was different. I wasn't exactly sure whether I wanted this particular guy. He was the last client of the night, so I had a couple of hours to come up with the perfect fantasy or talk to Logan about trading.

After my first two clients, I headed straight for Logan's office. I knocked on the door and waited for her to ask me in. No one barged in unless it was an emergency.

"Come in!" Logan shouted from behind the closed door.

"Hey, Logan, do you have a couple of minutes to help me brainstorm?"

She looked up at me with squinted eyes and a question forming around her mouth. I waited but when she didn't say anything, I proceeded.

"The new client, Max, has me kind of stumped. Honestly, the info he put down is so straightforward that a typical lap dance doesn't seem to jive for a VIP room, if you know what I mean."

She raised her eyebrows in mock surprise. "I read his sheet before I matched him up with you. You need to read between the lines if you want to work that room. That is why I gave him to you." She placed her hands in her lap and straightened in her chair. "I would have thought you would have picked up on that. Maybe I was wrong to pair you with him. I'll just give him to Jade."

"No need. I can handle him." I turned to go, as a smile appeared and smoothed out the hard lines of her face.

"You're the best dancer I've got, Candice. Don't let me down," she shrewdly instructed.

I wanted to slap that grin right off her face. Instead, I balled my fists at my sides and marched out before I said something I couldn't take back. I really didn't know what the hell she was talking about. I sure as heck didn't have much time to figure it out. I pondered the role I was supposed to perform while I was getting ready for my next client. This was way too frustrating. I had to clear my head if I was going to be present for Andy. He was a leather man. Assless chaps were his favorite. Now, that was a no-brainer and one I could figure out in a heartbeat.

Right in the middle of feathering my leather flogger along Andy's torso, the idea for Max's fantasy slammed into me. The idea hit me so hard I momentarily forgot where I was, a minor hiccup that Andy was clueless to. He was so wrapped up in his ecstasy he didn't even notice that I had stopped what I was doing.

I practically skipped out of the room when our time was up. I was elated to have a new role. I had forgotten the thrill that pulsed through me at a new prospect. A new role hadn't popped into my lap in a long time. It was a pleasure, albeit a tiny bit stressful, that I was happy to fumble my way through. Having regulars was great: it meant that I could perform on autopilot. Having to think outside of the box was liberating. It provoked my adventurous appetite. Another dimension would be added to Candy.

I scrubbed the makeup off my face and applied only mascara and a soft pink lip-gloss. I pushed the hanger around until I found the perfect red knee-length silky cocktail dress. I skipped the garter belt and stockings and elected for bare legs as I slipped my feet into black leather alligator stilettos. I twisted my long locks into a loose bun at the base of my neck. The finished product was of a striking high-class socialite ready to enjoy the evening with her lover. I said a quick prayer that I had read between the lines correctly as I went to meet Max.

I stepped into the dimly lit room. I immediately walked to the bar and poured a glass of Scotch, neat. I looked up at Max as I walked toward him. What I saw had my heart leaping to my throat and I paused in my gait.

My predatory smile never wavered and my momentary pause could only have been noticed if he was really paying attention. *I was a professional, for Christ's sake.* Up until this point in my career, I never have had this kind of reaction to one of my clients. Sure, many of them were good-looking and had cut bodies but there was something about this man that pulled me to him. I wanted him for me, not Candy.

For the first time, I was jealous of a stripper. This meant that Candy would enjoy this fascinating man but Candice would never have the opportunity. I did not date my clients outside of the club. You never mixed business with pleasure.

This man generated heat and power. It oozed from his pores. If I weren't careful, I'd lose myself in this room and abandon my carefully laid out rules. I needed to guard myself with him. He sat as if he was attached to a pole. His body was positioned at a perfect ninety degree angle. His long legs were bent at the knee with enough space between them for me to squeeze my body between.

I knelt and placed his Scotch into his wide palm. Long fingers wrapped around the glass. I tore my eyes away from the images of where I wanted those skillful fingers to touch. I looked up and into a chiseled jawline and wolf-like eyes. The colors of his eyes were unlike anything I had ever seen before. They were a mixture of a strong golden and yellowish color with a hint of copper.

They drew me in closer as they analyzed my every feature. They taunted me and yet entranced me at the same time. I was slowly losing the upper hand. These rooms were made to make the client feel as if they were in control. In reality, we were. I finally controlled my rapidly beating heart as well as my panting. *Shit, you'd think that I was a dog in heat the way I was lusting over this man.* I practically drooled all over his expensive pants. I loosened his tie, methodically giving myself time to regain my composure, and the upper hand.

He nonchalantly took a drink of his Scotch. I watched his Adam's apple slide down his throat as he swallowed. He seemed unaffected by my presence. His almost cold disposition challenged me. There was no way I was walking out of this room the only one sexually frustrated. *Game on, Max!*

I worked the knot out of his tie and slowly slid the silky material away from his neck and down his chest. I worked the material softly over his crotch as I pressed my stomach against his manhood. I pushed up onto my toes as I placed my hands on top of his muscled thighs and stood up. I laid the tie on the coffee table behind me.

I slipped out of my heels and glided over to the sound system set up in the corner of the room. I inserted the CD and pushed play. I turned back around. Once again, I faced Max as the Civil Wars crooned from the speakers. "Dust to Dust" began to play as I slowly walked toward Max.

I held out my hand. "Dance with me." My tone turned husky and deep. He enveloped my hand and stood up.

I turned and pulled him to an empty spot between the furnishings of the room. I stopped and twisted toward his body. We started with space between our frames. I demurely placed my left hand on his broad shoulder and my right lifted into his left hand. He stepped into my space as I stepped back. He led us into a cat-and-mouse chase. It was foreplay. "Eavesdrop" began to play as he stepped into me. I moved my left foot between his legs. I slid my hand from his shoulder to around his back and pushed him closer into me. I let my other hand slip from his grasp and wrapped it around the other side of his waist. He smoothly glided his hands to the middle of my back to caress down my spine to the small of my back.

Our movements slowed to more of an erotic dance. His fingers deftly pulled the zipper of my dress down. He pushed the material down my shoulders. The dress pooled at my feet. I stepped out of the dress and kicked it away from me. He smiled wickedly as I stood before him in only my sheer black shelf bralette and lacey thong. The track switched to "Poison and Wine." Which happened to be my favorite song by them.

He pulled me tighter into his body. My nipples grazed against his solid chest and ignited a fire in my belly. He skimmed his hands down my back to my ass. He gently squeezed and lifted me up. I wrapped my legs around his waist and interlocked my ankles together. My pulsating heat rubbed against his hardened cock as he led us back to the couch.

I was so turned on; I had forgotten that I was a paid stripper. He wasn't my lover. I had to quickly get that out of my head. I was here to please and fulfill his fantasy. I shouldn't even be turned on by him but try as I might, I couldn't tune him out.

My pleasure increased as he sat back onto the cushions and his length rubbed against my barely covered mound. His bulging cock pushed into my sensitive folds. The small patch of lace that covered my sensitive folds dampened as I unwound my legs to straddle his hip. He pushed his hips up, as he tasted my neck. He used his tongue and teeth along my neck to send tiny shivers throughout my body.

I ran my fingers through his perfectly styled hair. I pulled his thick locks as I nipped his earlobe. He groaned at the delicate bite. He moved his skilled fingers along my breasts to my peaked nipples. They erotically rolled each nipple; my hips ground into his pelvis both in pleasure and pain. He removed his hands from my breasts as I whimpered from the loss. Just as quickly, he laved up my breast with his mouth. I bowed back and moaned at the pleasure. He placed his fingers at the top of my panties and glided his thumb along the outside of the lace.

His thumb pushed into my still covered folds and circled over my clit. I circled my hips in tune with him. He scraped his teeth along my nipple; a ripple of desire shot right through my core. I circled faster and harder around his thumb, driving the need for release closer.

"Come for me," he commanded gruffly.

My orgasm exploded when his voice feathered lightly over my skin.

I placed my lips to his softly while my orgasm subsided. His mouth was addictive. He pushed his tongue inside as he mated with mine. Another wave of desire coursed through me. His thumb was lovingly fondling my womanhood from the outside of my thong. He used his fingers to push away the thin scrap of material and dipped his finger into my wetness. The shock of skin-to-skin contact had me sucking in air. My body trembled with pleasure. I was on the cusp of another orgasm. *Wait!* My mind shouted loudly, hurtling through my body's pleasure storm.

I scooted back away from his enthusiastic fingers. My eyes opened wide and I looked around wildly. I was just about to the point of panicking. *I never lost control, nor allowed a client to touch me so intimately.* I sure as hell never had an orgasm within these rooms. *Oh my gosh!*

Max had never gotten off. This was beyond the rules. Once Logan found out that I had broken them and left my client unsatisfied, I was going to lose my job. He would go right to her and voice a complaint. *Shit! Shit! Shit!* I had to get out of here and fast. Before I could scramble away, his baritone voice stopped me.

"It's our little secret." He swiftly pulled me back against him and assaulted my mouth. Before I could get swept away again, he pulled back. "You are so responsive and addictive. I can't wait to taste you the next time." He lifted me off his lap, picked up his tie, and walked out of the room.

I sat there in a stunned daze. I picked up his remaining Scotch and tossed it back. I picked myself up off the couch, hastily put on my dress, and left the room. There was no room for the walk of shame. I made sure to hold my head high, as if I hadn't broken every single one of the club's rules, let alone my own. I put on my street clothes and left to go home.

***

I crawled into a fetal position underneath the protection of the covers. I crossed the line. *How had this man been able to push against every one of my defenses and tear down my carefully built wall?* I was entranced the moment I locked onto his liquid amber eyes and powerful demeanor. Max had made my body soar with a simple dance. It was as if he had fulfilled my deepest fantasy. He had worked me as though he were the professional. With very little effort, I could seduce many men with a single look or sway of my hips. I had to put this out of my mind; no use on dwelling what I couldn't change. If he came back, I would make sure that I didn't melt like a stick of butter again.

***

I was running through the house, doing a quick clean, when the front door burst open. I squatted down with my arms held open to wait for the ball of spitfire to race into. With a whoosh, a thirty-pound blonde-headed tornado landed in my arms and knocked me on my butt. I laughed hard, as my precious daughter giggled at our silliness. I crushed her to my arms and smothered her face with yucky kisses.

"Enough, Momma! Wet me go," she squealed.

"Just one more. I missed you."

She pushed my face away as she rushed out of my arms and into the living room to play.

My mom held out her hand to help me off the floor.

She smiled. "Long night, kiddo? You look like you haven't slept well."

"Yeah." I sighed heavily. *If she only knew.* I turned on the coffee pot and grabbed two mugs.

"Was Riley good for you this weekend?"

"She was a doll. I love having her on the weekends. Your dad, on the other hand, is recouping!"

We both laughed. My father was an incredible man and loved Riley to pieces. Two days with her and he needed a break. I understood that completely. Riley could be a handful. She was a ball of energy and always running on an open throttle.

"I guess it's a good thing he has a couple more days to rest up." I rolled my eyes. He blew a lot of hot air about Riley spending the weekends with them but honestly, he loved the time she spent there.

"I'm going to sign Riley up for the tiny tots music class with Lucy once a week."

My mom looked briefly at Riley. "I think it will be good for her. She'll get to play with other kids her own age. Lucy's good with her and she will have a fun time." She drank the remainder of her coffee and stood up. She kissed my cheek and then put her cup in the sink. She went over to Riley to give her a hug and a kiss. "Love you, Riley. Be good for your momma and I'll see you this weekend."

"Wuv you too, YaYa."

She turned toward me. "Love you too, baby girl. I've got to run to the store. I'll give you a call later."

"Love you, Mom. Thanks again, for everything."

"Any time," she called over her shoulder as she left.

I gazed proudly at my wonderful daughter. I was extremely thankful for her. She was the only good thing that had come from Eugene. She was my reason for leaving him. I didn't want her to be tainted by his ugliness. Up until recently, we had shared custody.

***

One day, he had brought Riley home from one of his weekends with her and we began to argue. It was getting pretty heated. We never bothered to censor ourselves from Riley. Lucy came over that day, just in time to send Riley to her room. She rushed into the kitchen and tackled him as he was about to slap me. I had gone into myself and froze. She knocked him out cold and stayed until the cops came. Lucy was literally my hero. She shielded my daughter from the unpleasantness. I made sure I got a restraining order processed that day.

Riley didn't understand why she didn't see her father any more. If I had my way, she never would again. He never hurt her or was violent toward her in any way. He reserved all of that for me. Riley was, thankfully, blissfully ignorant of his darker ways. Plus, she was too young to understand all of it yet. One day, I would have to tell her but that was a long time from now.

I pulled her into my lap and inhaled her powdery scent. She was still my baby but at three going on four, she insisted she was no longer a baby. I kissed her quickly before she swatted me away. We sat on the floor and built princess castles out of her blocks for a long time.

3 FORREST

I had recently arrived in town and needed to blow off some steam. I wasn't ready to visit my brother yet. He would have a ton of questions and I wasn't ready to answer them yet. When I saw the sign for the Brass Ass, I decided to stop in. I'm not sure exactly what possessed me to go but I couldn't ignore the pull either.

Going to a strip club wasn't out of the ordinary but booking a VIP room sure as hell was. I filled out their little questionnaire, set up my time, and left to get something to eat. I cruised around town and took in the small city. There wasn't much to it, maybe four or five blocks. The center of town was littered with small shops, mom-and-pop grocery stores, and restaurants. One of those restaurants belonged to my brother.

The town may have been small but there was something about it that called to me. I could see why my little brother loved it here. He found the love of his life awhile back and followed her here. She didn't know it at the time but when her best friend left, it opened up the door for him to grab her up. They were getting married soon and I couldn't wait to see the sap become tied down. Phoenix was built for that life. I, on the other hand, was not. I'm not sure I would ever qualify as husband material.

I was curious to see who the owner had paired me up with. The owner was sharp and knew the business intimately. I would no doubt be satisfied with her choice. I knew the rules because she went over them in great detail. She had no problem throwing me out and barring me from the club indefinitely if I broke any of them. The dancers were loyal to her and she provided for them. The dancers wouldn't hesitate to press the panic button to call for the bouncers, for any reason. As long as I didn't touch any of the stripper's nether regions and didn't get violent, I was pretty much good to go. I may have a violent job at times but I never hit a woman. Women were meant to be cherished and worshiped, not brutalized.

I sat on the comfortable sofa in the dimly lit room and absorbed my surroundings. The room was designed to be inviting and intimate, as though you were in your own home. There was a lounge chair big enough for two comfortably to my right. A small table sat beside it. A sheet glass coffee table sat in front of me. The walls were decorated with soothing paintings. To the left of me was a small wet bar and a sound system. It was sparsely furnished. *Hell, how much did you need in a place like this?* I wondered whether all the rooms were decorated the same.

I heard the door open silently. The pulsating music from the club assaulted my ears for a brief moment and then disappeared as the door shut. Footsteps whispered along the carpet as the woman came into view. I sat up straighter when the tall, curvy woman walked silently by me. She walked gracefully in those fuck-me heels. Her long, muscled legs carried her perfect frame to the bar. Her slender hands expertly poured me a Scotch. My preferred drink of choice. *How she guessed that was fascinating.*

She picked up the glass and started toward me. When she finally looked at who sat on the couch, her movements faltered for a heartbeat. If I weren't paying attention, I would have never noticed the slight hesitation. She immediately regained her composure and professional demeanor. She was here to play a role for me but sometime between my drink and looking at me, she looked a little bewitched. Surprise rocked through her but she promptly pulled herself together.

As she drew closer, I was able to really look at her. Her large oceanic eyes swept me away in their current. They were so captivating that I had a hard time feigning a relaxed, almost distant position. She brought her tight body before me. She knelt between my legs and placed my drink in my loosely opened palm. I encircled my fingers around the thickness of the glass as though it were my lifeline. Her body intimately pressed between my thighs, barely touching my cock. If she continued to slither her body against me, she would find out how affected I was by the slightest touch from her.

I couldn't tear my gaze away from her expressive face. She licked her plump lips while she reached up to loosen my tie. Her breathing had become erratic. I could see her pulse beat rapidly in the curve of her neck. *It was getting increasingly harder for me to not touch her!* I wanted to see where she was going with this seduction. Thus far, I was on the brink of becoming her slave.

I took a drink of the Scotch, needing a minute to clear my head. She watched as though swallowing was the sexiest thing she had ever seen. Then a gleam of determination had her sliding my tie from around my neck and leaning into my crotch. I almost choked on the Scotch. Then she walked away. I didn't dare follow her. I needed to get myself under control. I thought of past missions and football stats. It was enough to settle my libido for the moment.

When I looked up, she had extended her delicate hand toward me and asked me to dance. It wasn't until that moment that I heard the seductive lyrics that serenaded us from the sound system. Whoever she had playing, sung with desperation and need. I let her lead me to the makeshift dance floor. At first we held a perfectly innocent frame. As we moved, I pulled her slowly into me. She fit so perfectly.

Her hands wrapped around me. I needed to see and touch more. I pinched the zipper between my thumb and index finger and pulled down. The material separated in the back. I ran my large hands up her back until the material bunched around the front. I slid the fabric to the floor. I sucked in a breath as she stood before me in a bra that only covered the bottom of her breasts. The tops of her breasts and pebbled nipples were exposed. It was the sexiest sight I'd ever seen. She was perfection, a mixture of hard and soft planes.

I moved my hands down her back and cupped her gloriously curvy ass. I picked her up and she locked her legs around my waist. I pulled us back to the couch. She straddled my hips and pushed her barely covered pussy onto my hardened cock. I licked and nipped along her neck. She pushed her hands through my hair. Roughly, she grabbed at the strands and pulled my head to the side as she used her teeth to nibble my earlobe. I groaned at the onslaught of desire that tightened my balls and made my dick painfully harder. I moved my hands to her dusty-rose colored buds. They begged me to touch and tease them. I placed the beaded nipple into my mouth. She arched back and moaned in pleasure.

I knew I was about to break the rules and I didn't give a shit. I needed to watch her come. She was so damn responsive. I could tell that she never lost control. I wanted to be the one to test her. I craved for her to come apart from my hands. I took a gamble and placed my thumb on the outside of her thong. I gently pushed my thumb through the cloth to her awaiting bundle of nerves. She withered beneath me. As my thumb circled her clit, her hips pushed into my thumb, imitating my movements. She moaned softly as her release built.

I couldn't remain silent anymore. I needed her to know just how unglued I was becoming.

"Come for me," I growled. No sooner did I command her than she bucked up into my circling thumb and came hard.

I could watch her orgasm all day long. She placed a soft kiss upon my mouth. Another rule broken. She tasted sweet and heady. I couldn't help but slip my tongue past her lips and tangle it around hers. I was getting lost in the sensation. I had to back away before I lost the last sliver of control I was hanging onto. Not yet. I had to have one more touch of her wet pussy. I slipped my fingers under the tiny piece of fabric and glided them along her slick seam. *God, this was heaven.* Before I could slip into her wet channel, she backed away. This was by no means the end.

Panic had replaced her desire and I knew not to press her any further. I didn't give a shit that I didn't get off. Hell, watching her was enough. What I wanted to do couldn't be done here but I would be back to pleasure her again.

"It's our little secret," I said to ease her frightened look. I picked her up easily and placed her on the couch beside me.

I stood up and walked toward the door. Before I

slipped out, I added, "You are so responsive and addictive. I can't wait to taste you the next time." I walked out feeling like a god.

***

I went back to the apartment I had recently rented. Phoenix was going to be pissed when I finally showed my face on his doorstep. He would expect me to stay with him. Finding out that I had an apartment and had been in town for a while would be hard for him to take. I wasn't exactly sure why I had yet to face him or why I was in this particular town. I had plenty of money and could afford a nice home. I just wasn't sure whether this place would lure me into setting down permanent roots. I was still in limbo. Not to mention, what the hell I would do for a job? For now, I would keep myself scarce and try to figure out what I was doing.

The apartment was sparsely furnished. All I brought with me were some clothes. Everything else was in storage near my parents. They didn't know that I was back in the States yet. Another thing I wasn't ready to deal with either. It's not like my life was uber secretive. They all knew I was in security. They just didn't know how high up the ladder my details were. I needed all of my missions to be top secret. They were primarily on a need-to-know basis.

I walked in the door, threw my keys onto the kitchen table, and stripped bare. I jumped into the shower, conjured the image of the exotic dancer, and found my own release. It was not how I wanted to come, but it was a necessary evil. It would be that way again. I would make sure I pleasured her without releasing my own the next time. After that I needed to figure out how to get her to go out with me. Better yet, to just come home with me after her shift. She seemed to be the type of woman who didn't date her clients. Then again, I brought her out of her carefully controlled shell. There was hope yet.

I smiled at the thought of chasing her as I stepped out of the shower. The thrill of a challenge was exactly what I needed. It had been a long time since a woman had piqued my interest enough to want to see them a second time.

4 CANDICE

"Riley, come on, baby. We have to hurry or we will miss your first class!" I shouted from the bottom of the stairs.

"Coming, Momma."

That was the only thing that I could hear. The rest of what she had said was muffled behind her closed door. I shook my head. *I'm pretty sure that hell would freeze over first before we were ever on time for something.* I knew I should have just gotten her ready as soon as she woke up this morning. *Oh well!* Lucy knew how we were so she wouldn't be surprised at our tardiness.

As soon as I set Riley on the ground and shut the car door, she bounced her way to the front of Treble. She waltzed in as if she owned the place. I walked through and said a quick hello to Nancy, the receptionist, as I breezed toward the back of the studio. By the time I sat with the other parents, the tiny tots class was in full swing. I blew out a puff of air and finally began to relax. Riley had a tendency to make you feel as if you were running a hundred miles an hour in a circle while trying to chase your own tail.

I smiled as I watched Lucy in her element. She was born to teach. She had such an easy way with children and well, everyone in general. She made wrangling ten three-year-olds look easy. They sat in a large circle with their instruments, just banging away. The music wasn't music at all. It was just a bunch of loud noises but the kids were laughing and having a good time.

Once the class finished, the parents gathered up their kids and tried to make a quick exit. I, on the other hand, patiently waited for Lucy to finish up so I could speak with her.

"Did you have fun, baby?"

"Oh yes, it was awesome. I wuv TiTi Wucy!"

"Me too. Why don't you go and play in the playroom for a bit while I talk to Aunt Lucy."

"Okay Momma."

As Riley left to go play, I walked up to Lucy.

"Hey, girl. Looks like your class is full. The kids seem to really enjoy it."

"Oh my goodness. It has been a complete surprise. Treble is taking off like crazy. I never imagined so many people would be interested in taking lessons."

"Come on, girl. Will you give yourself some credit? You are an excellent teacher and talented pianist. People would be crazy not to come and take lessons, not to mention attend your concerts every month. Hell, I live for them myself!" I told her truthfully. "It's time to realize how much talent you really do have."

"I guess. I just don't want to jinx anything yet. Treble is still so new. I love it and am so glad it has come to fruition."

"Have you been reading the dictionary lately or is Phoenix rubbing off on you? I sure as heck do not remember you having the best of grammar nor going this long in a sentence without saying the f-word," I said in mock surprise.

"Even I can turn over a new leaf smartass! Parents don't really like their kids coming home using that kind of language I reserve it for when I get home and use all my dirty words in the bedroom."

We laughed like a couple of drunken sailors. My cheeks hurt from my laughter and I wiped away tears. I finally caught my breath. "I needed that! You wanna get some coffee Sunday before my mom drops Riley home?"

"You betcha! This will be our last hoorah before the wedding and honeymoon. I won't see you for a couple of weeks," Lucy exclaimed.

That wiped the remainder of my good mood away. I completely forgot that the wedding was next weekend and that they were taking a long honeymoon. Damn, I was going to be lonely without her in my backyard. I grabbed Riley and we said our quick good-byes and plodded home.

I really didn't feel like cooking dinner, so I swung through the drive-through of Clucky's Chicken. *Yep, mother of the year award, right here!* I know fast food is bad for you but chicken is healthy, right? Who cares if we both like it extra crispy with mashed potatoes loaded with gravy?

"I wuv mashed potatoes," Riley mumbled with a mouth full.

"Try not to talk with your mouth full, baby. I don't want you to choke. Plus, it's not very ladylike to have food flying out of your mouth as you speak."

"I won't choke. See——awe gone." She opened her mouth wide enough for me to see the remnants of her mashed potatoes. I tried not to chuckle but she was just so dang cute.

***

The rest of the week went pretty fast and yet seemingly quiet. I was still waiting to hear from Eugene. He hadn't called since I put the restraining order on him. It wouldn't stop him. He would figure out a way to contact me or see Riley sooner or later. It was merely a waiting game with him. He'd lie low and wait for me to cool down with the hopes of me forgetting about the restraining order. I needed to be strong and keep him out of our lives for good. His silence was worrisome. I was not going to dwell on it for long. When he showed up, I would deal with it then.

During the week, I cut my hours at the Brass Ass to only four hours on Monday, Tuesday, and Wednesday. I took Thursday and Sunday off. My neighbor, Evonne, was in her sixties and enjoyed watching Riley. She liked to play bingo in the evenings so it worked out great for me. She watched Riley and I paid for her bingo time. It was a win-win for the both of us.

Logan, my boss, was pretty accommodating. She understood my circumstance and didn't fault me for it. Plus, I made most of my money on Friday and Saturday. Like I said: I was in high demand at the club. My VIP slots were always full. During the week, I worked the stage and lounge areas. I was a good employee and made the club a lot of money.

***

I walked into work and grabbed my client list for the evening. *What the fuck?* I started to sweat. *No fucking way!* Max was my last client of the night. I couldn't see him. He made me lose all sense of control. If Logan ever found out what happened last weekend, I would be out on my ass faster than you could shake a stick——or however that saying went. Lucy wasn't near me to correct me so whatever. *Crappy noodles.* This was not going to be a good night. How the hell was I supposed to concentrate on my clients if my mind was preoccupied with what Max wanted? Fake it until you break it or make it. Damn it—— he has got me all turned upside down.

"Looks like you did well with Max last weekend. He booked another time slot with you this evening, as well as tomorrow night," Logan said to my back.

I squealed in surprise. "Shit, Logan. You scared the crap out of me."

She raised an eyebrow at my sudden reaction.

"Sorry, I was lost in thought. Eugene has been MIA and I've been a little tense as to when he was going to show up." I quickly said so that she wouldn't read into anything.

She placed a hand on my shoulder. "I know how hard this has been on you lately but you can't let him deter you from your job. You have to be one hundred percent focused when you are here. If you are not, then you have the potential to lose clients and money. That cannot happen," she pointed out as she left.

She was right. I still felt as if my own mother had chastised me. I hated to let anyone down, especially my pocketbook. It was time to get my head in the game and make that money!

I was so engaged in my clients this evening that Max hadn't even entered my thoughts until this moment. I still had to figure out my outfit and what would play out in the room tonight. This time, I was not going for the elite socialite. I was going for the opposite of that spectrum.

I walked into the room, slipped my pumps off, and dimmed the lights. He sat in the same spot as last time, with almost the same posture; rigid and aloof. My nerves jumped up a notch. My normal high self-esteem had taken a nosedive the moment I saw him. *What the hell was I thinking?*

I wasn't sexy enough for him or professional enough. His presence was a complete mystery to me. I took a deep breath and collected myself. I was trying to drum up my courage to face him again. I silently counted to ten. I felt marginally better, so I crossed the room in my bare feet.

"Good evening, Max." I slipped my silk robe off as I walked by him.

I didn't expect a response from him. I was attempting to muddle his agenda and gain the upper hand. I was playing a childish game of cat-and-mouse. I feared that I was the mouse. The hunter-like gleam portrayed within his amber eyes spoke volumes. A shiver ran down my spine with the way his eyes intensely roamed over my scantily clad body.

I dressed purposely in the cliché stripper costume. I covered my pert nipples with stickered stars and left my breasts completely exposed. The only thing that was covering my lady bits was a small piece of see-through white lace. The audacity of my attire had him hiding a smirk. He was enjoying my choice thus far. I'm sure that what I thought was demeaning only encouraged him. I was truly playing with fire. I had come this far; I wasn't going to back out of my plan.

I seductively sashayed my hips as I walked over to hand him his Scotch. When our fingers touched, I felt the electric zing all the way to my toes. Which involuntarily curled into the carpet. His eyes raised in challenge. He wanted me to run. For the first time in my life, I was going to meet this challenge head on and call his bluff.

I slowly climbed onto his lap and rose up onto my knees to push my breasts into his face. I lowered back down and skimmed my breasts along his face. I almost expected the frat boy motorboat but he made no movement. I turned my lips to his ear and pulled the soft lobe into my mouth and sucked. I let it go with a popping sound. I used my lips and tongue to slowly kiss and lick my way down the side of his neck. Without losing momentum with my mouth, I circled my hips along his hardening cock. The contact felt amazing and made me wet. I continued to kiss along his neck as I moved my hips. I was on the brink of coming and needed to back away. He never made a sound, nor made a move to touch me, which had me worried. I needed to move onto the next part of my plan.

I slowly eased my body off his and walked to the stereo. I put on a good bass thumping song. The music assaulted my ears. It was all a part of my plan. I didn't want a seduction to take place this time. I wanted to show him the other side, a raunchy strip show. He may not have envisioned this when he paid for me tonight but this was what he was getting.

I sauntered over to the pole in front of the mirrors. I grabbed the highest part of the pole and leaned my body back. I tossed my head over my shoulder to look at him haughtily. He sat still as a statue on the couch. His eyes held no humor in them. As my eyes met his, anger shimmered in their depths. For a split second, I almost stopped this charade but I didn't.

I continued to piss him off by the second. I wanted him to feel as pissed as I was at myself last week. *Paybacks were a bitch!* I might lose him as a client but I had to maintain some amount of dignity. Some would say that I went about this the wrong way, but I had planned out this course. I was going to follow through with it. I grinned saucily as I wrapped my legs around the pole and hung upside down. *I was proud that I could still perform this maneuver at my age!* I moved my hands above my head and grabbed the pole tightly as I slid upside down the pole.

The music pumped loudly through the speakers. It pulsed through my body. I stopped my downward momentum and went into a sit-up position to take a hold of the pole and swing my body up while I placed my feet back on the ground. I walked to the front of the mirrors with my ass hitting the pole. I bent over and touched my toes as I flipped my hair around.

When I stood back up, I grabbed the pole above my head and swung my body around. The track switched to a provocative R&B song. I used my left hand to hold the pole and swiveled my hips, bent at the knee, and stuck my ass out. I dirty danced with the pole as if it were my greatest lover. In reality, it was. I was so lost in my dancing and swinging that I didn't even realize that Max had moved from the couch and was behind me.

When I circled my hips, ready to dip again, his hands slid around my waist. He pulled me in close to his body so that I couldn't get away. He moved with my body effortlessly. As we danced, he ran his hands along the sides of my rib cage. I sucked in a deep breath as his calluses scraped along my skin. His touch was slow and deliberate as he inched his way up toward my breasts. Instead of caressing them like I wanted him to, he only skimmed underneath as he traced slow, maddening circles up and down my quivering stomach.

He moved his hands over my lace-covered mound and pulled me harder against him. I threw my head back onto his shoulder. He took the opportunity to kiss along my neck. I could feel his hardness push along the crack of my ass. I wanted him to turn me around and thrust inside me. He purposely kept my back to his front to keep me from the very thing that I wanted.

He placed his fingers over my hipbones and underneath the strings of my thong and ripped the material away. I gasped at the shock and lust that coursed through my body. The scrap of material floated to the floor. The only thing that covered me were the star stickers placed over my hardened nipples. With one hand splayed across my stomach, the other reached up and tore the stickers off, one at a time.

I moaned in ecstasy at the mixture of pain and pleasure. Even in my lusty haze, I realized that I had lost control again. This time I really didn't care. All I could think about was the big alpha male behind me. The torrent of emotions that coursed through my body made me putty in his hands. I arched my ass against him, giving him permission to do whatever he wanted to me.

He slid his fingers along my wet folds. I bucked into his fingers and pushed them into the wet, sensitive flesh. I bit my lip as I thrashed my head from side to side, needing release. He caressed and teased my pussy as I breathlessly moaned and writhed around, trying to coax his fingers to my sensitive bud. His teeth grazed along my neck as I sighed out his name. He groaned as if in torture.

He turned me around gruffly and picked me up as if I weighed nothing. He gently laid me down onto the couch. Max stood over me, soaking up my flushed, naked skin. I closed my legs at the possessive look in his eyes. He assertively pushed my legs apart as he moved between them. I reached up to try to unbutton his shirt but he pushed my hands above my head and held them there, signaling his ultimate control over me.

He dipped his head to my breast and pulled the taut nipple into his mouth. His tongue made lazy circles around my nipple, which made my hips thrust upward to seek his cock. He moved on to my other breast and repeated the same motions.

"Please, Max. Make me come. I need you to touch me," I begged him.

He never uttered a word; he just placed soft kisses along my belly and down to where I wanted his mouth the most. He spread my legs farther apart to expose me, making me feel vulnerable. As if he knew I was a split second from shutting down, he spread my folds apart and licked my sensitive skin. I pushed my hips up as I grabbed his hair to hold him exactly where I wanted him.

His tongue swiped along my clit; bolts of electricity shot through my body. My legs shook at the sensual assault of his tongue. He gently pushed two fingers into my warm center as his teeth gently bit down on my clit. I closed my eyes, on the verge of the biggest climax ever.

"Look at me while I eat your pussy," he demanded.

Holy shit, his dirty words only fueled my excitement. "Oh my God, Max. I'm going to come," I practically screamed.

"That's it, baby. Let go. Come for me now."

The rush of his sweet command had me dropping over the edge. My orgasm tore through my body. Wave after wave crashed through my system, leaving me panting and utterly drained.

He kissed his way back up my satiated body. His mouth demanded entrance. I could deny him nothing. I met his hungry kiss for kiss. I traced my hands down his back, over his tight ass, to the front of his pants.

"No, Candy. Tonight was about you, not me."

He kissed me one more time, and then got up and retrieved my robe. He laid it over me and covered my nakedness. I felt completely loved in that moment. He took one last look at me before he left the room. I let out a breath that I didn't even realize I was holding. *Oh my fucking word!* I don't know how the hell I ended up in this situation but I was grateful in more ways than one. I wasn't going to taint what we just shared with negativity. I owned my own actions and choices. I wanted him to take me and he did. I knew what I was going to do tomorrow night. I smiled and left the room like a giddy teenager.

5 FORREST

I left the Brass Ass with a raging hard-on. I knew immediately what Candy was doing as soon as she walked by me in her barely there costume. It was comical until I realized what she was up to. Her coquettish look was meant to throw me off my game. I have to admit, at first, it did. I lost all semblance of a coherent thought as she drifted by me. All I could do was watch her glorious body seductively sway by. I was an entranced fool.

When she pushed her breasts into my face as a big fuck-you, I wanted to lash out at her. I didn't want to hurt her with my hands. I wanted to use my tongue and teeth to punish her. Honestly, I loved that she pushed those luscious mounds all over my face but it was done with condescension. She wanted control because she lost it with me last time. Most importantly, she wanted to cheapen last weekend and that really pissed me off.

I made sure to keep my emotions in check. I wouldn't touch her. I knew that she would second-guess herself even more. In some aspects, she was extremely easy to read and in others, she was a complete surprise. Her emotions would flash quickly across her face, revealing everything that she thought and felt.

One only had to look hard enough. I paid attention to the slightest nuances from people. Being able to detect the minutest gesture or tic could potentially save the job from utter disaster. It's what made me really good at my job. It's also what kept my clients and me alive thus far.

When she took her act to the pole, I became enraged. *How dare she belittle what we did in this room?* If she thought that I was going to instantly become embarrassed or pissed off enough to storm out, she was wrong. I would wait her out. I'd let her continue with her childish game. I did not want to sit here while she straddled a pole. If I wanted to watch that, I would have sat out in the lounge. I wasn't really sure what I wanted but her acting like a clichéd stripper was not it.

She finally quit her circus act and started dirty dancing. I sat up straighter and enjoyed the provocative movements. She ran her hands down her body and I could no longer sit and watch. I needed to be close to her and to touch her. When she seemed absorbed in the music, I moved silently behind her. I captured her hips and pulled her tightly into my body. I didn't need to think about how to move with her. It was an inherent dance. Both of our bodies instinctively moved in sync with each other. She threw her head back. Pleasure fueled her body.

I took the opportunity to lavish my mouth upon her delicate neck. I could no longer stop myself from touching her most intimate area. Once my fingers touched her slick pussy, I just about came in my pants. She was practically dripping. I twisted her around and laid her on the couch.

It was time for me to taste her. I felt as if I were in heaven once my taste buds sampled her sweet, earthy aroma. I could spend all day lapping her up. I enjoyed going down on women but Candy made it addictive. That was the exact vision I took into the shower with me tonight.

While I drove aimlessly around the small city, I spotted a for sale sign in front of an intriguing three-story Victorian home. I parked my car in the driveway. I wasn't sure why I sat here. I should just put the car in reverse and go home. Instead, my fingers slipped over the door handle and pushed the door open. *I guess I was getting out of the car to check the property out.*

From outward appearances, the house had been abandoned for quite some time. The yard was overgrown with dandelions and yellowish grass. After I did a cursory scan of the yard, I finally looked up at the house. The foundation and overall structure of the house looked solid but that's where all the homey traits ended.

The shutters hung on for dear life. The steps going up to the porch screamed at me as I ascended them. I stepped gingerly onto the porch. Any minute now, it was going to cave in on me. *At least it would be a short fall!* The boards of the porch creaked and moaned as I walked around and looked into the murky windows. I raised my hand and swiped the grime from the window so I could get a better look.

From what I could see, the downstairs had cherry-stained hardwood floors. They were dusty from years of neglect but could easily be redeemed to their former glory. I noticed a wide staircase with some kind of decorative carvings along the railing. I couldn't make out its detail but I was intrigued. I decided that it was smarter to just call the realtor than it was to brave a tetanus shot.

I entered the phone number while I walked to my car.

I left a message for the realtor named Gus something. Hopefully he would call me back this afternoon. I wanted to go through the house soon. With a cheesy smile plastered on my face, I drove over to my brother's house.

Before I could knock, the door burst open. A flurry of chestnut hair knocked into me. *Oomph!* The air rushed out of me as an elbow plowed into my solar plexus. I grabbed the other arm to steady the crazy woman before we both fell backward.

"Where's the fire?" I chuckled.

"Shit balls. I'm sorry. I am such a klutz sometimes," she said, embarrassed.

I laughed. "No harm. No foul." I held out my hand. "I'm Forrest and you are?"

"Lucy, the idiot, who doesn't look where she is going. Although, technically it's your fault, seeing as I wasn't expecting you to be standing right outside the door. So I'm pretty sure you owe me an apology."

She looked so serious and a little pissed off that I couldn't help but laugh at the way that she had turned the tables on me.

I fell in love with the ballsy broad in that very instant. Phoenix was one lucky bastard. She was sarcastic, beautiful, and klutzy. *Who in their right mind wouldn't fall in love with her?* I bowed, like a true Southern gentleman. "My sincerest apologies, Miss Lucy. I did not mean for you to try to jump into my arms. Although, I can see why you would. Look at me——I am utterly irresistible!"

Damn if she didn't punch me hard in the arm!

"Are you trying to steal my fiancée?" Phoenix

boomed from behind Lucy.

"Well, brother, I can't help it if she desires me! Hell, she threw herself right at me."

"I'm sure she did. Much like the plague."

We both laughed heartily and hugged each other.

"Now that the introductions are over, why don't we take this reunion inside?" Lucy walked back inside.

"Fuck, brother, you have a spitfire on your hands." I slapped him on the back as we fell in behind Lucy.

"Yep and I am enjoying every minute of it."

"I'm sure you are!"

We fell into one of the chairs in the living room and began our ritual of catching up.

Lucy handed each of us a beer. "Well, fellas, I'm out of here. Forrest, it sucked meeting you. I hope you won't be here when I get back."

I winked at her. "Of course, love, I'll still be here, waiting for your return."

She laughed. "I hope so! See you two later."

I watched her walk over to Phoenix. She gave him a sultry good-bye kiss. I had to turn my head for a brief moment. The amount of heat the two of them produced just from a kiss had a thin sheen of sweat break out over my forehead. I was a tad bit uncomfortable. I've never been privy to such honest affection. It was a little unsettling.

I had to admit that Candy popped into my head

about the same time. What Lucy and Phoenix shared felt similar to the combustible feelings between Candy and me. Only a couple more hours and I would see my erotic siren. Lucy gave me a quick kiss on my cheek on her way out the door. Her surprising act of sincerity brought a welcoming smile to my face.

"I can certainly see why it didn't take you long to get hooked on Lucy."

"As the age-old cliché goes, it was love at first sight," Phoenix replied with a glazed over look in his eyes.

"So I guess talking you out of getting hitched is out of the question?"

"Do I look stupid to you?"

"Stupid? No. A fool maybe!"

"I'm not the love 'em and leave 'em type, brother. That title is reserved only for you."

"There is my condescending little brother. Damn, I've missed you."

"Me too. When did you get into town?"

Shit! I knew it wouldn't take him long to ask that question. I was hoping to at least talk in enough circles that he would just leave it alone. I wished for too much.

"A week ago." I shrugged.

"A fucking week! What the hell, Forrest? And you are now just coming to visit? Where are you staying and why haven't you stopped by before now? What have you been doing all this time?"

"Slow the fuck down, Mom," I practically shouted at

him. My fists clenched. I needed to take a deep breath. I knew this was how he'd react. He took it personally that I didn't come straight here. More importantly, he was pissed that I wasn't staying with him.

"Look, I needed to decompress after my last job. I rented an apartment and have just been hanging around, trying to get my head on straight," I said seriously. "It had nothing to do with not wanting to see you or stay with you until the wedding." I breathed out slowly, making sure that my heart rate slowed. I didn't want to fight with him. I hadn't seen him or my parents in over a year.

"I get it, Forrest. I am sorry, man. What do you think about our little town?"

"It's starting to grow on me." Before I could elaborate more, my phone rang. Phoenix got up to get more beer, while I talked to Gus, from Lakeshore Realty.

I hung up and asked Phoenix, "You got anything pressing for the next couple of hours?"

"Nope, just work later this evening. Why?"

"You want to check out this house for sale? I'm going to meet the realtor in thirty minutes, if you're interested."

He looked at me inquisitively. "I'm game."

We pulled up to the dilapidated house. You would think that seeing it again would give me pause. It didn't; it only increased my curiosity.

"Hello. I'm Gus, from Lakeshore Realty. You must be Forrest." He held out his beefy hand.

"Nice to meet you. This is my brother——"

"Hey, Phoenix. How are you? You still planning on marrying Lucy?" he interrupted.

I could sense Phoenix tense beside me. He replied to Gus's dig as if it hadn't bothered him in the least. I wouldn't have been so nice, if that comment were directed toward me. I wouldn't have answered with words either. I would have just taken a swing at his smug face. I didn't want to work with him on this deal, even if it did come to pass. However, I should probably take a page from Phoenix's book and not let it bother me.

"Gus, we are on a tight schedule. If we could get started with the walk-through, that would be great," I stated dryly. I really wanted to shut him up. I wanted to look through this house by myself without him fawning behind us. I didn't have time to make idle chitchat with this dirt bag.

"Sure, no problem."

We scurried into the house, fearing that the porch would cave in with all of our weight. Gus took the previous hint and didn't speak. He let us wander through the house. Phoenix and I left him standing in the foyer as we began our exploration.

There were two rooms that opened up immediately upon entering. To the right was a decorative cherry-stained archway. We walked through the elaborate doorway into a spacious and airy living/entertaining room.

The stone fireplace ran from floor to ceiling. A worn, yet once beautifully carved, mantel ran across the width of the fireplace. Bookcases adorned each side of the fireplace. Two sets of French doors aligned the other side. They opened up to the side portion of the wrap-around porch, which encompassed the gazebo. It was stunning.

We walked out of the living area and across the foyer into another large doorway, identical to the other room. This room seemed to be a formal dining room. Hanging in the center of the room was a large crystal chandelier. One side had a large bay window that looked out the front side of the house. The other side also held two sets of French doors, which led to the opposite side of the porch and into another gazebo. There was a smaller doorway at the far end of the room. This, I assumed, led to the kitchen.

We walked through the swinging door, right into the kitchen. To my surprise, it had been updated. There was a wide island with barstool seating. Along the outer edges ran spacious countertops and updated appliances. There was a walk-in pantry that was large enough to fit two people in at the same time. Tucked into the corner of the kitchen was a breakfast nook. Surrounding the nook were multiple windows that overlooked the backyard.

Another large living area connected through the nook. A smaller stoned fireplace sat along the far wall. It wasn't as intricate as the front room was but still impressive. *What the hell were all these rooms for?* I didn't know enough people to fill this house up. We walked out of this room and stood in front of the extravagant staircase.

I raised my eyebrows at Phoenix. We were both speechless. This house, so far, was more than I could have imagined. The exterior of the home was dilapidated from abandonment. The interior seemed to have been sealed and untouched from neglect.

"You thinking what I'm thinking?"

"Race you to the stairs!" Phoenix shouted.

Phoenix ran through the living room and straight up the right side of the main portion of the staircase. I rushed through, charging behind him. I hit the other side of the staircase a second faster than Phoenix.

"Come on, little brother. You better climb faster or I'm going to beat you," I taunted.

"Please! You're old and out of shape."

I laughed at the fact that he was right but that didn't deter me one bit. I kicked it up another notch and barely beat him to the center of the landing.

"Should have bet on that!"

"Whatever! That was hardly a win. Not one I'd boast about!"

I rolled my eyes at him as we took in the vastness of the second floor. The two wings of the staircase stopped on this floor. The main portion of the stairs continued up to the third floor. We walked up the main stairs together. The landing opened up into the largest room I had ever seen. There were stained-glass windows along each of the walls. The glint of light cast colorful prisms throughout the room. This room alone had me mesmerized. I didn't even need to see the rest of the house.

On the opposite side from the windows was an entryway to another room. We walked through and into the biggest master bedroom that I have ever seen. I didn't own enough furniture to even fill it. The master bath had a huge clawfoot tub. His-and-her sinks aligned the opposite wall. An all tiled walk-in shower adorned the other end. The commode sat in a smaller room with its own door. That was my favorite piece of the bathroom next to the walk-in shower. I could live in this bathroom alone. The previous owners must not have paid too much attention to the rest of the house but they sure went all out in here.

When I walked of the bathroom, I noticed a set of French doors. I opened them up and walked out onto a private balcony. The balcony had enough room for a couple of lounge chairs and a table. It was the perfect spot to relax and watch the sunset. *Where the fuck did that idea come from?* I don't think I ever watched a sunset without an agenda.

There was so much more to the house. I could have spent days roaming the halls, continuously finding little hidden gems. We made our way back downstairs. We took a quick look at the backyard and then met back up with Gus.

"Gus, do me a favor and pull up the specifics on the house and what the owners are asking. I'll be by your office in an hour to pick up the information," I instructed. I didn't want this Neanderthal to ask any questions just yet.

I wanted him to know that I was interested in more but not interested enough to start talking about deals. Plus, I didn't want him hounding me every day about what I thought about the house. In general, he now knew that I would call him if I were interested and that I would not take kindly to unsolicited calls. I really didn't want to have any unnecessary contact with him.

Phoenix knew me well enough not to ask me any questions either. He would get the story when I was ready to tell him. That's one of the things I loved about him. He understood when to wait for an explanation and when to demand one.

"I liked the house. It had a really interesting floor plan. The master bedroom was by far my favorite. The only thing that was concerning was the fact that it needs a lot of work." He didn't add any more until we parked at his house "I'm not sure what's going on and I know you'll tell me when you're ready. On a side note, thanks for dragging me along with you."

"Thanks, Phoenix. I appreciate it. I'm not really sure what I'm thinking yet. As soon as I figure it out, I'll let you know." I smiled.

"You going to come in for a bit or head back to your place?"

"I'm going to head home. Talk to you tomorrow."

I beeped my horn as I left his drive and headed to the realtor's office. I grabbed the paperwork from his receptionist and drove home. I had plenty of time to snatch a quick shower and some dinner before my date with the lovely Miss Candy.

6 FORREST

I walked into the Brass Ass as if it were my second home. In recent days, it had become exactly that. I had become accustomed to seeing Candy on the weekends; it felt like our typical date night. *How fucked up was that logic?* With a predatory smile on my face, I opened up the door to my favorite room in the club. I strategically sat on the oversized lounge chair. This time I was going to observe Candy from the moment that she entered the room.

My body sensed her arrival before she even had a chance to open up the door. I automatically sat up straighter, my nostrils flared slightly, and my heart picked up speed. Even my damn dick twitched. This wasn't something that I did consciously. My head and body were at war when it came to Candy. My head told my body to simmer down and control my emotions. My body repeatedly told my head to fuck off. That's about as articulate as my body was going to get.

She stepped into the room. I felt as if I were sucker-punched as the air rushed from my lungs. The more I saw her, the more radiant she became. Tonight she wore tight skinny jeans with a flowing black tank top. She was not wearing a bra either. The material swayed in tune with her bouncing breasts as she walked. *How the hell was I supposed to maintain control when she walked around like that?* No sane man would be able to. I was beginning to believe that she was my kryptonite.

I'm probably delusional. It's all a part of her act. Maybe she acted this way with all of her clients. She made them believe that they were special. As my thoughts became muddled, I remembered our first night. Not even the best actress could fake the emotions that poured off her. I couldn't deny the strong feelings between us. I didn't know what it was or where it would go.

Hearing the Scotch being poured into the glass had my mind switching gears. I hadn't really taken the time to look at her tonight. I had focused too hard on the girly thoughts taking up residence in my brain. Candy had no makeup on. Her hair was up in a loose ponytail and she seemed relaxed. Normally she played up the part of whatever character or role she chose for the seduction part of the night. I wouldn't argue with any of them that she had chosen to play. Tonight, she seemed to have donned herself, which I found more exciting and sexier than the others. I got to see a portion of the real person. I'm pretty sure that I was the first——at least while on the job.

She turned on the same sweet, tortured singer from the first night as well. This must be her favorite group because it seemed to be her go-to. The duo's voices blended well together. It was hauntingly beautiful and soulful. I understood why she favored them. I began to like them myself. I mostly listened to old country like Merle Haggard and Johnny Cash. This new-wave country didn't do shit for me.

Candy stood in front of me and stepped between my

thighs. She seductively rose the glass to her lips and took a long sip of the Scotch. That intimate act alone had me gulping. She handed me the glass and sat on my lap, with her body sideways leaning up against the armrest, while her legs lay on top of mine and her ankles crossed over the other armrest. This new aspect caught me off guard. She had me all twisted up and nervous. I set the glass down upon the table so that she wouldn't notice how badly my hand shook.

She bent her head to my neck. I felt her warm breath caress my skin right before she placed small kisses up my neck and underneath my chin. Just as quickly as they started, she stopped and placed a gentle kiss on my mouth. My chest heaved from the anticipation of her next move.

"How was your day?" She spoke with sincerity.

It took me a moment to form a thought because I became tongue-tied. We never tried to have a conversation in here except for a couple of demands. *What the hell was she doing?* I cleared my throat. "It was productive. How was yours?" *Did I just fucking say that?* I mentally punched myself multiple times. I was such a moron. She genuinely laughed, which sounded like music to my ears. She had a deep, throaty laugh that was sexy and made you want to keep her laughing.

"I spent the day being lazy, doing a lot of nonproductive things." She made fun of my answer.

I laughed heartily because it proved to be an innocent, flirtatious move. I don't think that she realized that she did that. I loved that she didn't have to think about her reply. There was no motivation behind the honest response. She had said the first thing that popped into her head. No filter.

She unbuttoned my shirt with her skilled fingers. My breaths became shallow. Disappointment infiltrated my mind when our conversation abruptly ended. I craved the sound of her voice. I found myself trying to still her hands to hear more.

"Candy——"

She cut me off by laying claim to my mouth. She kissed me with passion and abandonment as her delicate fingers continued to unbutton my shirt. She used both of her hands to open the front and expose my chest and stomach. It became harder and harder to breathe. I couldn't concentrate as she kissed and licked her way down my body. When she got to the button of my pants, she looked up and into my eyes and smiled. I held my breath the minute her smile lit up her face. Her blue eyes swam with mischief and some other emotion I couldn't identify.

She tugged on my pants, signaling me to lift my hips up so she could take them off. I know I shouldn't have let her but I couldn't stop her either. She had all the control tonight. It seemed to be what she needed. I let her have the reins. My cock sprang free, happy to be released from the confines of my pants. She ran her hands up and down my legs, sending goose bumps over my heated flesh. She brought her mouth to the inside of my thighs and nipped the sensitive flesh. My desire kicked in another notch and my dick grew even harder.

She brought small amounts of pain with her teeth and then used her tongue to soothe the pain. Pleasure shot throughout my body. With her delicate hands, she cupped my balls with one and wrapped the other one at the base of my cock. I sucked in a breath at the intense sensation. I moaned her name as I ran my fingers down her ponytail. I needed to touch her in some fashion. I needed her to know how good her hands felt. She tenderly rolled my balls around her palm and tightened her grip along my shaft. She looked up at me one last time, smiled wickedly, licked her lips, and sucked my cock into her mouth.

"Oh, fuck. Candy." That was the last coherent sentence I managed to rasp out.

Right after that, she placed her finger along my taint and applied just enough pressure while she made small circles. Her mouth pulled my cock deep into her throat and pulled at my dick, commanding that I come in her mouth. It didn't take me long to grunt out a moan as I released my seed.

When I came back down from my intense orgasm I felt like a horny teenage boy seeing his first naked woman and prematurely ejaculating. *Holy fuck!* If I couldn't last long with her mouth over me, I wouldn't last a second buried deep inside her. She pulled herself up and sat on my lap again. She laid her head on my shoulder as she lazily drew imaginary circles along my chest and abdomen. Even though I had just come, my cock began to harden again. *Would I ever get enough of this woman?*

She quirked her eyebrows when she noticed me stirring again.

I laughed. "What can I say, Candy, I can't get enough of you."

She looked at me with a brief hint of sadness before she masked her gloom. "Please call me Candice. No one knows my real name in these rooms but you. I don't really want to hear my stage name anymore tonight."

That threw me for a loop. I smiled, more than happy to use her real name. It made the small amount of time I had with her seem that much more real. For my response,

I leaned forward and gave her a searing kiss. I nipped at her bottom lip. She moaned my fake name and I stopped.

"My real name is Forrest." Then I picked back up with tormenting her mouth and neck as I slipped my hand underneath her blouse.

She squirmed on my lap as I kneaded her breast. I continued to kiss along her neck and collarbone. I trailed my other hand to her jeans and unbuttoned them. She tilted her hips up and slid her jeans down. She conveniently forgot her panties. I sent a silent prayer of thanks to the big man upstairs. I gently stroked along her folds. Her legs opened wider so that I could easily slide my fingers along her silky pink folds. I dipped two fingers into her moist heat while my thumb rubbed her clit. She threw her head back in ecstasy. What I really wanted to do was replace my fingers with my cock. I wanted her so badly.

I continued to fuck her with my fingers as my lips and tongue made love to the rest of her body. I felt her tighten around my fingers as her orgasm pulsed through her. She moaned my name as she came. I gingerly slipped my fingers out of her and brought them to my mouth. I sucked her come off my fingers. "Delicious."

In a swift motion, she threw her legs over my hips and straddled me. Before I knew what she was doing, she slid onto my hard cock. She felt so good. Her body rocked back and forth and up and down. We both attacked each other. Our teeth clanged as we tried to devour each other.

"You are so wet and tight. I'm not going to last, Candice. Tell me you're close," I begged her. I wanted her to come one more time before I let my own release go.

"Yes, Forrest. Oh God. I'm coming," she gasped.

"Fuck," I growled.

I could feel her muscles tighten around me, gently coaxing my cock. The sweet torture had me come with such intensity that my hips pushed up forcefully and drove my cock even deeper. *Holy shit, she's trying to kill me.*

I kissed her sweetly as we both fell from our high. I cupped her face so she had to look me in the eye. I wanted her to see how crazy I was about her. Her eyes reflected the same emotions back.

That gave me the courage to ask, "Will you let me take you out on a date beyond this room?" Her silence was my answer. Before she could close the door on us, I said, "Please Candice. I don't want to keep coming to your work in order to get to know you. I know that you feel the same thing that I do. I think that we owe it to ourselves to find out what that is."

Candice shook her head, so I made one last-ditch effort.

"For the first time in my life, I have felt something real. I am not ready to throw it away. I enjoy coming here but we will get caught and I'll be banned. Most importantly, you will lose your job. Our time is almost up and you know that we can't be in here any longer than the allotted time. Logan seems to be an excellent observer and it won't take her long to figure it out. I can't keep doing this. Tonight is my last night here."

She kissed my mouth with such longing. I tasted her good-bye. I wanted to keep begging her but I had to hang onto what little pride I had left. I needed to hang on to it. I put everything on the line and she didn't want it.

"Thank you, Forrest, for what you have given me. I will cherish our time together. I need to keep my personal life separate from work. I met you at work, therefore I can't bring you home."

"Can't or won't?"

"Won't. I am sorry," she whispered, defeated.

I let her get up and fix herself before she left the room. Watching her turn and walk away without saying a word tore me up in more ways than I could've imagined. It took me a bit longer to pull myself together.

***

I threw my keys on the counter and kicked my shoes off. They landed haphazardly into the corner. Pissed, I wouldn't even touch the feelings that had me literally shaking with anger. I finally found someone I could see myself with long-term and she didn't want to be a part of that. Finally, I understood what Phoenix had talked about after he met Lucy. I always thought that what he said was a crock of shit. *Why her? Why now?* I was so confused. I wanted her more than I wanted my next breath.

The house I was excited about mere hours ago seemed as if it were a distant memory. The thought of living so close to Candice and unable to touch her gave way to thoughts of rage. I couldn't act as if nothing had happened between us. I could only imagine what would happen if I saw her with another man. I clenched my fists, ready to punch someone or something. *Fuck!* I needed to get control over myself. Losing my shit and punching the walls would not accomplish anything.

I held my breath and counted to ten. Slowly releasing the air helped. I no longer saw red. After a few hundred more deep breaths, I managed to grab hold of some rationality. For my sanity, I needed to walk away: away from her, this fucking town, and from these godforsaken crushing feelings.

7 CANDICE

Thankfully, Forrest was my last client of the night. There was no way that I could even attempt to see another client right after him. He turned me inside out. I knew going into the room as myself had been a bad idea but I couldn't stop myself. I didn't want to go in as Candy anymore. He brought out such carnal feelings that holding back with him would be pointless. I couldn't control myself around him. He would be so easy to fall in love with that it scared me.

I knew that if he didn't stop the appointments with me, I would be ruined at work. Even if Logan never suspected what went on behind those closed doors, I couldn't go and play coy with another man after being with Forrest. It felt wrong, as though I were cheating on him. I had never felt this intensely about a man or client; I'd never had to worry about how it would affect my job. After being with Forrest, it was obvious that being a stripper would no longer hold any interest for me.

I would have to either find another job——one that wouldn't come close to paying the bills——and have him, or keep stripping and let him go. When he asked me to see him outside of work, I wanted to say *hell yes* but I had to think about my daughter. *How would I support her if I couldn't return to my job and be one hundred percent focused?*

Another thing that held me back: what would happen when he left? He didn't come across as the type of guy who hung around for a long period of time. I mean he went to a strip club for entertainment, for goodness' sake. Commitment doesn't seem to register that high on his radar. I hated to assume anything about him but I couldn't rule the thoughts out either. When you worked in the club for a long time, you tended to become jaded.

What if Riley became attached to him? I had been so careful not to bring any guys home for her to meet. I don't want her to have to lose another man who she cared about. With her father out of the picture, it was imperative that I protect her from heartache. I really didn't date all that often or at all since my divorce. I put all of my time and energy into taking care of Riley and providing for us. That's why Rico came in handy! I would have to pull him back out now that I chose to walk away from Forrest. What a depressing thought. More importantly, I liked not having to answer to a guy. I could do what I want, when I want. I answered to no one. I don't have to worry about having backup when I disciplined Riley. What I say goes.

That was all good in theory but if I was honest with myself, I was lonely. I also wanted Riley to have a strong father figure like I have. She deserved to have two strong parents to raise her. All of these thoughts churning in my head had me restless. I couldn't seem to shut them down to sleep. I picked my book up, to try to escape. I put it back down, having no idea what I had just read.

***

I woke up feeling as if I had stayed out all night drinking. My tongue stuck to the roof of my mouth. The Mojave Desert couldn't be this dry. I had bags underneath my eyes and my head pounded. I haven't felt this bad since the night after my wedding. I can't really remember that night; it was all a blur. I wished last night was just as cloudy. After a nice hot shower, I felt almost normal. Some aspirin would fix the rest. I had a date with Lucy this morning.

I walked into Clyde's Bistro, grabbed our coffees, and waited for Lucy to stroll in. Forrest remained on my mind as Lucy plunked her vibrant self across from me.

"What's got you so pensive?" Lucy asked by way of greeting.

"Pensive? You sure are bringing out the big guns today. Are you dying? Is that why you are trying to clean up your language?"

She laughed at me as though I were crazy for asking such a question.

If you knew her like I did, you'd know that prior to Phoenix, her vocabulary was vulgar at its best.

"Hey, sugar breasts, what's got you so flipping tore up? Did a client urinate on your pasties?"

"Pasties? What the heck is that?" Lucy looked at me like I had hit my head or something.

Then all of a sudden, bam, it hit me. "Oh, crap. I get it now." I rolled my eyes at her and laughed. "That's better. Seriously, though, why the sudden change? It's driving me bonkers. I am not used to this cleaned-up version of you."

"It has nothing to do with Phoenix. He loved me before and he loves me now. I'm doing this for me."

"I call bullshit. What's the real reason?"

"Gage bet me five-hundred dollars that I couldn't go a month without using derogatory language. I intend on winning that bet, especially now that he is a big time pro MMA fighter." She laughed sadistically.

The gleam in her eye told me more than I needed to know. She was highly motivated to win the bet. The competition had grown fierce between the two of them. They had known each other for their whole lives.

***

Right before Gage moved to Vegas last year, she had told him that she loved him and asked him to stay. Well, you can see how that turned out. Gage went anyway. For a couple of months, they severed ties. During those months, Phoenix asked Lucy out and as they say, the rest is history.

From their separation, Lucy and Gage's friendship had only grown stronger. It became a force to be reckoned with. Phoenix, being a fairly secure man, hardly showed his jealousy over their relationship. After all, he got the woman he loved. He was secure in the knowledge that Lucy's romantic feelings for Gage were long gone.

***

It felt good to sit with my best friend and talk about the upcoming wedding as well as other trivial topics. I wanted to tell her about Forrest but there was nothing going on, so it was a moot point. We had been sitting in the bistro for so long that we ordered another coffee and a couple of muffins. I told her I would be at the golf course to help her get ready for her wedding. We hugged and went our separate ways.

My mom dropped Riley off not long after I walked through the door. She was one mass of energy. After a brief hug, she ran around and sang one of her favorite princess songs. Mom stayed long enough to give me her overnight bag. She kissed Riley good-bye. Out the door she bounced. I wasn't really in the mood to talk to her today anyway. I loved her but sometimes she was too perceptive for her own good.

"Momma, wook at this." Riley had grabbed her step stool and her princess wand. She made a grand production of stepping onto the stool and clearing her throat. I stifled a chuckle.

"Wet it go, wet it go, flying horses and dragons," she sang in her loudest voice. After that line continued multiple times in succession, she abruptly stopped.

She bowed. "Thank you. Thank you, vewy much."

I clapped enthusiastically and praised her for a beautiful performance.

***

Through dinner she proceeded to tell me in great detail her adventures over at YaYa and Pappa's house. She loved them to death. I was really lucky that they lived close by and took her on the weekends so that I could work. They never judged me for being a stripper. They treated it as any other respectable nine-to-five job. When anyone asked what I did for a living, they told the truth. They were proud of me no matter what. *What more could I ask for in parents?* They were my lifelines. I was grateful for them every day.

Once Riley had fallen asleep for the night, I indulged

in a nice, long bubble bath. The lavender oil, along with the warm water, helped relax my body. My thoughts automatically drifted to Forrest. I couldn't stop them from wondering what he was doing. *Was he thinking about me too?* It had only been one day since I had seen him but knowing that I never would broke my heart a little more.

It figured that the one guy I could see a future with turned out to be a client. I should say former client. *Could I see him and work at the club too?* When he asked, I was too scared to even think about it. Now that I had some time away from him, I thought that it might just be possible. The bigger issue now was how to contact him. *Shoot.* That's what I get for making rash decisions.

This week went surprisingly fast. Before I knew it, I walked into the clubhouse of the golf course. I carried my maid of honor dress over my shoulder. It was carefully nestled into its protective garment bag. With a toddler running around, you could guarantee that something tragic would happen to the beautiful dress. I didn't take any chances.

My parents had Riley. They would bring her by later. They would stay for dinner and then head back to their house until Sunday. For a change, I had the whole weekend off. I only asked my parents to keep Riley tonight. I would come get her in the morning but they insisted. Being the dutiful daughter that I am, I didn't argue. If they were watching her too much, my mother would tell me. They rarely went on vacation. They chose to spend most of their time with Riley. I felt slightly guilty over that.

I opened the door to the room designated for Lucy and me. She looked absolutely stunning. Lucy wasn't known for wearing dresses. She was a jeans and t-shirt kind of gal. Seeing her hair done in a loose fishtail and makeup made me get teary eyed. She sat on a padded bench and waited for me. She changed out of her tank and shorts and into her sexy lingerie. I helped her step into her wedding dress.

"You are always beautiful Lucy, but my God, you in this dress, takes my breath away. I know that your mom is looking down at this very moment with an obscene amount of pride."

"I love you, girl. Thank you. I needed to hear that. I miss her so much." She wiped her eyes, making sure she didn't smudge any of her mascara. "You and Riley are my family. Now get in your dress."

I slipped on the baby doll dress Lucy picked out for me. It was a tulle-lined dress swathed in an intricate garden of rosettes. I felt utterly feminine and sexy. Lucy wasn't a typical bride who picked out hideous dresses for her wedding party. I could look as gorgeous as I wanted and she wouldn't feel as though I stole her moment. Looking at Lucy in her dress and happy, no one could upstage her.

"You look gorgeous, Candice. That dress fits you perfectly."

"I love it. Thanks for not making me wear something hideous! This I can actually wear again!"

The closer we got to the ceremony, the more unglued Lucy seemed to become. I couldn't ease her nerves and everything I said seemed to make her more nervous. At that moment, I decided to head out of the room and directly to the bar. I made the bartender make up three different kinds of shots. I told him to make one sweet to get the first one down easily. The next two would range from a little harsh to can't feel your toes. I turned to take the drinks back and I ran into Forrest.

"What the fuck are you doing here?" I asked, surprisingly angry.

"Attending a wedding, the same as you," he joked.

"Well no shit, Sherlock. What side and relation?"

"Groom's brother." He snickered.

I sucked in a breath. I was glad I didn't mention him to Lucy. She would have immediately known who I was talking about. *Shit! Act normal.*

"My turn. What side and relation?"

I finally let go of the breath that I was holding in. Good thing, because I came dangerously close to passing out from my lack of oxygen. As my face slowly turned back to its normal color I answered, "Maid of honor. Lucy's best friend. Now, if you'll excuse me, I need to get back to the bride." I smiled as if I didn't give a shit one way or another.

I can't fucking believe my luck. Phoenix's damn brother. I had to be near him all night. He would drive me crazy before it was all said and done. Just bumping into him had my body tingling and my panties wet. I opened the door and brought the drinks in. I tried to shut down my inner turmoil but it didn't work very well.

"Okay, we have a Jolly Rancher to loosen you up and a Captain Coke to numb your nerves. Last but not least, the Mind Eraser to make you forget the last two!"

"Oh, my flipping goodness. I don't want to wobble down the aisle!" Lucy said, with just a hint of anxiety.

"Suck it up. We don't have much time. On the count of three: one-two-three." I picked up my shots one at a time and downed them like a professional. Lucy stared up at me in awe.

"How the hell did you do that and not puke all over me?"

"The verdict is still out. Now quit being a little bitch and get going," I told her with menacing glee.

I got a kick out of watching Lucy plug her nose to finish out the shots. She wasn't a heavy drinker so I knew that these shots would help relax her enough. All she needed to do was see Phoenix and she would have no trouble walking down that aisle. Lucy's uncles Sal and Enzo knocked on the door to let us know that it was time. I puttered around, fixing her dress, so that she wouldn't see the tears that pooled around my eyes. I knew if she saw me crying she would start. There was no time for a makeup malfunction.

I gave her a quick kiss on the cheek and told her I loved her. I started out the door ahead of them. We all lined up inside of the exit door to the veranda. Mendelssohn's "Wedding March" began. I slipped my arm through Forrest's outstretched arm. I felt as though I had finally come home. As we walked down the aisle to take our places, I had a brief fantasy. For a moment, I let myself believe that Forrest and I were the ones getting married. When he let go of my arm to stand beside Phoenix, my fantasy shattered like glass.

I stole a quick glance at Forrest. He caught me and smiled politely. I'm sure that he noticed the longing in my eyes. It was unbelievably hard to hide it. I sighed heavily. A flash of ivory caught my attention. I focused on the stunning beauty all but running down the aisle toward her future. Phoenix drank in the sight of his gorgeous bride. My heart twisted painfully when I thought of my lonely future. I smiled as I saw Riley clapping and yelling out how beautiful Lucy was. Riley had become my shining beacon, guiding me through the rough waters. She made my chosen isolation from men a little more bearable. I may not have Lucy's happily ever after but I did have a satisfying life.

The ceremony was quick and to the point. Lucy was not one to need fluff. She liked simple and to the point. Which made standing for the ceremony a breeze. Afterward, we witnessed them signing the marriage certificate and headed to the reception. Lucy and Phoenix made a beeline for the head table. They really weren't wasting any time in moving the reception along. They were equally eager to say their good-byes and hit their honeymoon. It surprised me that Lucy wanted a traditional wedding in the first place. She seemed more the justice of the peace or eloping kind of girl. I think she did it for her mother, even though she had passed away a couple of years ago. This would help her ease the pain of her mother's passing.

Dinner was excellent. Phoenix's restaurant, Luna, had prepared everything buffet style; fillet, chicken, potatoes au gratin, creamy spinach, sautéed asparagus, salad, and bread coated with honey butter filled the ivory-covered tables. Luna was a five-star restaurant. People came in droves just to taste the cuisine. Once the waitstaff had cleared the plates, I decided that it was time for our speeches.

I stood up and grabbed the microphone. I politely interrupted the crowd. "It's time for the maid of honor and best man speeches. Since I am the prettier one, I'll go first." Everyone laughed and then fell silent as I began to speak.

"My name is Candice Launer. Lucy is my best friend and savior. I have known Lucy, not for my whole life, but for the best part of my life. She always goes above and beyond to make sure everyone around her is happy, sometimes forgetting about herself in the process. She selflessly loves unconditionally. She is the godmother to my beautiful daughter Riley. She can cheer me up with a smile and her witty personality. She will literally give you the shirt off her back if you asked her. I should know because she has."

"I was sitting in the coffee shop in town, searching the classifieds. I wasn't paying attention to the lid when I raised my coffee to take a sip. Needless to say, I didn't realize that the lid wasn't on securely. The coffee spilled all over my nice button-down white blouse. I was completely mortified. My blouse was wet and stained with coffee. Before I could jump up to get a napkin, Lucy walked over to my table, and took off her sweatshirt and handed it to me. Never mind all of your perverted thoughts——she was wearing a tank top underneath. She was still modestly clothed. After I gave her a huge thanks, I asked her to join me. We have been inseparable ever since."

I took a calming breath as I looked over at Lucy and smiled with unshed tears in my eyes. I let them fall as I continued with my speech.

"When she met Phoenix, I saw her blossom into the stunning flower you see today. I know that I am not losing my best friend today but gaining a welcomed addition to our circle. Without further ado, please raise your glasses in congratulating Lucy and Phoenix. I love you, Lucy!"

"I love you, too, Candice." Lucy squeezed me tight.

I handed her the tissue from my bra so she could dab her nose. I sat back down and wiped the tears from my eyes as Forrest began his speech.

"Hello. My name is Forrest Walker. Phoenix is my baby brother as well as my best friend. Ever since Phoenix came home from the hospital, we have been joined at the hip. He is and has always been in my corner. He came back to college after a trip out here, just raving about a beauty with a trucker's mouth."

Laughter rang out to the truthfulness of his words. As the laughter died down, Forrest continued. "I couldn't believe that anyone such as this existed. To capture my brother's heart was no small feat. This woman sitting beside Phoenix most certainly did. I have to say that this is the first time that I have spent time with Lucy. To tell you the truth, she has captured mine as well. She swears better than any trucker I've ever met! Beautiful doesn't even do her justice. She is pure magic. Lucy, welcome to our family. I am one of many who can't wait for your lives to unfold. Let's raise our glasses one more time to congratulate my little brother and Lucy."

Phoenix stood to bro-hug his brother. I went to retrieve my tissue but had forgotten that I gave it to Lucy. As Forrest hugged his brother, he discreetly slipped me his handkerchief. He was being a gentleman to me, even though I had treated him poorly.

After the cake was cut, I snagged a double portion for myself. I cut another small piece for Riley. I sat down between Riley and my mother. I handed her the plate and she greedily dug in.

"Are you having a good time, baby?"

"Yes. T-Ti Wuce is so pwetty. She wooked just wike a pwincess."

I chuckled. "She certainly does and so do you."

We sat there enjoying our dessert and talking for a bit.

I gave her a kiss on her cheek and told her to be good for YaYa and Pappa. We gave our hugs. My dad carried a tired Riley out to the car. My mom blew me a kiss as she followed them out.

Lucy hugged me. "I want the details soon."

"What are you gibbering on about?"

"You'll see," she said secretively.

What the hell was she talking about? That's when I noticed Forrest walk toward me. *Damn it.* He looked as if he were on a mission. I looked around for someone, anyone, to save me. *Nada!* I had wasted precious minutes looking for a scapegoat so now I had no time to flee.

He sat down next to me. His cologne intoxicated my senses with his delicious scent. My breath hitched as I greedily inhaled him. His brow quirked as a smirk played along his skilled lips. He knew that his close proximity wreaked havoc on my body. I'm sure he could see my throbbing pulse beating double time along my neck. He hadn't touched me or said anything and I wanted to pounce. I used all the willpower I had to remain seated.

"Hello, Forrest. Are you having a good time?" I tried for nonchalant but sounded breathless instead.

"I am. Are you?" he asked in a husky voice.

"Yes, it is a lovely wedding."

He laughed boisterously. "Since you are being purposely brusque with your answers, maybe I can get your body to exchange more information with me."

I looked at him suspiciously.

"Come on, this won't hurt a bit," he teased.

He grabbed my hand and pulled me to the dance floor. The song had changed to a slow number. As he predicted, my body wouldn't shut up. What I couldn't say with words, my body conveyed easily, and without remorse. *Traitor!* We danced as one. Our bodies were very much in sync with each other. I sighed as I laid my head on his shoulder. My imagination couldn't have conjured up a better man. I should know. I spent many long nights fantasizing.

We moved silently along the dance floor. I looked up at him and became lost. Desire seeped from my body in heavy waves.

"I miss you," he whispered into my ear.

Goose bumps erupted all over my skin. "Take me home, Forrest."

He placed a kiss on my forehead and abruptly let go of me. I'm pretty sure he misconstrued the meaning of what I said. I didn't want to explain what I meant in front of everyone. I would just show him when we got back to my place. My body hummed with nervous energy. I had never brought anyone back to my home. It had become my sanctuary. I didn't want it tainted with thoughts of previous lovers. This time, I would break my rules. I wanted him in my house as well as my bed.

He retrieved my clutch from the table and led the way out to the car. He seemed distant even though I could easily have reached my hand out and touched him. I allowed him to continue to believe that I just needed a ride home. It gave me plenty of time to gather my senses. It also gave me the option to back out of my plan if I needed to at the last minute.

8 FORREST

Tension within the car lay heavy between us. The air grew thin and suffocating. I cracked open my window in order to let in the cool night air. I gripped the steering wheel so tight that my knuckles had turned white. I wanted to reach over and touch her in some manner but I knew if I did, I wouldn't let her go. She demanded that I take her home. I didn't have to but I didn't want anyone else to either. For a brief moment, I thought that we had connected again. Her body sent me a plethora of powerful messages. I had hoped that once I got Candice to shut her mind off and just feel, I could sway her to change her mind about us.

I had a hard time wrapping my mind around the fact that she had a daughter. I would never have imagined that she had a kid. It made more sense for her to break off any potential relationship than the excuse she gave me at the club. Dating a client could make her job more stressful, especially if they were the jealous type. I wasn't but I guess she wouldn't know that. It's not as if we had heartfelt conversations the moments we did see each other.

My mind seemed caught in a whirlwind of thoughts

as we pulled into her drive. I shut the car off and went to open up her door. I could be mad as a rattlesnake and still act like a gentleman. She stepped out of the car gracefully. Her long legs ate up the distance to her door. I put my hands in my pockets to keep them from pulling her into me. She unlocked the door and stepped partly into the entryway.

I looked up at her. "Good night, Candice. You looked stunning tonight. I'm glad that I had one more opportunity to see you." I turned to walk away but stopped when she spoke.

"Come inside, Forrest. Have a drink with me before you go."

I must have had a stunned expression on my face because she laughed heartily at me.

"I won't bite, I promise. That is, unless you want me to," she said coyly.

I must have entered the twilight zone because her behavior was fucking bizarre. Either that or she was a tad on the crazy side. Which, I really couldn't rule out. I stood at a life-changing intersection: forward into the arms of a woman who made me feel or turn around back to a lonely existence. I hesitated for a moment. *Fuck it*. I followed her the rest of the way in.

I didn't let her get far. I wasn't in the mood for a drink. I grabbed her arm and spun her around and into my body. She fit seamlessly against me. I gently lifted her chin up so she had to look at me.

"Are you sure that this is what you want? If we go forward, the next time you try to kick me to the curb, it won't be so easy."

"Okay," she answered breathlessly.

I smiled as I placed a gentle kiss to her lips. The kiss turned scorching in a matter of seconds. I picked her up and carried her to the bedroom.

I set her feet back on the floor and slowly undressed her. Her skilled fingers attempted to unbutton my shirt but I lightly swatted her hands away. I was in control tonight. I unzipped the skimpy dress and let it fall to the floor. She stood before me timidly in a white lacy bra and a hi-cut thong. She was adorable and sensual as she stood on display for me. I wanted to take my time soaking her in but I couldn't wait. I needed her with a desperation that I had never felt before. In one swift motion, I picked her up and tossed her on the bed. She let out a squeal of delight.

I pounced on top of her. "Sorry, baby. I'm going to give us both a quick release. Next time, I'll make sure we take our time. I can't wait any longer to be inside you," I growled.

"Shut up and take me." Staking her claim, she bit my lip.

I didn't even pull my pants past my knees. Just low enough to be free to slip inside of her wet heat. I was no gentleman. I took her fast and hard. When my orgasm drew near, I circled her clit and we peaked at the same time.

I landed heavily on her. As our breathing slowed, I rolled off her and tucked her into my side.

"I needed that." Candice laid her head on my shoulder and wrapped her arm and leg around me.

"Glad to be of service." I chuckled. She swatted my chest playfully. I didn't want to ruin the mood but we had to discuss an important detail she forgot to mention. "So you have a daughter, huh?" I know——not very eloquent but how do you broach this type of topic postcoitally? You just spit it out, that's how.

She sighed heavily. "Look, Forrest, I didn't mention her because it wasn't necessary. Not to mention those types of conversations do not take place at the club. It's my personal business. You were a client, not my boyfriend. This thing between us is not serious; there is no need to involve my daughter. If or when our relationship becomes more serious then you can meet her, but not until then. This is not open for further discussion."

Her tone made it very clear that I wouldn't be a fixture in Riley's life at this point. I had a hard time rationalizing the need for me to be. Until I knew for sure that I would stay put, I would not try to change her mind. I still felt slighted but understood that she didn't want Riley hurt.

Her chest heaved and her nostrils flared. I wished it were from sexual tension. She was getting pissed. So I did what any sane man in my position would: I distracted her. I kissed from her neck down to her toes, purposely avoiding her intoxicating pussy. I let her squirm before I indulged in her silent pleas. I made sure I left no piece of her silky skin untouched before I slipped inside her. Our moans of desire grew with every thrust. Fuck, I could stay in her tight pussy forever.

We managed to get out of bed long enough to eat something and quickly return. Of course, after we had tested every hard surface in the house. Two blissful days in her company wouldn't be nearly enough. My typical MO was a wham, bam, thank-you ma'am. However, the more time I spent with her, the harder it became to leave. Riley was due home in a couple of hours so I had to leave. I really wanted to meet her but knew it wasn't wise. This was neither the place nor the time. Not now but soon. I gave her a saucy kiss and told her I'd give her a call later.

I wanted to head over to my brother's house and talk to him but he was gone on his honeymoon. *Damn it.* Instead, I headed back to the old Victorian. I walked around it one more time, hoping to find some kind of answer as to what my future held. I couldn't remember a time where I felt indecisive and unsure of where I was heading. I felt close to panicking. Which, in my line of work, would get you killed. This did not ease my mind about future assignments. *Shit! If I couldn't do my job, what the hell would I do?* I had plenty of money saved but not nearly enough for early retirement.

I sat on the rickety step and put my head between my legs as if my life depended on it. Finally, the roaring that filled my ears had eased enough for me to gain some semblance of control back. I stood up slowly so I didn't get dizzy and headed to my car. Then it hit me, like a bolt of lightning. My body froze for a moment. I turned back around to face the Victorian as though it had called my name. I smiled as though the old house had whispered its secrets.

I drove straight to the realtor's office. I went to step out of the car and remembered it was Sunday. No way in hell would that greasy bastard be here. I left him a quick voicemail, telling him to call me first thing Monday morning. I wanted to call Candice but would wait until everything was in place. Our relationship was too new to reveal anything remotely serious.

Who the hell was I kidding? I had already picked up the phone and dialed. Before I could change my mind and hang up, she answered.

"Hello?" she asked hesitantly.

"Hey, beautiful. Long time no talk!"

"It's only been an hour. You miss me already?"

I swallowed as her voice dipped an octave and went husky. I looked down at my pants and sure enough, my favorite appendage stood at attention. *Down, boy! It's just her voice.* My dick couldn't comprehend that piece of info. Shit, her voice alone drove my loins wild.

"I do. I'm not sure if I'll be able to last until this weekend without seeing you," I said honestly.

Somehow she had wormed her way in. I teetered the fence line, contemplating a serious relationship. But, she had a kid to worry about. Hell, I wasn't sure I could do commitment, let alone become a father. I had to derail this train of thought; it went nowhere. I kept stressing myself out for no reason. It's not as if she made any demands. *I was the one who called her!*

Candice cut into my thoughts. "I have to work this weekend. I won't be home until late both nights. I'm not sure that I'll be able to see you."

"Well, what if I pick you up Saturday afternoon and we go get some lunch? I promise to have you home in time for your shift."

She became silent. "Okay. That will work. Riley stays with my parents on the weekends while I work and my mom brings her home on Sunday. This way I won't have to answer a bunch of questions or introduce you to Riley."

Excitement bounced its way through my chest cavity until I realized what she had said about me meeting Riley. I had to admit I wasn't ready to meet her either but fuck!

Did she have to put it as though I were a secret? I slapped myself upside the head. *Slap on a dress and call me Nancy.* I was being a freaking girl. Worrying about stupid girly nonsense right now. I needed to slow down. There wasn't any hurry.

***

I walked into my rental and threw the car keys on the kitchen table. I turned on the TV for some noise. I didn't enjoy the quietness. I wanted to talk to Phoenix but he had to go on a stupid honeymoon. What a loser! Boredom came knocking and sat comfortably on my shoulder. This has been the longest down time I've ever had. I didn't know what to do with myself. I sat down at the computer and started to draw up some plans for the house. Without an inspection, I wasn't completely sure what would have to be fixed. I could make an educated guess: just about everything. I could do some of the minor repairs but I would have to hire someone to handle the major ones. I couldn't explain why I felt the need to invest my time into a project that I might not undertake.

9 CANDICE

After I hung up with the ever-persistent Forrest, my mom and Riley walked through the door.

"Did you have a relaxing time this weekend?" My mom gave me a peck on the cheek.

"I did. Thank you again, for keeping Riley. I enjoyed not having to do anything!" I lifted Riley onto my lap and squeezed her tight as I rained kisses all over her.

She squealed with delight. "No mowe, Momma. I too big foe that now." She wiggled out of my grasp and ran to her room to play. It pained me to know that soon she wouldn't need me anymore.

"She will always need your love." My mom echoed my inner turmoil.

"I know that. It's just that she is growing up too fast for my liking."

"They all do. I still miss those days with you sometimes. Riley helps to ease the emptiness."

"Mom? You and Dad should be traveling and enjoying your retirement. Why aren't you?"

"Honey, we are enjoying it. We don't need to go anywhere at the moment and if we want to, we will." She placed her hands over top of mine. "You are not holding us back. We love to keep Riley. So you can just get that right out of your head."

She knew me too well. That's exactly what I alluded to. Mom usually doesn't stay long after she drops Riley off, but today she did. She had a good knack for knowing when I needed to talk. A good quality conversation was long overdue.

Riley rushed into the kitchen with her tea set, demanding a tea party. Mom took her leave as Riley set the table. While Riley occupied herself, I ran to get the boas and tiaras.

"We need to be properly dressed for our tea party." I held out a boa and a tiara. Riley clapped her hands gleefully. She snatched the pink boa from my arm and wrapped it around her shoulders. I gently laid the tiara on her head. "For the beautiful princess." And then I bowed.

"Thanks, Mommy." She purred her appreciation.

I wanted to squeeze her tight but if I did, she'd say that I babied her. Teatime was serious business. Conducting ourselves like true princesses was extremely imperative.

Tea corresponded well with lunch. We sat at her little white table with pink and blue chairs, while we ate hot dogs smothered in ketchup. We drank lemonade in the tiniest cups known to man. My fingers could barely hold the handle as I sipped. I wouldn't pick up her spilled drink; this time, it would be mine. *Slippery little suckers.*

I looked over at my sweet baby and busted out laughing.

"What so funny, Momma?"

"You have ketchup smeared all over your cute face." I reached over to wipe her chin. She promptly swatted my hand away.

"I'm saving that foe latah."

"Okay, baby, if you say so." I couldn't help but chuckle. It was a complete mystery as to where she had heard that saying. Not! I bet a dollar that it had come from Lucy.

When we finished lunch, I decided that we needed to get out of the house for a while. "Hey, baby, you want to go to the park for a bit?"

"Yes. yes, and yes," she shrieked with joy.

"Alrighty. I'll grab the water while you get your shoes on."

"Okay, Momma." Her feet slapped against the tile as she ran to get her sneakers.

I strapped my now hyper child into her car seat.

"Momma, don't foget to put the belt on."

"Thanks for reminding me. I won't." I turned around in my seat and smiled lovingly at her.

She was too smart for her little britches. The park wasn't far, only a couple of blocks from the house. We could have walked but it would be late by the time I dragged her away from the slide. I didn't mind the walk, but with her father potentially lurking around, I didn't want to run into him.

I parked the car and unbuckled Riley. She ran as fast as her little legs would carry her. I loved this playground. It was small and not many people used it. It had just enough equipment to keep Riley entertained. I sat on the most uncomfortable metal bench that faced the slides. Riley spent most of her time sliding. For hours, all you would hear was her sweet voice yelling at me to watch her. When she got tired of going down the slide, she would run over to me and grab my hands and pull me toward the swings.

"Push me higha, Momma."

"You got it. One underdog coming right up." She never really got the true underdog but she would giggle every time I did it.

The swings didn't hold her attention for long. If she couldn't do something on her own, she would abandon the one thing she needed help with pretty quickly. Riley didn't like having to ask for my help. She was at that stage where she liked to do everything herself.

As I watched her run, the back of my neck broke out in goose bumps. I scanned the play area to look for someone or something that seemed out of place. I didn't see any animals and we were the only ones here. I walked around the playground as I tried to keep my eye on Riley. For the life of me, I couldn't spot or see anything out of the ordinary. *What the hell was giving me the creeps?* I started to panic. My skin began to crawl and I had an insane desire to grab Riley and run.

I didn't want to scare her but we needed to leave right now. "Come on, baby. It's getting late. We need to get home," I called to her as I walked back toward the slide.

She didn't answer me and I couldn't hear her little

squeals. As I picked up my pace, I called to her again. "Riley. Answer me now." Silence was my only answer. I picked up into a run as I shouted for her. "RILEY. Where are you?" *God, please let her still be there and okay.* A million thoughts ran through my panicked mind. *Where could she have gone? I only looked away for a split second.*

Damn it. The park was not that big. I could see all sides of it, no matter where I stood. I came up to the slide, still shouting for her. There——I saw her legs. *What the hell is going on?* I moved in front of the slide. There she lay safe and sound, staring up at the sky with her hands placed behind her head. Waves of anger rolled off me.

"Riley, why didn't you answer me? You scared Mommy. I thought something bad had happened to you." I was breathing heavily from my mini marathon, but mostly fear.

"I was being weally quiet. I didn't want to scawe the cloud away. Isn't it pwetty?" She looked up at me with those big baby blues and pointed her chubby finger at the sky.

My anger slowly receded. Relief filled my lungs and I exhaled the rotten feeling of fear.

"Yes, baby, it is but next time please let me know where you are when I call you. I was really scared."

"I pwomise, Mommy."

I gathered her little body into my arms and inhaled her sweet powdery smell. She wrapped her soft body around me. Even with my eyes closed, the adrenaline continued to flow through me. I carried her to the car with my heart still pounding in my chest like a runaway freight train. Total relaxation would be a long time coming.

***

I breathed a sigh of relief as I eased my body into the hot bath water. After only one story, Riley fell fast asleep. Now that she was tucked in, I let my mind wonder over the feeling that I had gotten in the park, right before I thought I had lost Riley. My skin crawled, as though someone were watching me. I couldn't describe the sensation; it had come on out of the blue. I shrugged it from my mind. It wasn't worth trying to figure it out. Everything had turned out fine. Since I couldn't explain it, so I washed it away, along with the bubbles in the tub.

I slipped into bed right as my cell phone lit up.

"Hello," I answered lazily.

"Hello, beautiful. How was your day?"

His voice brought a smile to my lips. I hadn't realized how much I missed him until I heard his sexy voice. I sighed and wished that I were snuggled into his hard body. "It was good until it wasn't."

"Want to talk about it?" Forrest said with concern.

"I just feel like I got the mother of the year award presented to me" I joked.

"Mother of the year award?"

"Yeah. It's an imaginary award given to moms who do stupid shit."

He laughed huskily. "Really? I am not aware of such an award nor why you would be given one. I know you are a great mom."

His sincerity made me crave his strength. Pain

punched me right in the heart at my stupidity. "I thought I lost Riley at the park today. I got this really weird feeling. I got caught up searching for the reason and momentarily took my eyes off her." I took a deep breath and continued my embarrassing rant. "When I couldn't figure out why, I called for her. Multiple times, I yelled her name but she never answered me back. I couldn't see her and I panicked. I was terrified, Forrest. She never moved. I am her mother; she is my responsibility and I failed. Oh God, Forrest, what if somebody had taken her?" I took in a deep breath, trying to control my emotions. I was on the verge of tears.

"Baby, please don't beat yourself up over this. It could have happened to anybody. Remember that she is safe and tucked into her bed, none the wiser."

"Don't let me off the hook that easily. It very well could have turned out differently."

"But it didn't. You are a wonderful and loving mother——focus on that. Now, tell me about what got you all scared prior to that."

I ran my hands through my hair and lay back on my pillow. "I really don't know. It was just a feeling I got. Something wasn't right. My skin broke out in goose bumps and I had an eerie feeling. I can only describe it as though something or someone were watching us. Forrest, we were the only ones in the park. It's a small park connected to an elementary school. It's open to the public but most of the time it's empty."

He didn't say anything for a minute. "Are you still there?" I asked.

"Yes. I am thinking."

"You believe me, right?"

"Absolutely. I trust my instincts and you should too. I am just as stumped about what made you feel uneasy as you did."

"I didn't stick around. As soon as I found Riley, we left. Once we were home, the feeling went away."

"Promise me the next time you visit the park or get that feeling again, you will call me."

"Yes I promise I will."

"I wish I were there to hold you."

"Me too," I whispered.

"Candice?" he asked uncertainly.

"Yeah."

"I can be there in less than ten minutes. I promise to leave early enough so Riley doesn't know that I was there."

"I'll leave the door unlocked. Please hurry. I need you."

I snuggled deeper into my covers and waited for Forrest. I couldn't believe that I allowed him to come over. I was a total fool. I couldn't resist him and I didn't want to. This man had the potential to severely break my heart. I heard the front door open and his footsteps come up the stairs. He would be worth every broken piece.

Forrest stopped in the doorway and gazed at me. I was completely covered and still his eyes roamed all over me. He made me feel as though I were the most beautiful woman in the world. The predatory look in his eyes made my body hum with anticipation. He slowly walked to the other side of the bed and stripped. I licked my lips at the sight of his washboard abs and strong, muscular arms. He drew back the covers and pulled me into him.

He kissed me passionately. He held onto me as though I were made of porcelain. He gently unwrapped me as though I were a cherished gift. Forrest worshiped my body adoringly.

I lay curled into his side, feeling exquisitely treasured. "I'm glad you came over tonight. I've missed you."

"Me too. Thank you for allowing me to come over." He kissed my forehead as I lay my head on his chest. "Sleep beautiful. I will keep you safe."

10 FORREST

I laid awake most of the night, gazing at Candice. She fit perfectly into my folded arms. Her curves nestled seamlessly along my body. Electric currents shot along my limbs, straight to my heart. I had the strongest urge to make sure that she and Riley were always protected.

* * *

Protecting people came naturally to me. I literally fell into the line of work. I was at the right place and time and saved a high-profile individual from a potentially fatal gunshot wound. A team of skillfully trained private security surrounded him but the gunman had found a tiny hole. I easily could have been shot from the private security as well as the gunman. Once I saw the tiny red dot, my reflexes took over.

I became immediately drawn to the thin red line of the laser. My eyes followed the threadlike beam right to the barrel of the gun. The gunman's position was only a couple of feet from me. I twisted my body to the right and lunged for the man. My right hand cuffed the assailant's wrist and knocked the gun out of his unstable hands. While he was momentarily stunned, I used my momentum to throw us both to the ground. I landed on him hard. His breath whooshed out of him, freezing him on his back. While he was immobile, I flipped him onto his stomach, brought both of his wrists behind him, and jammed my knee into his back. I leaned all of my weight onto him until the bodyguards rushed to my aid. One of the bodyguards secured the firearm. The others took over securing the guy.

I was held in interrogation for hours, with nothing much to say except for what little I saw and what happened afterwards. No matter how they tried to spin it, my story held up. Between the eyewitness accounts and my own, it was evident that I did not work with the assailant. I later learned that the guy I saved was Grey Larson, a business tycoon.

He offered me a job as one of his bodyguards. He put me through rigorous training. Apparently, I had surpassed his expectations. Six months after I signed on with his hired guards, he demanded that I become his personal bodyguard. I stayed with Mr. Larson for four years before I decided to become a freelance bodyguard. After my stint with him, I became one of the most sought-out bodyguards and I loved every minute of it up until this last mission.

***

I shook off the memories. I didn't want to relive my last mission. It was best left under lock and key. So I shoved it back into the recesses of my mind. I didn't want this night with Candice tainted. I wasn't sure when I would be able to hold her all night again. I wanted to savor this night. Morning would come soon enough.

I awoke before dawn. Candice had wrapped her entire body around mine. Her long limbs snaked around me like an anaconda wrapped around its prey. I contorted my body every way I could think of but couldn't escape. I wasn't trying that hard. She was strong but in my arms she felt more like fine china, exquisitely beautiful and treasured. The more I moved, the more I became aroused. *Shit!* I didn't want to wake her up. She looked so peaceful and I didn't know when Riley would make an appearance.

It became increasingly more difficult to keep my touch platonic. At first, my hands cautiously trailed over her soft skin, gently trying to wake her. She was deliciously naked which further complicated my current arousal. I placed a kiss on her forehead and whispered in her ear. She stirred, murmuring in her half-awakened state, and rubbed her body along mine. In my mind, I knew she wasn't deliberately trying to turn me on. My body, however, had already short-circuited. All of my blood flowed directly south.

"Baby. You need to turn over so that I can go."

"No. Don't leave. So comfortable."

I laughed. "Seriously, you need to move over. It's almost morning."

She mumbled something incoherently and rolled over. Her perfectly round ass rubbed against my throbbing cock. I choked back a groan. I needed to move from this bed right now. Instead, I reached my hand over her luscious ass. She moaned and squirmed from the contact, driving my need for her into a burning inferno.

She subconsciously pushed her ass into my hands as I caressed her curves. Little breathless sighs escaped her lips, urging my hands to continue their journey. I massaged both of her cheeks as I made my way down. She voluntarily rolled onto her stomach and spread her legs. Her shaved pussy glistened. It beckoned me. Her head moved to the side and over her arms. Coquettishly, she smiled at me.

I slowly moved over her and kissed my way down her back. I licked down her spine as her ass pushed up into my chest. Her squirming drove me wild. I had to taste her.

"Get on your knees, baby." She did as I asked without question.

I grabbed onto her hips and lifted her higher. She opened to me, completely dripping wet. I licked her moist folds and drove my tongue into her pussy. She cried out as my tongue fucked her. I could feel her walls tighten. I stopped right before she could orgasm.

"Forrest. Don't stop. That feels so good." She whimpered.

I couldn't if I wanted to. She tasted heavenly. I flipped her onto her back and spread her legs as wide as they would go. I gazed up at her and almost came from how sexy she looked. Her eyes were glazed and hooded. Her chest heaved, pushing her ample breasts out. Her cheeks flushed to a rose color. Her tongue darted out and licked the bottom of her lip. I took one last long swipe along her pussy, savoring her sweetness, before I pushed my throbbing cock inside her.

She cried out as I thrust into her. "Harder, Forrest."

I lifted her legs onto my shoulders, elevating her hips, and delved deeper. She bit her bottom lip as her walls tightened, milking my cock. She dug her nails into my back as she came.

I couldn't hold out any longer. "Fuck, Candice," I hissed. I placed soft kisses along her neck and gently brushed my lips over hers. "I don't want to leave you but I need to go before Riley gets up." I kissed her again. "I'll come back in a couple of hours with breakfast. How does that sound?"

"Sounds incredible. Donuts and coffee from Clyde's?"

"For you, anything." I got up quietly and slipped on my clothes. I silently padded down the stairs and let myself out the door. I grinned the whole way to my car.

It was too early for the coffee shop to be open so I drove home. I took a shower, hating the fact that I wiped Candice's scent from my body. I donned some well-worn jeans and a sweatshirt and headed to the coffee shop.

I arrived at Clyde's just as they were opening up. Being the first customer granted me the freshest donuts. *Shit. How does she like her coffee?* I could call her. Nah, I'd take an educated guess. With her personality, she probably liked it hot and sweet. As for the donuts, I got a dozen assorted. I didn't know a lot about kids but with chocolate icing or jelly filled, at least one of those would be a winner.

I pulled into the drive and grabbed the breakfast. As I walked up the drive, the hair on the back of my neck stood at attention. I did a cursory glance but saw nothing out of the ordinary. I wasn't at all familiar with her neighborhood, so I couldn't really rely on that alone.

Something caused my unease. I just didn't know what or who it was. Adrenaline coursed through my body as I walked up to the door. I wanted to make sure that my body language stayed neutral. No sense tipping off whatever was out there. I wouldn't alarm Candice just yet.

I would remind her when I left to keep the house locked up at all times, even while she was home.

I rang the doorbell with my elbow. While I waited for Candice to come to the door, I tried to formulate a plan for keeping them safe. The door swung open and the sexiest rumpled blonde stood before me. I wanted to immediately grab her, throw her over my shoulder, and hightail it upstairs. *Who was I kidding, that was way too far. The wall inside the entryway would work nicely!* "Good morning, beautiful."

She smiled shyly at me. "Morning."

I loved that her voice had dipped an octave and turned husky. Her nipples had hardened and became so stiff they were trying to tear through her thin tank top. Lord help me, she wasn't wearing a bra. The need to kiss her soft plump lips turned out to be overwhelming. Claiming her mouth was only a fraction of what I conveyed. Naughty promises filtered through as I slipped my tongue past her soft lips.

Using all of the willpower that I possessed, I severed the connection before I lost all sense of control. I had to think of Riley now.

The pitter-patter of little feet running toward me echoed in the small entryway. Candice opened the door wider so that I could come in. The cutest little blonde-haired, blue-eyed, little girl skidded to a stop right behind her mother She wrapped herself around Candice's leg, squeezing with all of her strength. She peeked at me from around her mother's leg but didn't release her hold.

I bent down so that I was level with Riley. "Hi. My name is Forrest. I'm a good friend of your mommy. It's nice to meet you. Will you tell me who this beautiful princess is?" I pointed to her so she knew I meant her.

She unlatched herself and walked right in front of me. She squinted her tiny eyes, angled her head to the side, and examined my face. I had no idea what she was searching for. I waited for her to find the answer.

A huge toothy grin spread across her face. "I'm Wiley. Nice to meet you, Fowwest." She held out her small pudgy hand. My larger hand swallowed hers up as we shook.

She looked up at her mommy for praise. Candice did not disappoint her. "Riley, that was such a grown-up way of introducing yourself. I am so proud of you." She picked her up and swung her around. "Come on, baby. Let's wash our hands up for breakfast. Forrest was nice and brought us donuts." She set Riley down.

"Yes." She pumped her hands into the air and did a little jig on the way to the sink.

I laughed heartily. "She is smart and sweet, just like her mother."

"Already trying to brown-nose me, Mr. Walker?"

"Is it working?"

"I'll never tell."

"Seriously. She is cute as hell and I can see what a ball of energy she is. She's really smart for her age. I don't know a lot of children to compare her to but she is pretty articulate for her age. You should be proud of yourself for that."

Candice caught me by surprise; she turned in to me and kissed me. "Thank you."

"Welcome. Now let's eat. I'm starving." I winked at her.

We sat at the table and ate our donuts. I had guessed right about the coffee and beamed brightly at having guessed correctly. Score! Major points in my favor. Riley grabbed two of the jelly-filled donuts. She split one of the donuts in half.

She stuck her finger in the middle and scooped up a bunch of jelly. "Yummy. I wuv jelly. Thank you, Fowwest."

"You are most welcome. Me, too, but I love the maple nut frosting ones better." Candice and I both grabbed for the maple nut. "I relinquish the donut to you for this one time. Next time I won't be so nice."

"You shawed. I'm so pwoud of you, Fowwest."

I chuckled. "Thank you, Riley. It is nice to share, isn't it?"

"I don't like to but Mommy says it is."

I laughed so hard that I spit out some coffee. I received tiny fairy giggles from Riley and a deep, husky laugh escaped Candice's potent mouth. Even if it were at my expense, I would take Riley and Candice's sweet laughter every time. I vowed that before I left, I would do a bunch of dumb shit just to hear them.

We played rescue the princess. How I got roped into sitting in the ivory tower (couch cushion) with a purple tiara on is a mystery. Riley, of course, was the prince, slaying dragons. Candice tried to play too, but Riley had none of it. "I play with Fowwest wight now. I play with you wata."

Candice laughed, threw up her hands in defeat, and slinked off. "He is all yours, Riley. I'm going to go get ready. Play nice, you two. I don't want to have to put anyone in a time-out."

"We will. I pwomise!" She was so serious that I had to hide my grin when she turned back around. "Okay. Now scweam so I can save you."

"Argh."

"No, that's too low. You have to scweam wike a gwil."

I chuckled. "Help me. I need a prince to save me," I cried in the highest pitch I could squeal.

"I'm hewe, Fowwest. I save you."

"Ah. Thank goodness, you found me. I am forever in your debt. Please take my hankie, kind sir." I handed her a dishtowel.

"Thank you. I will chewwish it fowevea."

I bent over and placed a kiss to her plump cheek. "My hero." She became real silent for so long that I thought I had hurt her feelings somehow. I was about to apologize when she flashed me one of her megawatt grins.

"Let's play blocks."

I sighed heavily, glad that she wasn't hurt from something I said. "Lead the way."

We spent the better part of the morning playing and I was reluctant to leave. However, I didn't want to intrude on whatever plans Candice had for the day. I gave Riley back the blocks that I used to build with. "Okay, princess,

I have to get going."

"No—stay!" Riley grabbed my hands to prevent me from standing up. *Brilliant move!* This kid had already won me over today. She just tipped the scales to one hundred percent and owned me with that restraint trick.

I looked over at Candice for help. She just chuckled and shook her head. "You're a big boy. You handle it."

"How about I come back tomorrow? If it's okay with your mom, then I'll take you to the park?"

"Mommy, pease say yes. Pwetty pease."

She looked absolutely adorable. Her lips pouted as she jumped up and down. It was a cross between a potential tantrum and Disney World excitement. In the near future, she will have perfected the well-known pout. The word would become her playground.

"Pretty please." I aided Riley's cause. I even threw in some eyelash batting for a grander effect.

Candice's laughter rang throughout the living room. Music to my ears. "Alright, you two quit ganging up on me. Yes, you can go to the park with Forrest tomorrow." We both hooted and hollered. "One more thing before you guys get too excited. I'm going too. I'm not so sure that I should leave you two alone yet. I see major trouble in your future."

"We pwomise to behave and not get into any twouble. Pinkie pwomise." The both of us held out our pinkies and we shook on it.

I looked at Riley. "No troublemaking. We made a pretty serious promise. Pinkie promises cannot be broken."

"Yep. I only use it when I won't bweak it."

God help me, this child was incredible.

11 CANDICE

After Forrest left, Riley bounced off the walls, chanting *Forrest did this* and *Forrest did that.* I hadn't heard her talk this much about anyone else, except for Lucy. Lucy was her favorite person and after today I'm convinced that Forrest ran a close second. Which scared the crap out of me. *What happens to Riley if we don't make it?* She'd lose another male figure in her life. I really fucked this situation up. My hormones have officially kidnapped my brain cells. The sudden piercing pain in my heart told me that there'd be no way that I could walk away from him. I would have to tread lightly.

I walked Riley over to Evonne's and then headed into work, dragging my feet. Unfortunately, the bills didn't pay themselves Tonight I worked the stage and the floor. I didn't have the energy to hustle tonight. I sighed heavily as I got ready for my shift.

Tonight I wore a purple thong, see-through matching bra, and sky-high silver stilettos. The bass pumping out of the speakers pulsated through my body as I stepped out of the dressing room. This would be a long night. Even the music couldn't jolt my enthusiasm. Reaching into my reserves, I marched out onto the stage and waited for my

cue. "Hopelessly Devoted To You" by Dubstep played
and I stepped onto the dimly lit stage.

I exaggerated my steps toward the pole. I pointed my
toes out as a ballerina glides along the stage floor. I walked
around the chrome beam and extended my legs, and then
abruptly brought them back, until my back butted up
against the hard metal. The coolness of the metal sent
shivers down my spine. The lights brightened as the lyrics
seductively serenaded the patrons. I inhaled deeply, pushed
my breasts out, and my ass into the pole. I slowly slid
down the pole and bent at the knee. I pushed back up the
length of the pole. My hands caressed the cold metal as
they journeyed above my head. I tossed my long hair to
the side and picked up my legs from the floor. I held onto
the pole with my hands as I used my body to maneuver a
snake-like slither while suspended in the air.

I could hear the catcalls from the gentlemen in the
crowd. I drew them to me like moths to a flame. I stared
straight ahead, never looking at any one particular patron.
As the music's beat pulsated throughout the room, I
gyrated around the pole as though a seasoned acrobat. In
many ways, I was. It took strength and grace to move my
body around the pole sensually.

The song beat halfway through; I moved into a split
with my hands on the pole between my legs, and twirled
my body slowly around and around until I touched the
floor. As the song wound down, I slid to the floor on my
knees. I tossed my head back and touched my body as I
made love to the surface of the stage.

I turned over onto my back and pushed my shoulders
into the floor. My ribs jutted into the air and my hips
hooked onto the floor as though it were an anchor. I
stayed in that position for the last seconds of the song.
With my act finished, I got up and gathered the money

that lay strewn across the stage.

I can't say that the evening flew by but it sure didn't drone on like I thought it would. I put my street clothes back on. I needed a foot massage after wearing the devil's heels all night. Before I drove off, I sent a text to Forrest.

How about another sleepover?

He immediately responded.

Definitely. Call me when Riley is down for the night.

K.

I smiled to myself. She should already be in bed by now. Evonne usually took her back to my house after she ate dinner so that Riley could sleep in her own bed. I wouldn't have to wake her up to take her home. Their routine ran as smoothly as clockwork. This would give me the time that I needed to take a quick shower before Forrest arrived.

Feeling slightly normal, I pulled on my most comfortable pajamas. I would not seduce Forrest. That's what I did all night to strangers for money. I wanted him to see the average daily me. So my nightwear consisted of an oversized tee shirt, with comfortable panties, and no bra. The butt floss torturous panties were mainly worn for work and the occasional going-out type dress. Thongs, along with heels, were highly overrated.

Just as I was getting ready to send Forrest a text, the text box lit up.

I'm in the driveway. Let me know when the coast is clear.

Someone's eager. You are a little early, aren't you?

By my calculations, I'm a few years late.

Butterflies instantly sprang into action. My insides were in utter chaos. My body coiled tightly with anticipation and resounding need. *Would it always be like this?* I didn't have time to dwell on the fact that I couldn't answer that question. I flicked on the porch light and opened up the door. Forrest quietly shut the car door and strolled toward me. He stopped midstride and just stared at me.

Thank goodness for the porch light that illuminated his facial features. Otherwise, I would have assumed that his hesitation was from my frumpiness. His teeth pressed tightly together, making the muscles along his jaw dance. The liquid amber color of his eyes glowed bright. A predatory gleam had my nipples puckering as they slowly marked my body. He held himself rigid, as if he didn't dare move a muscle. Before I could second-guess myself, I ran and launched myself into his arms.

I wrapped my body securely around his. I licked, bit, sucked, and grazed along his neck as if he were my salvation. He was the one gift I would ever let myself indulge in. *Consequences be damned!* He carried me inside stealthily. Even with me nibbling at his neck, we were still quieter than a mouse. He smelled and tasted delicious.

One minute, I was attached to his body. the next, I was airborne. I bounced as I landed on the bed. I tore my shirt over my head and tossed it haphazardly. I bent on my knees in the middle of the bed. "Get your sexy ass over here so I can take what's mine."

He didn't waste any time in shedding his clothes. He

was magnificent. His strong Adonis body emitted so much sexual power that I felt as though I would combust.

He climbed up onto the bed and gently shoved me backward. I lay on my back as he hovered over my body. His eyes roved up and down my body, taking in their fill. He left no part unscathed. He hadn't touched me and yet I could feel his heat surround every inch of my skin. I burned and withered in urgency.

His massive hand cupped my cheek delicately. I turned in to his hand and placed a tender kiss on his palm.

"You have no idea how much I need you. You are my next breath. Without you, I am nothing."

My breath hitched and I swallowed the lump that had formed, threatening to choke me. At a loss for words, I leaned up and kissed him with a fervor that I didn't know I had possessed. I sucked on the bottom of his lip and pushed my legs farther apart, enabling him to nestle deeper against me.

"Forrest, rip off my panties." I thrust my hips ardently. I was soaking wet and throbbing with need.

His growl vibrated along my skin, sending tiny jolts of electricity to my core. My whole body was wound tight. He skimmed his rough hands over my breasts. My nipples drew tighter. I moaned his name in ecstasy. The closer he came to my panties, the heavier I panted.

In one quick movement, the thin material tore away from my body. "Please. I can't wait anymore. I need you inside me."

"Soon, baby. I have to have a taste of your mouthwatering pussy first." He spread my legs as far as they would go. "Fuck, Candice. You are so wet. You're practically dripping." I sucked in a breath as he licked along my inner thigh. He used his tongue to trace my outer folds. I squirmed underneath him as his teasing continued down to my other thigh.

"Forrest!" I hissed. That did nothing to increase his pace. It had the opposite effect, in fact. He continuously nibbled and licked my inner thighs and folds until I clamped my legs around his head. "You better fuck me now or I'll finish myself off." It was an empty threat.

Forrest looked up at me and grinned naughtily. Already on the brink of an orgasm, he used his wickedly skilled tongue to drive me off the cliff. My orgasm tore through my body in delicious waves. I wanted to scream aloud but had to bite the inside of my cheek. As my orgasm subsided and my body relaxed from its adrenaline high, Forrest slammed into me.

"Ah, Candice. You feel so good. I can still feel your pussy tightening around my cock."

I couldn't speak nor did I want to. I only wanted to feel his fullness rocking into me. It was sweet torture. He drove me literally insane. I pulled at my sensitive breasts. I raked my nails along his back. I grabbed his ass painfully. All the while, he thrust in and out of me. Pleasure slowly built inside. He pulled out and teased my clit with the tip of his dick, bringing the smoldering pleasure to a roaring fire. He slid his dick along my folds and then drove into my center, filling me up even more. I couldn't hold out any longer. "Shit, Forrest——I'm going to come."

"That's it, baby. Come all over my cock while I'm fucking you."

My walls constricted and squeezed his cock.

"Holy fuck." His cock twitched as my orgasm surged

through me.

Forrest placed a delicate kiss to my forehead. He rolled onto his back and dragged me to him. No words were exchanged as we silently enjoyed being in each other's arms. I placed my head over his heart and listened to its steady beat. The hypnotic drumming became my bedtime lullaby.

***

I rolled over and reached for Forrest but only encountered cold sheets. I reached for his pillow so I could feel closer to him. It was a poor substitute and left me feeling lonely. Wallowing in bed would not be permitted. I quickly washed my face and brushed my teeth. I wanted to get downstairs and start making breakfast before Riley woke up.

The bacon began to sizzle as the doorbell rang. I ran as quickly as I could to get the door for Forrest. I opened it up and froze. The man on the other side was not Forrest. He looked possessed. Dry, cracked, reedy lips rose up into a sneer. The whites of his eyes were tinted yellow, with thin red lines winding throughout. A thin sheen of sweat beaded over his upper lip. I could have fried my bacon with the grease from his hair.

"Miss me?" he spit at me.

My mind finally snapped out of the fog. I wiped the spittle off my cheek in disgust. "You are not welcome here. I have a restraining order against you. Get off my property or I will call the cops." I enunciated just in case he didn't get the hint of disdain from my tone. A healthy dose of fear ran through my veins and my heart thumped loudly against my chest.

"You are my wife. I most certainly belong here.

Aren't you going to let me in?"

The stench of rotting meat flowed out of his mouth and permeated my nostrils. "No. Now get the fuck out of here!" I screamed at him.

I couldn't help it. He was scaring the shit out of me. I wouldn't allow Riley to see him like this, all strung out. If I had it my way, she would never see him again. He slammed his palm onto the door; I jumped. He used his body weight to move the door wider. His eyes enlarged at my fear. He always took pleasure from frightening me.

"Lucy isn't here to protect you this time."

"Is there a problem here?" Forrest bellowed.

Oh, thank the heavens! My eyes pleaded with Forrest to help me.

Eugene turned around to face Forrest. "Nope. Just visiting my wife. So you can mosey the fuck on."

"Ex-wife. And I told you to leave."

"You should probably do as the lady says and move on."

"Fuck you. Who the hell are you to tell me what to do?"

"Nobody you want to mess with right now. I suggest you leave immediately or I will help you leave."

He looked Forrest up and down, weighing his options. "Fine. I was going anyway." Eugene shoved past Forrest. "See you around, cunt."

I watched him walk away until I could no longer see him. Forrest pulled me into the house. Once inside, he shut and locked the door. My body shook like a leaf blowing in a windstorm. He wrapped his strong arms around me until the tremors died down. I took a lung full of air and expelled it slowly.

I couldn't look him in the eye. I was so ashamed that he had to witness that. "Thank you, for helping me."

"No need to thank me. I'm glad that I showed up when I did." He gently cupped my chin. "Are you alright?"

"I'm much better now. Shit! The bacon."

I ran to the kitchen and shut the burner off. Pieces of burnt bacon seared into the pan, stinking up the house. I'd soak the pan later. I'm surprised Riley slept through all of this. Thank God she did.

Forrest came into the kitchen. "I take it that was Riley's dad."

"Yeah." I looked up at him with determination. "He wasn't always like that. I mean, he has always been a controlling son of a bitch but never that strung out."

Forrest walked over and enveloped me into his strong arms. He placed his chin on top of my head. "It's okay—you don't have to tell me right now. Someday, I want to know the whole story." He kissed me lovingly and held onto me until we heard the pitter-patter of little feet rushing down the stairs. He placed a kiss on my forehead, quickly stepped away from me, and sat in one of the kitchen chairs.

Riley skidded to a stop when she noticed Forrest. "You came back. We go to the pawk now?"

"You just woke up and haven't even eaten yet. Let's fill up our bellies. Then we can go to the park."

"Okay." She hesitated for a moment and then jumped onto his lap.

I watched in awe as Forrest hung onto Riley as though she were a natural extension of him. Tears sprang to my eyes as I looked at the two of them carry on as a father and daughter would. Forrest caught me wiping my eyes. He winked and blew me a kiss. *Fuck, I was in love with him.* It hit me like a ton of bricks. I felt as if I was going to hyperventilate. I was glad for my mini audience——or I would have.

12 FORREST

The three of us walked hand in hand to the park. Riley giggled and skipped the whole way there. I loved the feel of her tiny hand enveloped in my much larger one. That tiny display of trust made me feel like a superhero. Nothing could touch me. I never once dreamed of having children. I loved my freedom too much. I never wanted to be saddled with any responsibilities. Especially those that involved a mother and a child who wasn't biologically mine. As callous as that seemed, it was true. However, upon meeting Riley, my whole outlook turned upside down.

Right at this moment, I couldn't think of anything better to do then play and be silly with her. Being with Candice was the ultimate gift and Riley made it even better. I may not have helped create such a sweet child, but in my heart, I knew without a doubt she belonged to me. I had to make sure that I protected them both from that piece of shit. I would do everything in my power to make sure that he never again hurt either one of them or I'd kill him.

***

The minute Riley let go of my hand to run to the slide, I immediately felt a sense of loss. Candice looked up at me and replaced Riley's hand with her own. Once again I silently pounded my chest. I looked down at our joined hands. I lifted hers to my mouth and placed a soft kiss to the back of her knuckles. For her to allow this moment of affection, knowing that Riley could be watching, drove my love for her even more. I kissed Candice's cheek and took off after Riley.

"Wait for me, squirt."

"You awe too slow." She climbed to the top of the slide as fast as her little legs could carry her. "I win."

"Yes you did. You are super fast."

"Watch this, Fowwest. No hands." She threw her hands up in the air and slid down, squealing the whole time.

I had to physically remain rooted so that I didn't try to catch her if she fell. *Where the hell did that come from?* I had no idea and I really didn't care. She just made me instinctively want to protect her.

I didn't want anything to mar her perfect little personality. *But hell, she was a kid; she would eventually get hurt, right?* I couldn't, nor could Candice, save her from everything. Oh, but I could most certainly try. The only thing that I knew for certain was that I needed both of them in my life.

I ran from apparatus to apparatus with Riley until she plumb tired my ass out. I slumped onto the bench next to Candice, needing to catch my breath. "How the hell do you keep up with her? I'm a pretty fit guy and I'm worn out after an hour."

Candice smiled at me patiently. "The key is to let her wear herself out. You wait for her to call you over when she needs help. Otherwise, if you run around like a maniac trying to keep up with her, you just burn out." She laughed heartily. "She is three and with boundless amounts of energy. We have limits and I sure as hell know mine. You'll learn." She playfully patted my cheek.

I couldn't help myself. I leaned over and placed a kiss along her plump lips. They called to me, begging for my attention. I couldn't ignore them any longer. I wanted to dive in deeper but knew that I had to keep this G-rated. I pulled away just before my hormones kicked my sensible side to the curb. "Maybe later I'll be able to kiss you properly."

"That was perfect. I wouldn't want it any other way. But, if you are a good boy, I'm sure that I can arrange for that later."

"Yes, ma'am. I will be on my best behavior."

"I have an idea. Why don't you let me stay with Riley tonight while you work? Give your babysitter the night off. When you get home, I'll be naked and in your bed waiting for you." I laughed at the look on her face. It had gone from hell no, to shocked, and finally to shy with a hint of blush shading her cheeks. "You look so cute right now. I'm only kidding about the last part. Well, partly kidding." I put my hands up before she could say no. "Candice, in all seriousness, I would love to stay with Riley. It——"

She cut me off. "Okay. I would really like that."

She completely stunned me. I thought for sure she would have said no. "What? Really?"

"Yes, really. I trust you, Forrest. I like going to bed in your arms. I'd really like to wake up in your arms too. How about not sneaking out in the morning this time?"

"Deal. Pinkie promise."

"Are you really going to make me pinkie promise you?" She chuckled.

"Heck yes, I am. I'm not letting you back out on me."

She rolled her eyes while she stuck out her pinkie. "You are so juvenile."

"And proud of it."

We held hands and watched Riley play. I felt like a teenage boy again, on my very first date. My stomach leapt with nervous energy at holding her hand in public. She was such a private woman. I didn't want to ruin anything. I wanted Riley to become accustomed to her mother and me slowly. I never wanted her to feel as if she didn't belong right there next to us. Riley had no reason to be jealous or possibly think that I would take her mother's attention away from her. I adored Riley. All I wanted her to know was that I loved her as fiercely as I loved her mother. Of course, I wasn't going to go shouting it on the top of a roof. Hell, I had to tell Candice first. I hesitated to tell her because she wasn't ready to hear it yet.

Candice called for Riley. "It's time to go, baby. We need to get home and eat some lunch."

"Okay, Momma. I'm coming."

She sprinted from the ladder and tripped over her feet. She landed spread eagle with her face smushed into the tire shavings. No sound escaped her lips. Then the air broke with a blood-curdling scream. I sprang from the bench and ran to her. I picked up her tiny body and held her against me as tears slid down her cheeks like tiny streams.

She looked up at me pitifully. "I got a boo-boo on my knee and it huwts." She hiccupped.

"Let me take a look at it." She lifted her leg up for me to inspect. "Hmm. That doesn't look so bad. I bet it does hurt." I bent my head down and gave her red skin a kiss. "That is a magical kiss. It will heal your knee up in no time."

Her blue eyes got as big as saucers. "Weally, Fowwest?"

"I promise."

She wrapped her little arms around my neck and squeezed with all of her strength. "Thank you foe my magical kiss."

"You are most welcome."

I stood up with her still wrapped around me. I held onto her with one arm and with the other, I took Candice's hand. We walked back to her house, a now solemn bunch.

***

Riley finished up her lunch in record time. "Can I go watch caw-oons? Pease."

"Go ahead, munchkin. Me and Forrest are going to sit at the table and finish our lunch."

The TV must have already been set on her favorite channel because some cartoon began to play in the background and Riley was as quiet as a mouse.

"Thank you for what you did with Riley today. I was

a little taken back when she didn't want me."

"I'm sorry. I didn't mean to intrude. I just reacted."

"It was a fleeting feeling. I'm so used to it just being Riley and me. I'm the one who fixes all of her bumps and bruises. There is no one else who helps dry up her tears. It's hard to let you intervene but I'm glad I did. A huge weight lifted off my chest. I can't tell you how relieved I was that you had inserted yourself and took over." I sighed heavily. "Raising Riley by myself is harder than I thought it would be. I love her to death and would do anything in my power for her. Sometimes, it's nice to have someone to share the load."

"I'm glad that you let me. I know this is crazy because I haven't known her for very long, but she has me wrapped around her little finger." What I really wanted to say was that I had fallen in love with the both of them. "Why don't you go ahead and relax before you have to go into work? Let me hang with Riley for a little while."

"Are you sure? You've been with us all day and you will be with her all night too."

"Yep. Go ahead. I've got this." I smiled at her. I got up and cleared the table. I walked back over to Candice and pulled her up and into my arms. I grazed my teeth along her neck and then playfully swatted her ass. "Get. I'm going to hang with Riley."

She chuckled and shooed me away. "Fine. I've got things I need to get done before work anyway."

My head felt as though it would explode from all of the instructions that Candice threw at me. I had a list of five emergency numbers now taped to the fridge. I also had the directions to Evonne's house and Riley's car seat strapped into my truck. *Holy, fuck me!* There was a shit ton of stuff I needed to know. Candice kissed Riley and me good-bye.

"See you waater, Mommy."

"Love you, munchkin. Be good for Forrest."

"I know. Bye."

"Are you sure about this, Forrest?" She looked as if she was about to say fuck it and call in to work.

I smiled and kissed her reassuringly. "Yes. Now off with you, before you are late. I will see you when you get back."

With a final wave, she walked out the door. I turned to Riley. "You got any Play Doh?"

"Yep. Come on, I show you."

We played nonstop until dinner. I had Riley go wash up while I fixed our peanut butter and jelly sandwiches. I had no desire to whip up a gourmet meal. That's not my area of expertise. I never claimed to excel in that area. I left that nonsense up to Phoenix. Frozen dinners were my go-to. I made sure to cut the crust off. Most kids I've encountered hated crust on their bread. I set our plates down and waited for Riley.

She plopped down in her chair and stared at her plate for a moment. She looked at me in awe. "You awe my hewo. Thank you foe cutting off the cwust."

I mentally patted myself on the back. "You are most welcome. Now eat up before it gets cold."

She giggled. "It aweady cold."

I lightly slapped the side of my head. "Duh."

Her face lit up when she cackled at me. "You funny, Fowwest."

***

I wasn't quite sure about the proper protocol for little girls and bath time. "Riley, why don't you go get your swimsuit on and we will take a little swim in the bathtub?"

"Yay. Mommy neva wet's me have my bathing suit in the tub."

I shook my head at her excitement. By the time Riley was squeaky-clean, the bathroom looked as though a tornado had hit it. I quickly changed her into her favorite pajamas and then wiped up all the bubbles and water that had splashed onto the floor. "Come on, squirt. Let's go read some books before bed."

We read almost her whole bookshelf before she yawned. "Okay, it's officially time for bed." I covered her tiny frame up and bent down and kissed her forehead. "Good night, Riley. Thank you for the best day of my life."

"Welcome. Wuv you, Fowwest." She closed her eyes and was out in no time.

My heart lodged into my throat. I stood rooted in the doorway, just watching her sleep. She evoked such strong emotions from me that I felt raw. I finally turned out her light and cracked her door. I didn't feel right shutting it all the way. I wanted to be able to hear her if she cried out during the night. I made my way downstairs to pick up any mess that we had made.

I shut off all of the lights, locked the door, and headed up to the bedroom. If Phoenix could see this domestic goddess that I portrayed right now, he would keel over laughing. I chuckled to myself at the image. I stripped down and climbed under the covers. I planned to wait up for Candice but once my head hit the pillow, I was out.

13 CANDICE

My mind was not focused on work at all. My tips certainly reflected it. All I could think about was being at home with Riley and Forrest. I wouldn't be surprised if Logan called me into her office tomorrow. Oh well. I would deal with it if it came to pass. My shift was over and I was getting the hell out of Dodge. Ben waited for me when I exited the building.

We walked silently to my car. "Thanks, Ben. See you tomorrow night."

"Yep. Be careful."

"Always."

I hit the unlock button on my key fob. The lights flickered. I happened to look down just as the interior lights came on. *Fuck!* My front tire was as flat as a pancake. I turned around and called out to Ben. "Hey, Ben. Wait up."

He turned around and waited for me to catch up to him. "What's up?"

"I got a damn flat."

"Do you have a spare?"

"It's already on the car. I forgot to replace it awhile back."

"Can you call someone for a ride?"

"Not without having to wake up my daughter. Do you think that you could give me a lift when your shift is over?"

"Let me go talk to Logan. It's not that busy and Mark can keep an eye on things. You don't live that far do you?"

"Thanks. No, only about fifteen minutes."

"No problem. I'll be right back."

It didn't take any longer than five minutes before Ben and Logan were striding my way. My armpits began to perspire the closer they got.

Before I could get a word in, Logan spoke. "I'll take you home, Candice. I don't want to leave Mark by himself, even if it is a slow night."

"Logan, please don't go out of your way. I told Ben I would wait until his shift was over."

"Don't worry about it. I'm taking you home and that's the end of it." She smiled at me to cut some of the sting from her abruptness.

I thanked Ben and followed her outside. The next fifteen minutes would define the rest of the night. I really liked Logan but with my performance tonight, I would get an ass ripping from her. I buckled my seat belt and patiently waited for Logan to tear into me.

"What's going on with you tonight? I don't think I've

ever seen you give such a piss-poor act since I've known you."

I squeezed my eyes shut and regulated my breathing. "I'm sorry, Logan. I know I didn't put forth my best effort. I have no excuse and it won't happen again."

"Look, Candice, I'm not coming at you as a boss right now. I'm trying to be your friend. I'm concerned because you have never been vacant up on stage. You are always intensely animated. It's hard to focus on anything else when you are up there."

I sighed heavily. "I really don't know what to tell you. I'm having a hard time focusing on work."

She looked over at me skeptically. "And that's all. Nothing else on your mind?"

"No. Nothing at all."

She ground her teeth together. That was her trademark for when she got pissed. I had no doubt that she knew that I was lying to her.

"Alright. I'll let it go for the time being. As your boss, I better not see you slip again. I also know about what happened in the VIP room with your client, Max."

I sucked in a breath and prepared to take the tongue-lashing. "How did you find out? Oh fuck, the cameras in the corner of the wet bar. Shit. Logan, I am truly sorry and that only happened with Max. I know I broke the rules and by rights should be fired right now."

"Shut up, Candice. I didn't watch. I saw the writing on the wall and shut off the camera to that room. I turned the camera off every time you met with Max. Technically, I don't know what went on in that room. This is why I am giving you one more shot. Do not make me regret it."

Mortified didn't even begin to cover how I felt. "I won't, Logan. Why are you not firing me? Not that I want you to but I sure as hell would understand if you did."

"Because you remind me of myself. You normally don't bring your problems into work. The men love you and you're cold on the inside. The job, up until now, didn't affect you one bit. You did your job and moved on to the next. You are the best dancer the club has. You are an asset to me and it's in my best interest to keep you on the payroll." She pulled in to my drive and turned to look at me. "That's not to say that I won't fire you if you don't start toeing the line. I've given you more chances than I would any of the other dancers. Start thinking about your daughter and her future, not with what's between your legs."

Ouch, that stung. "Yes, ma'am. You have my word." I opened up the car door and leaned back in. "Thank you again for giving me another chance when I don't deserve one and for the lift home. I appreciate it."

"See you tomorrow."

I shut the door and marched inside. I wanted to slam the door and stomp up the stairs but I didn't. My tantrum could wait. I quietly walked up the stairs and peeked in Riley's room. Her deep breaths assured me that she was still sleeping. I tiptoed up to her bed and softly placed a kiss on her cheek. I recovered her and gently shut the door. As I neared my bedroom, my palms became sweaty and my heart rate increased. I was eager to see Forrest and yet so pissed at myself for wanting this man.

Before I opened the door, I took a minute to compose myself. It wasn't his fault that I couldn't control my actions when he was my client. It's my responsibility to be the professional in those rooms. I had let myself down. It wasn't fair to be angry with him. I took a deep breath and turned the knob.

The faint glow of the moon silhouetted his body. He lay motionless on his back, with his arm bent at the elbow and tucked underneath his head. His muscular chest peeked out of the covers, making my mouth drool. I silently walked into the bathroom and washed my face. I tossed my clothes into the laundry basket and slipped under the sheets, naked. The coolness of the fabric sliding over my skin further aroused me. I hesitated for a split second. I was torn between waking him up and letting him sleep. He was painfully sexy. It would be a waste to allow him to sleep.

I crawled farther down the bed. I threw the covers off us. His naked torso threw my lust into overdrive. I froze when Forrest murmured in his sleep. I didn't want him to wake up just yet. I wanted to fulfill my fantasy first.

I carefully nudged his legs apart. He hadn't moved yet. I held my breath as I glanced up at his gorgeous body. *How did I get so lucky?* He was all sharp curves and chiseled lines. One of my favorite parts of him lay flaccid at the moment but I would change that. I really loved that he manscaped. There's nothing worse than going down on a guy and having his pubic hair vying to floss your teeth. It made the whole action seem like a chore.

I slithered between his legs. I placed my arms along the outside of his hips for leverage. I bent my head between his thighs. My tongue snaked out and licked him from the bottom of his soft sack up the length of his veiny shaft. I continued my journey along the ridge, just under the tip. I wound my tongue around the edge and then swirled the tip with my tongue. Forrest moaned. I smiled.

My desire grew as quickly as his cock did in my mouth. I opened wider and drew his length deep into my mouth. His cock grew even harder as I swirled my tongue around his length while I drew him in and out of my mouth. I lightly wrapped my hand around his balls, slightly squeezing, and fondled the sensitive skin.

His fingers sensually teased my scalp as my lips sheathed his cock. "Mmmm. I better not be fucking dreaming."

His cock slid through my lips with a popping sound. "As long as I'm the dream girl, you can dream all you want."

With one last lick, I rubbed the length of my body up his torso. My breasts staked their claim along his chest while my lips seared a path up his neck. My teeth grazed his defined jawline, toward his eager mouth. I licked the seam of his lips. When they granted me entrance, my tongue darted inside. Our tongues mingled with a bone-tingling potency.

When I raised my mouth from his, I gazed into his molten eyes. His unspoken invitation issued a passionate challenge, hard for me to resist. I buried my face in his neck, and breathed a kiss there. My feelings for him intensified. I burned out of control with desire.

I pressed my lips down the length of his shoulders. My tongue explored each nipple. I followed the ridges of his abs, farther down. His tormented groan had me heady with arousal.

Sitting up swiftly, I swung my leg over his hips, and straddled him backward. I slowly lowered myself onto his thick cock and moaned in ecstasy. His hands explored the soft lines of my waist, my hips, and the length of my spine as my back faced him.

"Candice, you are so fucking hot."

I angled my head coyly to my shoulder and seductively smiled at him, as I drew him deeper inside. He sat up and placed his chest against my back. It was flesh against flesh. His lips traced a sensuous path along the sensitive skin of my neck. I swiveled my hips around and around, taking him deeper and deeper each time. The stroke of his fingers along my taut nipples sent toe-curling jolts throughout my body.

His fingers whispered along my stomach, down to my swollen nub. I gasped with sweet agony. His thumb circled my clit and I exploded.

We lay entwined with sweat glistening off our naked bodies. I slipped into unconsciousness, completely satisfied and thoroughly loved.

The sounds of laughter had me stirring from a deep sleep. The smell of buttery pancakes and sausage had my lazy ass running down the stairs. I stopped dead in my tracks as I eavesdropped on them. The kitchen looked like a complete disaster zone. Pancake batter dripped from the bowl, on to the counter. Riley's cheeks were speckled with the goopy mixture. She stood on a stool with the spatula in one hand and watched the circular batter bubble while it cooked.

My frilly apron was tied around Forrest's waist. He shielded Riley's body away from the heat of the stove. I could no longer stand by and watch dry-eyed, so I stepped in and placed a quick kiss on the top of Riley's curly head. I snuggled into Forrest's back while I wrapped my arms around his trim waist.

"Morning, Momma."

"Good morning, sweet baby. What are you two doing?"

"We awe making you bwakfast." She shook her head as though it were obvious.

I chuckled. "It smells delicious. It's a good thing that I am starving. Shall I get the plates?"

"That would be awesome. Thank you." Riley turned to Forrest. "Fwip that fwap jack, Fowwest. It's going to buwn if you don't."

Forrest's body shook with laughter. "Yes, ma'am. While I finish these up, why don't you help your momma set the table?"

Her pudgy hand swiped at her forehead in a mock salute. "Yes sir." God, I loved this child. She had smeared batter all over her forehead.

I used almost a whole package of wipes trying to clean Riley up from breakfast. I shooed her out of the kitchen while Forrest and I cleaned up the rest of the mess.

"Breakfast was delicious."

"You are most welcome." He brushed a gentle kiss to my nose. "I don't like to cook but I really had a lot of fun with Riley. I'm glad that she didn't freak out when she woke up and found me here."

"I'm honestly surprised she didn't come and wake me up." I sat back down in the chair and put my feet up.

"She wanted to but I asked her to let you sleep some more." He lifted my feet into his lap as he sat in the chair. His strong hands massaged the pads of my feet.

"Would you mind taking me to Phoenix's house this morning? They got back late last night. I'll leave you my car and I'll have him take me to get yours fixed."

"Oh shit. I forgot they were coming home. Yes that would be great. I'll hang with Lucy for a while and if you don't get back before I leave then I'll just use your car for the night if that's okay?"

"Perfect. I'm going to get cleaned up and then we can head out."

He bent over me. I parted my lips as I raised myself to meet his kiss. I quivered at the sweet tenderness of his kiss. *My goodness, he was going to be the death of me.*

14 CANDICE

Riley sat in the back, chattering a mile a minute. My legs bounced up and down nervously, the closer we got to Lucy's. *Craptastic.* I haven't told her a thing about Forrest and me. Guess I wouldn't have to. Showing up together would paint a pretty clear picture. It would be pointless to try and ceny anything. Plus, as soon as we walked in the door, Riley would be telling her that Forrest stayed the night and that they made breakfast together.

Forrest placed a soothing hand upon my knee. I turned toward him. He smiled reassuringly at me.

"Don't worry so much. Lucy is your best friend and Phoenix adores you." He stared at me and then burst out laughing "I'm the one who will get pummeled for chasing after you."

His laughter was infectious. I found myself calming down instantly. His eyes held me captive. "I love you."

No, No. No. No. I didn't just say that out loud. I slapped my hand over my mouth. Sheer terror seized my body as the shock of discovery hit me.

The smile in his eyes contained a sensuous flame. He shot me an irresistibly devastating grin. "I love you too."

My lips parted in surprise. I quickly clamped them shut as I stared at him in astonishment. I had no time to recover. We had pulled in to Lucy's driveway. Before I could walk to the other side to get Riley, he had already unclipped her. She bound up the front steps and pounded on the door with her tiny fist.

The door swung open and Riley rushed into Lucy. "TiTi Wuce, we come to see you."

"I'm so glad. I've missed you." She twirled her around and around, planting tickling kisses all over her face.

"No mowe. You make me pee my pants." She wiggled free from Lucy and plowed into Phoenix.

"My turn." He plucked Riley up and threw her up in the air. Her little body shook with laughter.

"Unci Phoenix, put me down."

"As you wish, princess." He gave her a smacking kiss.

"Ewe, gwoss," she cackled and ran inside to bang on the piano keys.

Forrest pulled my hand in his confidently and gently pulled me along. I didn't have to look up to know that Lucy stared at me. I could feel her questioning look bore into my skin, bordering on tiny pinpricks along my flesh. I bit my lip nervously and looked up into Lucy's triumphant face. I let go of his hand and ran into my best friend's open arms.

I hugged her tight. "You are a smug bitch!"

"I missed you too." She squeezed me back. She flung her arm around my shoulders and we flounced into the house. We left the menfolk to themselves. We had a lot of catching up to do.

We lounged on the couch while Riley pounded on the keys. I cringed at the ruckus she made. That poor piano. I wondered whether she would break such a fine instrument.

"Quit scrunching up your face. She won't break it. It only sounds like it's dying."

"Are you sure? She is being awfully hard on it."

"Please——you should see what Phoenix and I do on it."

"Oh my goodness. Could you be any louder? You know she repeats everything she hears."

"She can't hear me. Why are you being so uptight? Are you all puckered, waiting for me to grill you about Forrest?"

"Fuck you."

"That's better. Now dish it, sister."

Where the hell do I start? "Why aren't you surprised to see me with him?" I huffed out. "Seems to me that you already know what's going on."

"Don't get so defensive. I don't know a damn thing. Quit peddling and fucking tell me already before I lose interest."

She may have rolled her eyes nonchalantly but she was dying of curiosity. I'm going to let her stew for a bit longer. "Tell me all about your honeymoon first."

"Seriously?" She threw her hands up in mock frustration. "Fine." She smiled to herself as she spoke. "It was glorious. We were going to go to Ireland but opted to stay in the States instead. Girl, we traveled to Vegas. Gambled, ate at fancy restaurants, and fucked like rabbits. Then we went to Montana. Rode some horses and rode each other some more. There were a lot of other places we visited but all I can remember is his naked body." Her eyes sparkled.

"Kill me now. You win. I will tell you." My hands flew in all different directions as I recounted the story. I closed it up with blurting out my love for him on the way over.

"For shits and giggles. Do you love him?"

"What kind of fucked-up question is that? I told him I did. Do you think that I'd make that shit up?"

She bounced up and down on the cushion, acting like Riley on a sugar high. "I figured something might be going on from the way he marched in your direction at the wedding."

"Wait. So that was what you were talking about? I didn't understand a flipping thing you said until now. It all makes sense." She grinned at me as though she was a proud parent and I just aced my test. *That observant bitch!* Sometimes I wanted to hate her.

She enveloped me in a bear hug. God, she was stronger than she looked. "Let it happen. Don't overanalyze every little nuance from him. He is made from the same cloth as Phoenix. Which means he has got to be amazing in and out of the bedroom."

I shook my head in disbelief. "There is something wrong with you. Not all of your neurons are firing."

She shimmied over to Riley. "Come on, princess. Let's give the piano a break and go get an apple fritter. Aunt Lucy needs some Clyde's coffee."

Thank goodness for small miracles. Not a soul in line. For the first time since we've been coming to Clyde's, it was a ghost town. I gave Riley the freedom to skip around the empty café. No dirty looks would be directed my way today! Right as we sat down, my cell phone chimed.

Hey baby, letting you know that I have your car. I'll be by in time to stay with Riley and you can take your car to work. If you want, I'll stay again. Love you.

My heart overflowed with love.

Sounds like a great plan. I love you.

He made it so easy to utter those three powerful words. They tied me to him but my free will and independence stood equally strong. He freed and liberated me more than ever.

"Lover boy has got you seeing stars, girl."

"Yep I can't deny it. He is the real deal. I have never felt this way before." I looked over at Riley as she chomped her muffin without a care in the world. "He cherishes the both of us. I loved him before he met her." I angled my head toward Riley. I didn't want her to know that we were talking about her. "He tipped the scales when he treated her as his own. Not many men would do that. That's why I kept so many of them at arm's length." I closed my eyes in defeat. "I tried to shut him out but I couldn't. Every hour away from him became agony. Lucy,

I've got it bad."

"That's putting it mildly. Remember to breathe and take it one day at a time. Try not to think about the worst. He is the type of guy that even if things didn't work out with the two of you, he would still be around for the little princess."

I lay my head in my hands. "I know and that would be the kicker. I'd die a little more each time I saw him. I'm hoping that it won't be an issue. I am enjoying our time together. I'm not seeing a chapel yet. I honestly don't want to get my hopes up."

She placed her hands on top of mine. "Even if you were, that would be okay too. Just continue to be you and it will work out."

"I a pwincess. Fowwest be my new daddy?" She smeared the crumbs of her muffin across her face with her petite hands.

I turned toward Lucy, openly gaping at what Riley had just uttered. *Fuck. How the heck would I explain this one?* I couldn't ignore her. Thankfully, Lucy took over for me.

"Sweetheart, Forrest won't replace your daddy. He loves you and your mommy and would never come between you and your daddy." She rumpled Riley's hair.

A tear slid down her cheek. "Fowwest doesn't want to be my daddy? I wuv him and he has to be my daddy. My ova daddy weft me."

I pulled her into my lap. "Oh, baby. Your daddy loves you very much. He has been extremely busy lately and hasn't been able to see you. Forrest loves you too. He can be a daddy to you as well if you want him to." I cradled her in my arms until her sniffles died down. She crawled off my lap and climbed back into her chair.

"I want him as my daddy. He wood neva weave me."

She continued to finish up her muffin as if that was the end of the conversation. I, on the other hand, had been shaken to my core.

15 FORREST

Phoenix and I stood in front of Candice's car. I swiveled my head toward him. "You thinking what I'm thinking?"

"I believe that I am." He slapped me on the shoulder and squeezed the tense muscle beneath.

"I'm going to kill that motherfucker. He sliced her tire. It's so fucking obvious. He might as well have left the fucking knife sticking out. Candice didn't see it because it was dark and she only saw that it was flat. What kind of game do you think he is playing?" My hands fisted at my sides. I ground my teeth together, trying to gain control over the blind anger that rolled through my veins.

"Probably only trying to scare her because she has a restraining order against him."

"He came by the house the other day. I came up on the two of them in time. He was furious at her. I'm positive that if I hadn't come along then, he would have roughed her up. He was strung out on something. Not sure what, but he was hard up. My God, Phoenix, Riley was upstairs sleeping." I huffed out a breath and stalked around the car. "I need to get that house fixed up. I don't want Candice and Riley living there a minute longer."

"I know just the guys who can handle the job. They are quick and reasonable. I know for a fact that they would jump at the opportunity to help. They renovated Treble for Lucy. It didn't take them long, either. I'll give them a call right now."

"Thanks, man. I'm going to call a tow service and get this fixed." I continued to stalk the parking lot while I hammered my instructions to the tow company.

I wanted to punch something so bad. Everything seemed out of my control. I couldn't go looking for Eugene. What the hell would I do when I found him? Beat him to a bloody pulp and threaten him to stay away? He'd press charges so fast that my head would spin. It would only create more problems for Candice. I couldn't protect her from the inside of a jail cell.

Once the car was towed, we hopped back into the car.

"Hey, can you take me to sleazy Gus so that I can buy this house?"

"You got it. Let's go buy you a house. Should we stop and look at rings while we are at it?"

"Ha, ha, ha. You are a real comedian."

We stormed into the realty company as if we owned it. I asked the receptionist whether Gus was available. Luck was on my side today. We didn't need any formalities. He brusquely pulled us into the conference room.

"I've been waiting for you to show up. I've already

got the paperwork ready to go. I figured you wanted it and wouldn't balk at the price. It's already below market value. You are getting a good deal on it."

"I don't have time to dick around with prices. Whatever it is, I'm willing to pay it." I grabbed the pen with gusto and started to sign.

As I flipped each page, peace overtook my body. The rage cleared out and my body relaxed. This was meant to be. I could feel it deep in my gut. I always trusted my intuition. An hour later, the paperwork was signed and we headed to the bank to get a cashier's check. I couldn't believe that I was a homeowner. Thinking about settling down would normally have me antsy. This time, it felt as natural as breathing. I wanted to have a family. Not just any old family, but one with Candice and Riley.

"Alright. It's all set. Lucy's uncles Sal and Enzo will meet with you first thing tomorrow."

"Great. Thanks!"

"Where to now? Maybe I should get a second job driving a taxi."

"You are one sarcastic bastard. Thanks for all of your help. Now I just need you to take me to my apartment so I can pack a bag and then back to Candice's."

"Yes, sir. It's going to cost you."

"Doesn't it always!"

***

I waved bye to my brother. With my bag in my hand, I knocked on the door. This wasn't my house so I couldn't just walk in. Hopefully it wouldn't be theirs much longer.

That is, if Candice agreed to move in with me. I heard the locks click. Good to know that she took me seriously when I told her to keep her doors locked.

My angel opened up the door. "You are a sight for sore eyes." I placed my hands on her hips and hoisted her up in the air. She wrapped her legs around my waist. I used whatever time we had kissing her senseless.

"I could get used to this kind of welcome. I've missed you."

"Hope you don't mind. I brought a bag with me. I plan on staying with you for a while."

She cocked her head to the side. Her blue eyes dilated to the point of turning black. "Is everything okay? Not that I mind a bit. I want you here." She unlocked her legs and slid down my body.

"Where is Riley?"

"She is in the living room, playing with her Legos. Why? You are starting to scare me."

"I'm sorry. I don't mean to. Do you think she will be all right for a minute so we can talk outside? I don't want her to hear this."

"I'll leave the door open while we sit on the porch."

I guided her to the small bench and had her sit. I had to stand for this conversation.

"Somebody slashed your tire. I have a pretty good idea who but can't prove it."

She raised her hands to cover her mouth as she sucked in a breath. "Do you think it was Eugene? He came

147

here to scare me. He accomplished his goal. You saw me; I was frightened."

I clenched my jaw together as the memory engulfed my mind. "I can't confirm it but I believe that it was him. Who else would want to hurt you?"

Her shoulders sagged with defeat. "No one comes to mind besides him." She shook her head in disbelief. "He is so strung out that he is liable to do anything at this point." Her body shook as silent tears rained down her cheeks.

I pulled her in to me and encased her with my strength. I softly trailed my fingers through her hair as her tears drenched my shirt. "I promise everything will be alright. I won't let him hurt you or Riley."

She raised her head, pleading with me to be right. "You can't be here all the time." She steeled her back. "I will not let him run my life anymore. I will not play his victim. I owned that role for far too long. First thing tomorrow, I will go to the police station and report what happened."

"Mommy, whewe awe you?"

"I'm outside talking to Forrest. We are coming in."

"K, Mommy. Have Fowwest come and pway wegos with me."

"You got it, princess. I'll be right in." I placed a soft kiss upon her lips. "We will figure this out together. I love you."

"I love you too."

I played with Riley while Candice made dinner. Not much was said; we were both lost in our own thoughts.

Even Riley was quiet. I hated that she could sense our worry. She's bundle of energy and to watch her melancholy broke my heart. Frustration fueled my dark mood. We each gave Candice a kiss good-bye. I tried everything I could think of to perk Riley up but nothing worked. She didn't even play in the bathtub. I began to worry about what was going on with her. This was so out of character.

I propped up a bunch of pillows on her bed. How do I get her to talk? I climbed in next to her. The wood frame groaned with our combined weight. Mainly mine. I prayed that it wouldn't split apart.

"Scooch over, baby girl. Before we read, is there anything that is bothering you? You haven't been acting like yourself today. Are you feeling sick?" She was only a baby and here I am, trying to have an adult conversation.

Sometimes she acted much older. You had to be careful around her because she picked up a lot, even when you thought she wasn't paying attention.

"I not sick. I just sad." She hugged her knees, unsure of herself

I pulled her into my side and squeezed her tight against me. I would slay every dragon that came across her path. If I could keep her safely cocooned in my arms forever, I would. "Sweetheart. Will you tell me what is making you sad?"

She snuggled deeper into my side. Almost as though she were trying to disappear. "My weal daddy doesn't wuv me. He neva come to see me anymowe." She sniffled, trying to hold back her tears.

My heartstrings constricted from her confession. My chest compressed painfully. What a large burden for her to

149

carry. I vowed to lighten her load. No little girl should be sad or heartbroken.

"I know for certain that your daddy loves you. How could he not? You are the cutest princess around. He has been busy lately and I'm sure that as soon as he can, he will come and visit you." What else could I say to her? I wouldn't shatter her illusion of him.

"Weally?"

"Yes. Really. You want to know a secret?"

She crawled out of my arms enough to peer up at me. Her eyes shone with excitement. "Yes. Wight now."

My heart soared with her lifted mood. I couldn't take away all of her sadness but I could help her forget about it for a while. "I love you."

She covered her mouth and giggled. "That not a secwet."

"Oh, but it is. I haven't told anyone but you. So whenever you feel sad, you remember that I love you to pieces." I strengthened my hold on her for a moment and then let her go.

"You want to know a secwet?"

"Absolutely, I do."

"I wuv you too," she whispered.

I lay back on the pillows and tugged her into the crook of my arm. I was afraid that if I spoke, my voice would betray me. This little girl had rocked me to my core. I picked up her favorite book and read to her. Halfway through the book, I felt her breathing even out. She was fast asleep. I hated to move her. She appeared peaceful. Honestly, I didn't want to let her go. I pulled the covers over us with my free hand and stared at the ceiling. My eyelids felt heavy as her tear-free lavender shampoo lulled me to sleep.

I woke up a couple of hours later, drenched with sweat. I surveyed my surroundings, somewhat confused. I peered down at the sweet bundle curled into my side. Holy cow, what a heat box; she could heat the entire house in the winter. I gently rolled her to her side and slowly slid off her bed. I recovered her and brushed a gentle kiss upon her tiny cheek. She murmured something I couldn't understand and fell quiet again. Positive she wouldn't wake up, I silently stepped out of her room.

I lay in Candice's bed and wondered how parents dealt with the constant worry over their kids. It was a never-ending battle. Fear for her safety and overall well-being consumed my thoughts. *Did my own parents go through this torture?* They seemed sane enough last time I talked to them. Maybe I would get through it too. My biggest fear; would I be a good father to Riley? I didn't want to replace Eugene——fuck yeah, I did. Insecurities tormented my mind until I drifted off to sleep.

Candice's body brushed up against mine as she crawled into bed. I instinctively dragged her against me. She released a heavy exhale. I could feel the tightness in her muscles as she tried to relax. I gently rubbed her back and shoulders. Inch by inch, her skin became more pliable against my hands. She whimpered as my fingers kneaded the taut muscle. My body yearned to make love to her but my mind processed her need to be held. My dick simmered down and I turned out to be highly satisfied with my arms draped around her middle. Loving her in any form made me one lucky son of a bitch.

She whispered her love as she drifted off. I lay there and held her for quite a while. Her golden hair spilled over her shoulders like a blanket. I feathered my fingers through the silky strands. The methodic movement soothed me to sleep.

***

Candice softly snored as my eyes adjusted to the morning light as it peered through the blinds. I scanned the clock on the end table. Still plenty of time before I had to meet up with Sal and Enzo. I snuggled deeper against her body, nuzzling my chin stubble in the crook of her apricot and milky colored neck. She fidgeted and moved her firm ass over my now very alert cock. My fingers moved aside her golden locks to reveal her slender neck. I softly placed my lips along the elegant lines. I nipped along the spot where I could feel her heartbeat flutter. Her ass continued to grind into my pelvis; making my dick twitched with anticipation of entering her warm center. Her arm reached behind and fisted my hair. She moaned my name huskily as I fondled her pink nipple until it became marble hard. Her breast heaved at the intimacy of my touch. My hand seared a path down her abdomen. I slipped my fingers inside. She bucked her hips and clenched around my fingers as I teased her inner walls.

"Feels so good. Don't stop."

"Never. You are so wet. My fingers are soaked. Are you ready for me, baby?"

"Please. Don't make me wait any longer."

I nibbled the sensitive skin along her neck as I eased my fingers out and replaced them with my throbbing cock. I pounded into her until her body tensed. She dug her fingers into my scalp, pulling my short hair as her orgasm rippled through her body. I closed my eyes and growled as my seed shot into her.

I would never get enough of this woman. Each time got more intense. She lay cuddled into my side. "I love you."

I could feel her lips form into a wide grin. "I love you too. You are the best thing that has happened in my life, aside from Riley. I didn't realize until now that I've been waiting for you. To think, all you had to do was seduce a hardened stripper."

"I'm not going anywhere. Hardened and cautious are two totally different things. You had Riley to look out for. I'm thankful that you let me into your life. I adore her. I know that she isn't biologically mine but one day I'd love the chance to make it official."

"Are you asking me to marry you?" her voice squeaked out.

"Not yet. You will know when I do." Her delectable lips puckered in a mock pout. I feathered a kiss along the seam. "This is a good time to tell you that I bought a house yesterday."

"Congratulations. That is incredible." The twinkle in her eye dimmed marginally.

"It's on the verge of being condemned but Phoenix talked to Sal and Enzo and they agreed to meet me there this morning. We are going to walk through to see what it will take to bring her back to life."

In a blink of an eye, she sat up on her knees, the twinkle sparkling again. Her oceanic eyes swam with excitement. "Forrest, that is exciting. Those two are miracle workers. You should have seen what they did with

Treble. They are phenomenal. You will love them. They work fast, too, especially if you pitch in."

I leaned my back up against the headboard and motioned for her to come closer. "What do you think about moving in together when it's all finished?"

She straddled my thighs. She cupped my cheeks with both of her hands and gave me a smacking kiss. "Seriously? You want Riley and me to move in with you? Don't you think that we are moving too fast?"

Her palms fell to my chest and I ran my fingers through her soft hair. "I'm assuming the renovations will take awhile. It's not like we can move in tomorrow. I don't give a rat's ass if we have only been dating an hour. I want you and Riley to share a home with me. I want it to be our home."

She bathed my face with tiny kisses. I chuckled at her eagerness. "So is that a yes, you will move in with me?"

"Unequivocally a yes."

"I want you to be absolutely sure. You can think on it if you need to. It's a big step for you both. What would you do with this house?"

"Shut up, Forrest. This is what I want. I am positive that Riley will be excited. I don't give a shit about this house. My home is where you are."

"I fucking love you." I gave her one last possessive kiss. "I have to get over to meet the guys. I'll get a ride so you have my car in case you need to do anything. Once your car is done, I'll pick it up and bring it back." I twisted back around. "If you get bored later, text me, and I will send you the address. Come see your new home."

Her grin grew bright enough to light up an entire city. My chest expanded at her delight. It would be my mission to do everything in my power to keep that expression on her face.

16 FORREST

Fuck! I slammed my hands on the dash of Phoenix's car. "Damn it. I hate not knowing what that son of a bitch is up to."

"Take a couple of deep breaths. There is nothing you can do about it right now. He will slip up, eventually and get caught."

I rubbed my face with my hands. Shit. I didn't like her being alone. Eugene was a loose cannon. There was no telling when he would pop up or what he would do when he did. *I shouldn't have left them alone.*

I blew out a frustrated breath. "You're right. There is nothing I can do about it now. I'll have to wait and see what happens next."

We pulled up to the curb, squealing the tires as he slammed on the brakes. I jutted forward into the locked seat belt that forcefully propelled me back into my seat from the sudden stop.

I narrowed my eyes at Phoenix. "You are a fucking

moron."

His shoulders shook with obnoxious laughter. "You should see your face right now. It was so worth it."

I got out of the car and slammed the door just to piss him off. "Paybacks are a bitch, little brother," I sang out.

I stormed over to the two guys who stood by the front porch. They talked animatedly back and forth. As I got closer, they both turned in my direction.

I stuck my hand out. "You must be Sal and Enzo. It's nice to meet you. I'm Forrest and you all know the idiot behind me." I shook each of their hands.

They both grinned. Enzo spoke first. "It's nice to meet you." Then he inclined his head toward Phoenix. "How's our baby girl?"

"She is doing well. Ready to go back to teaching." His eyes gleamed at the mere mention of his beautiful wife. Subconsciously, he twisted his wedding band. He could hardly believe that they were married.

"Tell her we said hi and to go see Momma Rose," Sal remarked comically.

Phoenix openly laughed at the comment because he knew how Momma Rose could be. She liked to meddle in her family's lives and that was putting it mildly.

I was eager to get this walk-through over. I wanted to get started on fixing up the house, like yesterday. "Alright guys, are we ready to do this?"

"It's your show, kid." Enzo chuckled.

I led everyone up the porch steps. They moaned

under our weight. I had the urge to jump the fuck off them before they collapsed. Sal and Enzo split up and walked around the sagging porch in different directions. I unlocked the front door, eager to get onto solid ground.

Phoenix followed behind me. Once we were safely inside, he looked over at me with raised eyebrows. I shrugged. Our silent communication, although brief, conveyed an entire conversation. We didn't know what the fuck to do, so we took a seat on the bottom step of the staircase and waited.

After the longest ten minutes of my life, Phoenix nudged me with his shoulder. "So, you and Candice, huh?"

"Are we in middle school?"

"Jesus, you are fucking testy today."

I ran my fingers through my hair gruffly. "I'm sorry. This whole thing with Candice has got me nervous." I craned my neck toward him. "I'm afraid he will get bolder and I won't be there when she needs my help." I put my head in my hands, frustrated that it was out of my control. "My gut is telling me that it's going to get worse."

"Tell me what your plans are for this house."

I knew exactly what he was doing. Sitting here, stewing over things that I couldn't control, would drive me crazy. The distraction he offered would be enough for me to settle my nerves.

"At first I wanted to use the downstairs for the security business and live upstairs. But I've changed my mind."

"You still want the house, right?"

"Yes." A grin appeared on my face just thinking about them. "I asked Candice to move in with me this morning. Now, I don't want my personal life so close to my business."

Phoenix slapped me on the back. "You sly dog, you. I can't believe you are actually going to settle down." He laughed out loud. "You better be serious about Candice because if you hurt her, Lucy will have your balls fried on a platter for dinner."

"You let her fight your battles now?"

"Nope, but this time I will gladly sit back idle and let her whup your ass."

"She could too." A deep chuckle escaped. "Good to know you're on my side, little brother."

Sal and Enzo descended the stairs. I held my breath and waited for them to speak.

"You want the good news or the bad news first?" Sal inquired.

"Bad news." I swallowed hard as I braced myself for the worst.

"The siding of the house needs to be replaced. The front portion of the porch is shot. We have to replace the whole thing due to the support beams underneath. The back portion will eventually break down. It's better to replace it all at once. Updated electrical wiring needs to be done throughout the house. You might also want to install a new heating and cooling system. The current one will cost you an arm and a leg to heat and to keep cool."

Those didn't seem too bad. "Okay. Hit me with the good news."

Sal and Enzo both looked at each other. "The good news is that it can all be fixed. The rest of the house is in pretty good condition, considering the length of neglect. You can restore most of the shine on the inside," Enzo pointed out.

"Hope you're not on a tight budget. These repairs aren't going to be cheap," Sal commented dryly.

I crossed my arms over my chest. "Whatever needs to be done, let's do it."

Enzo placed a hand on my shoulder. "The inside is all cosmetic. Restore and update as you go. It doesn't have to be done all at one time." He smiled at me reassuringly.

I liked them both. Enzo was the optimist to Sal's pessimism. "I'm game. When can you start?"

"It just so happens that both of our schedules are wide open." Enzo looked intensely at Sal with some kind of secret expression as he spoke to me.

"Enzo's right. We are free to start first thing in the morning if you want." He gave a forced smile and a tense nod of consent.

Confusion settled over my features as the two of them glared at each other. "Great. I'll be here too. I'll help out wherever you need me. I'm not skilled but I'll do my best to help and not be in your way."

Enzo held out his hand. "Looks like we have a gentlemen's deal, boys."

I shook both of their hands. "Thank you and I'll see you first thing tomorrow."

Wow. I shook my head and let my shoulders slump.

This was too good to be true. Everything came together way too easily. I got the girl. I got the house. It was hard to comprehend that everything was going this smoothly—almost too smoothly. I hoped to hell that fate wasn't gearing me up only to take it all away.

Phoenix rested his hand on my shoulder and cleared his throat. "Do you want to call Candice? If you want, I will take Riley home with me so that you guys can go through the house."

I cracked my knuckles. "Yeah, if you don't mind keeping her for a couple of hours?"

***

I swiveled away from Phoenix as I heard the car pull in to the drive. My palms began to sweat and my heart raced as I watched Candice and Riley get out of the car. A thin sheen of sweat formed along my spine and soaked into the back of my shirt. Having to wait for Candice's impression of the house gnawed at my tightly strung nerves.

Riley sprinted toward me, screaming with excitement. "Fowwest."

I bent down and opened up my arms. "Come here, princess." She took a flying leap into my outstretched arms. Her little arms wrapped snuggly around my neck and cut off some of my air supply. This felt right. I beamed proudly, just as any father would. I stood up with her still cradled in my arms to greet Candice. I switched Riley to my hip so that I could pull Candice into my other side. She put her arm around my waist and lifted her head. I responded to her invitation by covering her soft lips with mine.

She tasted like sin and strawberries. I licked my lips

after I pulled away. "Yum." I scanned her delicate features and soaked in all of her beauty. A squirming Tasmanian devil pulled me out of my trance-like state.

"Put me down, pease. I have to see Unci Phoenix." She practically jumped out of my arms and flew at Phoenix like a spider monkey. "How come you hewe, too?"

"I came to see if you wanted to come home with me." He brushed a golden curl behind her ear.

"Is TiTi Wuce home?" She scrunched up her face as if to say, she better be.

"Yep and waiting for us. So why don't you say good-bye to your mom and Forrest while I switch out your car seat." Phoenix set her back down.

"Bye." She caught up to Phoenix before he even got to the car. He chuckled at her eagerness.

Shaking my head with laughter, I hugged Candice tightly and softly kissed the top of her head while we watched them pull away.

She drew back from my embrace to look over at the house. My stomach clenched into a tight knot as I waited for her reaction. At this point, the house wasn't much to look at. A hint of panic welled into my throat. Softly, I spoke to her, unsure of what she was thinking. "I know it's not much right now."

With a deliberately casual movement, she turned and faced me. She reached out and clutched my hands. I swallowed the icy fear that threatened to latch on to my throat and waited. The beginning of a smile tipped the corner of her mouth. I let out the breath that I had been holding. I tugged her into me almost violently.

She brought a hand up to stifle her giggles. "It's beautiful, Forrest." Her graceful hands cupped my face as she rained chaste kisses all over my face.

I threw my head back and let out a great peal of laughter. "I can't believe you held me in suspense for that long. You are cruel."

"You bring out my devilish side." She enjoyed the tender sparring as much as I did.

"Let's take a look inside."

"Lead the way." She gently pushed my shoulder in the direction of the house.

We strolled up the rickety steps and into our home. After her feet crossed the threshold, she stopped. Her gasp echoed throughout the foyer.

Her hand automatically covered her heart. "Holy shit."

I laughed at her shock. "There is more to the house, you know."

She lifted her arms and covered her breasts. She stared at me defiantly. I chuckled at her retreating back. I silently followed in her wake as she oohed and ahhed. My smile grew wider the closer we got to the master bedroom. She ran up the stairs, curiosity fueling her body. She stood in the middle of the room and turned her body in every direction.

"This is absolutely breathtaking." She looked briefly over her shoulder at me.

"You haven't even seen the best part." I walked up next to her and covered her hand with mine. I tugged her willing body into the bedroom. She separated herself from me and marched into the bathroom. I could hear her squealing with delight. I couldn't help but grin to myself as I looked out the balcony doors.

Lost in thought, I didn't hear Candice behind me. She wrapped her arms around my middle with her chest firmly pressed against my back. She laid her cheek between my shoulder blades.

"Thank you, Forrest." She sniffled.

I twisted in her arms so that I faced her. I gently lifted her chin. Her beautiful icy-blue eyes shimmered with unshed tears.

I brushed my lips against hers as I spoke. "Are those happy tears?"

She sputtered out a laugh. "Yes. They most certainly are."

"Thank God!" My face split into a wide grin. "Let's go get Riley." I let my arms fall to my side and moved to the right toward the door.

Her hand snaked out and snagged mine. With strength I didn't know she possessed, she twisted me around. An expression of satisfaction glimmered in her eyes. The confidence that shimmered around her made my blood sizzle with desire. I crushed her into me and devoured her mouth. I ran my tongue along the seam of her luscious lips. Her body went limp, succumbing to my demands.

She raised her hands up in the air, motioning for me to remove her top. I skimmed my hands up along her exposed skin, bunching up the material until I pulled it over her head and tossed it to the floor. I placed a tantalizing kiss in the hollow of her neck that had her moaning in bliss. I trailed my lips down her ivory skin over her covered breasts. She threw her head back as I grazed each hardened nipple with my teeth through the thin material. I continued to tease while my hands reached around and unclasped her bra.

I reclaimed her mouth as I slipped the straps down her arms She stood before me with heavily hooded eyes. I lowered my mouth to her shoulders. Between kisses, I whispered how beautiful and sexy she was. I slid my hands inside the waistband of her pants. I pulled them down slowly, inch by tantalizing inch, until she stepped out of them. Standing back up, I pinched the silky fabric of her panties between my fingers and tore them off her. She gasped in sweet agony. Her heavy breathing combined with her soft cries of pleasure shot more blood to my dick. The overwhelming urge to claim her had me ripping off my clothes.

I held her gloriously naked body to me for a brief moment and relished in the feel of her pert nipples as they rubbed against my chest. I gently eased her down onto the thick carpet. I took my time exploring her responsive body. She withered beneath me. Small mews escaped her lips. I had to be inside her. I couldn't hold out any longer.

I drove into her moist heat. I growled as my cock thrust in and out of her. "This is my pussy," I commanded as I delved deeper.

She cried out, "Only yours."

I teased her with slow thrusts until she begged me to fuck her harder. I lowered my lips to her nipple and sucked it into my mouth. With each flick of my tongue, her pussy clamped tighter around my cock. I switched to the other breast. I glazed the hardened peak gently with my teeth before I drew my mouth over it. I pulled it into my mouth and rolled my tongue around the sensitive flesh. Her back arched upward as I lavished her supple breast.

Her inner walls clamped around my cock as tidal waves of ecstasy rushed through her. My own explosive release followed closely behind hers. I rolled to the side and tucked her into my ribs. We lay there, catching our breaths. I angled my head down and brushed a kiss into her hair.

17 CANDICE

I kept my eyes glued to his body as he sauntered over to my side of the car. My heart soared as though it were an eagle in flight. Every minute I spent with him increased my hunger. My appetite was insatiable.

I had given up on pure love a long time ago. My mind had told my heart that fairytales didn't exist. Forrest had easily destroyed the armor placed high around my heart. He was it for me. My love for him was so strong that I felt as if our souls were tied together as one.

A silly grin appeared on my face as he held open the door for me. He reached his hand out for me to take. I linked our fingers together as he helped me out of the car. I rose up on my toes and kissed his mouth adoringly. "I love you. Thank you for today."

His eyes smoldered. "You are the best thing that has ever happened to me. I can't imagine my life without you." He whispered a kiss across my lips. "Let's go get our princess."

We didn't stay long. We still had to pick up my car

before the shop closed. Riley spoke animatedly all the way to pick up my car and all the way home. I could only get one or two words in throughout her whole story. It quickly culminated into a minute-by-minute commentary. She was wound as tight as a six-string banjo. Forrest would have a hard time getting her to settle down for bed. I chuckled to myself at the image playing through my mind. Irritation gnawed at me, knowing that I only had a couple more hours to spend with them.

***

I kissed them both. "Riley, you be good for Forrest."

She looked up at me with innocent eyes. Then she saluted me. "Aye, aye, Mommy."

I ruffled her hair, grabbed my bag, and headed for the door. I turned my head and looked over my shoulder. I smiled to myself as I watched the two of them snuggled together, watching cartoons.

The drive into work seemed long and arduous even though I only lived fifteen minutes away. My mind was curled up, watching TV with my two favorite people. I had to get my head in the game. Any more screw-ups and Logan would can my ass. I had some money set aside but not enough to carry me through until I found something else.

I sat at my vanity and tried to psych myself up to shake my ass for a bunch of strangers. If I was honest with myself, it felt as though everything that Forrest treasured was out on cheap display. Disgust trampled on my frame of mind even more.

I lifted my chin and squared my shoulders. It was a job, just like any other. I would get through this night.

***

I heaved a sigh of relief once I put my street clothes back on. I made it through. I met Ben at the door and he walked me to my car. "Thanks, Ben."

"Night, Candice. Be careful driving home."

I waved him away. "Always."

I put my belt on and started up the car. From the corner of my eye, I noticed a slip of paper underneath my wiper blade. I unlatched myself, opened up the door, and grabbed the piece of paper. I threw it in my purse that sat in the passenger seat, backed out, and headed home. I'd look at it tomorrow. I was eager to get home.

I slipped in beside Forrest, bone-tired and with a heavy mind. As soon as I felt his arm slip around me, all my worries melted away. His heat and strength cocooned my body in a protective layer. My eyelids became heavy. I shut the world out and let my mind wander into dreamland.

***

Riley bounced on the bed and startled me awake. I only had a split second to gain my bearings before my exuberant child flew on top of me. I rolled on my back and stuck my arms straight out. Riley didn't disappoint; she jumped right into them. I squeezed her tight and then commenced to tickle the hyper right out of her.

She laughed and screamed until she couldn't catch her breath. "Mommy, no mow. Fowwest tode me to come get you foe bweakfast."

I laughed. "We better go downstairs before we get in trouble then." I grabbed onto her legs and pulled her closer. "But just one more tickle before we go."

She giggled as she kicked out at me, climbed off the bed, and ran from the room. I didn't dare chase after her. If she knew I did, she would certainly trip and fall down the stairs, too busy looking behind her. I walked into the kitchen. They both sat at the table with a stack of pancakes. I grabbed a plate.

I kissed the top of Riley's head. She smiled up at me. "I won."

"Yes, you did. You are too fast for me to catch."

I sauntered over to the empty seat next to Forrest. I leaned over with my stinky morning breath and caressed his mouth with a kiss. "Good morning."

"Morning, beautiful. Did you sleep well?"

"Always, when you are next to me." I smiled and piled my plate with delicious buttery goodness. Saliva pooled in my mouth as I slathered on the sticky syrup. This was so much better than cereal. "Yum. These are scrumptious," I mumbled with my mouth full.

"It not powite to tawk with mouth fuww." Riley parroted my favorite saying.

Forrest chuckled. "You're right, Riley. Should we let it pass just this one time? Mommy was paying me a compliment."

She placed her tiny finger to her chin and tapped. "Hmm. I think we wet it pass."

I leaned over and kissed her on the top of her head. "Thank you. I won't let it happen again."

Forrest shoveled his breakfast down in a hurry to meet up with Sal and Enzo. Riley and I took our time eating. I had the night off and I wanted to enjoy my time with her. Lately, it seemed as though I hadn't seen her much. The weekend would come soon enough.

I wondered whether my parents were going to keep her or whether Forrest wanted her to stay with him. I didn't want to take her away from my parents but if Forrest wanted to, I would let him. He jumped into daddy duty with both feet. What he didn't realize was that he was a natural. *Damn, I am one lucky woman!*

Riley went to play while I cleaned up. It didn't take me long. One thing I detested was cleaning the house. Forrest had scored another point for keeping the place picked up while I was at work. *God, could this man have a flaw somewhere?* Not having to clean freed up a lot of time. I threw in some laundry and sat on the floor with Riley and played until the washer dinged. I tossed the clothes in the dryer. I quickly packed a bag of snacks and drinks for the park. It was too nice out to waste it playing inside.

"Alright, baby girl. Get your shoes on while I load up the car."

"We going to the pawk?" Gleeful hope shimmered in her eyes.

"You got it, turkey." I gently pinched her cheek.

"I not a tuwkey. I Wiley." She thrust her chin out.

Laughter bubbled out. "Yes, baby, that you are."

We drove up to the empty playground. Sometimes I wished that there would be more kids here. Riley needed friends her own age. It wasn't fair that she had to hang with adults all day long. Then again, I really liked the quiet park. It made keeping an eye on her a little easier. And I didn't have to watch other little monsters knock into her or not wait their turn. I couldn't stand when certain moms let their child roam free without any regard for the other children playing. They were the type who never reprimanded them when they did something hurtful. I had a hard enough time disciplining my own child, let alone someone else's.

I reached into my purse for a piece of gum. My mouth felt as though I tried to swallow a couple of cotton balls. I didn't want to drink a bunch of water because then I would have to pee. The only bathroom was a porta-potty and I'd rather squat in the grass before I used one of those. Sure, it's okay for Riley. I have sanitizer. Plus, the child would eat off the floor——nothing grosses her out.

My fingers sought out the pack but brushed over the slip of paper from last night. Intrigued, I forgot about the gum. I pulled the small sheet out. The side I pulled out held nothing. I flipped it over. The other side contained barely legible print. I immediately recognized the penmanship.

The paper fluttered in my hands as they shook. The child-like scribble blurred the longer I stared at it. My heart skipped a beat and my skin broke out in a cold sweat. The hair on the back of my neck stood at attention. Goose bumps marched along my skin as I scanned the words again.

Did you get my last message? I am watching you. Soon I will take what's mine.

What the fuck kind of game was Eugene playing? What could I possibly have that he wanted? Money? It was possible but highly unlikely. I didn't own any good quality jewelry. I put my engagement ring and wedding band in the safe. They weren't worth much but maybe one day Riley would want them. My hand flew to my face and covered my mouth. *No, I don't believe it. Why would he? Fuck, he wanted Riley.*

Hell, I knew he loved her in his own warped mind. I scanned the playground to ensure that we were the only ones around. I couldn't see anyone but that didn't mean that he wasn't lurking around somewhere. *Shit, shit, shit. What was I going to do?* I had to protect her. She couldn't stay with me until Eugene showed himself. And God as my witness, he would.

I had to get Riley home, where she wouldn't be out in the open for him to take. I doubted that I could stop him physically but I would sure as hell die trying before he snatched Riley away from me. If he got the chance, I would never see her again. I shook my head fiercely as I tossed everything in the bag. Nope, not going to happen. He would not gain access to her——ever.

Riley's giggles kept my hysteria at bay. My voice barely shook when I called for her. "Riley. Come on, sweetheart, it's time to go."

She stood at the top of the slide with her hand cocked on her hip. "Not weady. One moe time. Okay!"

I plastered on a tight smile. "Slide down one more time. Then we have to leave."

"Okay," she sweetly sang out, oblivious of my fear-laced tone.

I stood in front of the slide and caught her on her way down. The only way to distract her from running up the ladder again was for her to think we were playing a game. I picked her up and threw her up in the air and caught her again. She screamed excitedly. I tossed her over my shoulder, picked up our bags, and headed to the car. Riley's little giggles filled the air. Her laughter was infectious. Being silly with her helped ease a little part of the anxiety.

It took me forever to buckle her in because I kept searching around to make sure that Eugene didn't pop out and surprise me while I was preoccupied. I jumped at every little sound. I huffed out a breath of frustration. *Come on; keep it together for a few more minutes.* Finally, it clicked into place.

We pulled in to the drive and I unclipped Riley. I turned on my heel and called behind my shoulder. "Race you."

Riley's competitive side drove her need to win. She barreled past me, onto the porch. "I win."

"Oh, man. I can't believe you beat me."

She jumped up and down as I unlocked the door. "I did last time."

"Winner has to wash their hands."

"Okay. I go clean them up." She dashed into the bathroom.

While she was busy, I pulled out my phone and sent a quick text to Forrest.

Will you be home for dinner?

He replied instantly.

Yep. See you later. Love you.

A genuine shit-eating grin lined my face.

Love you too.

I wanted to tell him but I couldn't make my fingers type it. He deserved to have his time away. Fixing up the house made him happy. At this point, there was no reason for him to worry. I'd tell him about it tonight.

Forrest came through the door as I put the pasta into the boiling water. "Smells good in here." He picked up Riley and gave her a bear hug laced with a growl.

She growled and grunted back, communicating something that I didn't understand. He answered her back with grunts and groans. With her sitting on his hip, he walked over to me and covered my mouth with a simple but heart-warming kiss.

This is what I had dreamed my first marriage to be but it had turned out more along the lines of a nightmare, where Eugene continued with his starring role. A sigh of yearning for freedom escaped my lips.

18 FORREST

Something bothered Candice. She had told me it was nothing when I asked her earlier. I only had to look at the way she stiffly held herself, as though she were uncomfortable in her skin. She leaned heavily into me at times and didn't veer from my side for long. For the first time, I wished for darkness to fall and Riley's bedtime to come. I felt compelled to find out what the hell was going on. I was torn between wanting to play with Riley or fawn over Candice.

I waited downstairs for her while she tucked in Riley. It felt weird not being able to do our nightly ritual. I didn't know what to do with myself while I waited. I sat up straighter when I heard the door close. Her footfalls were light as she descended the stairs. She tiptoed into the room as though she were trying to avoid me.

I patted the cushion next to me. "Come here."

She plopped onto the cushion next to me and sighed with relief. Her body sagged into mine. I encircled my arms around her, giving her the strength she needed as she collected her thoughts.

She took a deep breath in. "I found a note tucked underneath my wiper last night. I thought it was an advertisement of some sort so I threw it in my purse and forgot about it." She closed her eyes and gathered up more courage. "I took Riley to the park this morning. While we were there, I rummaged through my purse. I pulled the paper out and on the one side was a warning."

My body tensed the more she spoke. *Why was she telling me this now? She should have said something earlier today.* I forcefully uncoiled my body. "What did it say? Who was it from? Do you still have it?"

She raised her fingers to my mouth, effectively shutting me up. "I'm trying to tell you." She slipped her hand in her pocket and pulled out the crinkled paper. She handed it over for me to read.

I snatched it from her hands as though it would disintegrate once she had read it. I remained impassively relaxed and cold as I read the few lines.

I raised my eyes up from the paper and peered right through her. "I'll take care of this."

She slid off my lap and stalked around the room. "That's not what I want you to do. I want to do this together. I'll take it to the police and…" She stopped midstride. "Was the slashed tire the previous message?" She crossed her arms.

"That's exactly what I think. Unless there is something else that happened." I looked at her questioningly.

"No. You know as much as I do." Her eyes sparked with fire.

I blew out a frustrated breath. "He is toying with you.

He will continue to play this game and I don't know how far he will take it."

Her blue eyes turned midnight and her brows drew together. "Are you in this with me or are you just playing house with us?" She spread her arms out wide and swung them from side to side. "Are we your pawns in this so-called game?" Her chest rose rapidly as her anger mounted. A flush reddened her cheeks.

What? How did this get turned around on me? I stood up and walked confidently in her direction. She backed away from me and inched closer to the wall. I continued to stalk her until her back hit the wall. She had nowhere to go. Goal accomplished. She needed to hear what I had to say. I cupped her cheeks with my hand. She turned her head to the side, not looking at me.

I gently turned her head back and forced her to face me. "In no way am I playing house with you and Riley. I am one hundred percent entirely yours. I don't want a family with anyone but you. I want to be Riley's daddy. The one she looks up to. I want to be the man who deserves your love."

I placed my mouth close to her ear and whispered, "I only see you." I sucked the tip of her earlobe between my teeth. She gasped at the rough teasing. I moved my lips down her delicate skin, across her rapidly beating pulse, to the hollow of her neck. "I crave your soft skin. I'm addicted to your cries of pleasure. I ache for your touch."

I fisted the collar of her shirt and tore it in half, exposing more of her creamy skin. My lips continued their downward path and paid special attention to her hardened nipples. I grazed each one with my teeth as I pushed the bra up. Her breasts sprung free. I swirled my tongue around one nipple. It pebbled more from my attention. My fingers rolled the other nipple. She cried out with pleasure and squirmed under my touch.

She whimpered as my lips left her aroused buds. I grabbed the waistband of her pants and pushed them down around her ankles. I kneeled as I lifted each leg and slid her pants over each foot. I leaned up, my face aligned with her belly button. I kissed the top of her shaved mound. "This is mine," I growled. I possessively shoved my tongue in her slick pussy, marking her with each swipe of my tongue. I pinned her hips to the wall as I devoured her sweet nectar. I hummed and licked until I could feel her orgasm pulsate around my mouth. "You taste exquisite. I will never get enough of you."

I moved up the length of her body. I stood before her with a hunger so intense I thought I would burst. I placed my hands along her ribs and hoisted her in the air. She automatically wrapped her strong legs around my waist. I pushed her back up against the wall for more leverage as I pushed my throbbing cock into her wet center. Her head thrashed from side to side as I drove in and out of her.

I bit and suckled each nipple. They erotically bounced in my face as I thrust harder and harder. She bit her lip to keep from screaming aloud. With one hand holding onto her and the other braced against the wall, I plunged even deeper.

Her inner walls tightened around my cock, coaxing my climax closer. "Fuck, Forrest. I'm going to come." Her walls constricted around my cock and I was lost in my own release.

When my legs felt as though they wouldn't give out, I scooped her up and carried her upstairs. I gently laid her on the bed and crawled in beside her. I tucked my arm behind my head. "Come here." She scooted over until her head fit perfectly into my shoulder and chest. "I love the way your body molds to mine." I let my arm fall down around her shoulders and pulled her tighter into me. I breathed a kiss along the top of her head.

"Forrest," she whispered into the silent room.

"Yeah."

"Do you think that I should send Riley to my parents for a little while? Just until things with Eugene get resolved?" She raised her chin up so that she could look at me. Concern danced in the recesses of her face.

My heart broke at the thought of having to send Riley away. She had a valid point. Eugene wasn't going away. All of his actions thus far pointed to desperation. He would come looking for her. She shouldn't be placed in harm's way. I sighed heavily, hating to admit that it was the right thing to do for Riley.

"Yes, baby. I think that is exactly what you should do. I don't want Riley caught in the cross hairs. Eugene is unstable and unpredictable. She needs to be far away from him and us. Especially since he is watching you."

I smiled to myself as an idea formed. I hoped that Candice would agree to it. "What do you think about me taking her to your parents before you go into work tomorrow? I'll take Riley out for ice cream or something and then head to their house. If Eugene is watching you, then he probably knows your routine. Hopefully he won't be watching the house and realize that when I come back she isn't with me. I'll make sure that your parents take Riley some place far from here, at least for the week. We will figure it out from there."

Her voice wavered with uncertainty and fear. "Do you think that she will be safe?"

I wasn't sure whether she would be but I trusted the fact that Eugene just wanted to scare Candice and he wasn't through with that yet. He wouldn't try to go for Riley until Candice feared for Riley's life.

"If you trust me, I'd like to book a flight for the three of them to visit my parents. They would love to meet Riley, and your parents will get some help with her."

A resemblance of a smile traced her sweet mouth. "I trust you with Riley and my life. I think it's a brilliant plan." She leaned up and placed her sweet mouth to my cheek. The tenderness with which she presented me had my heart signing all rights over to her.

19 CANDICE

For the first time in a long time, I woke up feeling rejuvenated. My limbs felt as light as my heart. Lately, I took advantage of Forrest's early morning hours and slept later than I normally would have. I used the excuse that it gave Riley and Forrest much-needed quality time. They didn't need it because they both took to each other as though they were kindred souls. I bit the corner of my mouth as I tried to suppress my giggles. Forrest was rugged and commanding. When he played with Riley, he became gentle. His whole body melted as soft as room temperature butter when Riley folded into him. He turned into an adorable pushover.

I silently glided down the stairs so I didn't disturb their morning. Actually, I wanted to eavesdrop on them. I loved to watch them interact. It was one of my happiest pleasures to indulge in. Especially when they were unaware of me. I hid behind the entryway of the living room. Riley sat, curled up into his lap. He had covered her in her favorite blanket. She had her head resting in the crook of his arm, using him as her pillow.

Her sweet innocence captured my breath. A slice of

reality but into my conscience. We would have to say good-bye to her in a few short hours. A mixture of fear and anger coiled in my belly. My fingers curled into my hand. I could feel the sting of my nails cut into my flesh. The spark of pain thrust me into action. I bent down and ruffled Riley's hair before I placed a kiss upon her forehead. Still bent over, I angled my shoulders toward Forrest. I rested my hands on his chiseled chest as I leaned in for my morning kiss. He secretly slipped me the tongue. I reveled in his naughty behavior. I pulled back before Riley could take notice.

"Are you guys hungry? How about French toast for breakfast?"

"Pease," Riley mumbled, never taking her eyes of the screen.

"Yummy. I'm starving." The glint in his eye conveyed his hunger and it wasn't screaming for waffles.

I squeezed my legs together to remind my lady bits that it was not the time to ravage him. It would have to wait until later.

I couldn't eat, so I let the two of them wolf down their breakfast while I called my mom.

"Morning, sweetheart. How are things?" she asked with a cheer to her voice.

I sighed and basked in her happiness before I destroyed it. There was no need to sugarcoat things. She would appreciate me being blunt. "Eugene has come around and made some threats. It has gotten serious enough that I am frightened for Riley's safety."

"What!"

I pulled the receiver away from my ear. "Look, Mom. I need you to be calm for me. Flipping out on me is not helping." I could hear her breathing as her anger mounted. "I need you to do me a huge favor. You aren't going to like it but it's all we could come up with for now."

She interrupted me. "Just say it, Candice."

"Forrest will bring Riley over to your house. We will make plane reservations for the three of you to go and visit his parents in California."

"I will do no such thing. Riley will be safe here with your father and me," she adamantly stated, not leaving much room for me to convince her otherwise.

I had to give it one last-ditch effort. "Mom, please listen to me. Eugene showed up to the house and threatened me. Forrest got there at the right time and made him leave. Then he slashed my tire while I was at work. A couple of days later, he left me a threatening letter. I'm really scared that he is trying to take Riley." My voice shook. "Mom, please, I am begging you to do as I ask."

Her soothing voice helped to keep my tears at bay. "Okay, baby, we will. How long will we be gone? And who the hell is Forrest?"

Oh, shit! That was how wrapped up in my own little world I was. I hadn't told her anything about Forrest. *I am such a bad daughter.* "I'm hoping only for a week but I don't know for sure. Eugene is seriously unhinged and strung out. There is no telling how far he is willing to go."

"Whatever you need us to do, we will. Now tell me about this Forrest." Her voice held a hint of a smile.

I sighed longingly at the mere thought of him.

"Forrest is the guy I've been seeing for a while now. Actually, he's Phoenix's older brother. Riley and he are close, and I trust him with her life as well as my own. I promise that when all this settles down, I will clue you in. Will you and Dad take Riley to stay with his parents? I will keep you updated with what is going on here and when it's safe to come home."

"As long as he stays with you and keeps you safe. I love you so much. The thought of you being hurt terrifies me. Be safe, Candice." She tried to mask the tears that emerged through her voice.

"I promise. I won't be able to say good-bye before you leave. Please keep Riley safe and unaware of what is going on. I love you, Mom." My voice caught as I tried to swallow my tears.

"Love you too, baby."

I hung up the phone and gave myself an extra minute to find my composure. I couldn't go back into the house and have Riley notice my sadness. She was a pretty perceptive kid. I wanted her to go away happy. In case anything happened to me, I had no doubts that she would be loved and cared for. I fucking hated Eugene with such a passion. I hoped to hell he sought me out so that I could kill him with my bare hands. I would end this shit once and for all.

I slipped back inside with a renewed determination. Riley was dressed and cleaned up from breakfast. *God, I adored that man.*

"I'm going to go make a call to my parents. I already arranged flights. They fly out tomorrow morning. I printed up their boarding passes and everything." He placed a gentlemen's kiss on my cheek and took the same path to make his phone call.

I tried to act as normal as I possibly could around Riley. I'm sure she had an idea that something was going on because she clung to me. Every room I puttered in, she came right along. That was fine by me. I cherished every second I had with her. I had the two of them come up to her room while I packed up her suitcase. I wanted Riley to know that Forrest and I were a team and what I conveyed to her, he would maintain the charade.

"How come you pack so much?" her little voice questioned.

I stopped what I was doing. I picked her up and sat her on the bed. "Well. You, my lovely princess, are going on a big trip with YaYa and Pappa."

"Whewe to?" Her excitement fluttered through her tone.

"You are going to go visit Forrest's mom and dad in California. Doesn't that sound like fun?" I made sure to add extra cheer so she wouldn't be afraid. "You get to fly in a plane and everything."

Her blue eyes turned as big as saucers. "A weal pwane? Do the piowit know whewe he going? I couwd hewp him."

My laughter bubbled out. "Yes, baby. The pilot knows the way."

She held up her petite hand to interrupt me. "Can I caw them YaYa and Pappa too?"

I looked over at Forrest for some reinforcement. "Their names are Daisy and River. Why don't you call them Miss Daisy and Mr. River for now. That way, when you meet them you, can come up with another name. They may like Grandma and Grandpa among other names. I bet if you ask they will help you figure them out." He looked over at me as if to ask if that was the right response.

The love that poured off me could have drowned a lesser man. "After I get you all packed up, do you want to go get some ice cream with Forrest?"

"That be awesome." She looked up at me. "Are you done yet?"

I stole a kiss from her elfin nose. "Yep. You are all set to go get some ice cream."

She trotted out of the room to go find her shoes. I slumped onto the edge of the bed, feeling lost. A sharp pain ravaged a path through my heart. Tears stung my eyes as they slipped down my cheeks.

Forrest engulfed me in his masculine arms. "I love you. She will be safe with my family and yours." He moved my hair from my shoulder and placed a soothing kiss.

I nodded, unable to speak. Forrest went to help Riley while I mentally told my feet to move. I quickly swiped the tears from my face and went to say good-bye to my little girl. I prayed that it wouldn't be the last time I laid eyes on her.

20 FORREST

Candice gave Riley one last squeeze before I loaded her up. There was nothing I could say to ease her pain. So, I placed a comforting kiss to her quivering mouth. Riley chattered away and didn't notice the tears streaming down her mom's face as we backed out of the drive. That image of her would haunt me for days to come, quite possibly forever.

My hands gripped the steering wheel so tightly that my knuckles had turned white. Anger coiled through my veins at the thought of Eugene using his own flesh and blood to torture Candice. I wasn't naïve——there were parents out there who used their children to get their spouses to adhere to their will. It was inconceivable for me to imagine what kind of monster would entertain such an idea.

I adjusted the rearview mirror so that I could glance at Riley and still maintain my focus on the road. "Would you like to get some ice cream before we head to your YaYa and Pappa's?"

Her smile lit up her whole face. "Pease."

Her grin was infectious. "Okey-dokey, princess."

I pulled into the first ice cream place that I saw. The place displayed small round tables outside on a square concrete slab. The place was open but deserted, which was perfect for me. I didn't want the distractions of other patrons to intrude on my time with her. It might be selfish on my part but I didn't give a rat's ass. I adored the little firecracker. When it came time to turn her over, I would lose a piece of me until she returned.

We walked hand in hand up to the counter. I picked her up so she could look through the frosted glass and choose her flavor. "Know what you want?"

She tapped her pointer finger against her chin. "Hmm. It's tough caw." She paused dramatically. "I think stwabewwy in a cone, pease."

My laughter shook her whole body. I looked at the high school kid behind the counter. "Two strawberry ice creams in a cone, please."

She looked at me with bored eyes. "One or two scoops?"

Riley and I looked at each other and grinned. "Two."

We took our cones outside. The metal chairs scraped along the concrete slab as we slid them out from underneath the table. Before we walked out, I had made sure to grab a fistful of napkins. I'm glad I did because Riley had melted ice cream all over her face. How she managed to get some on her forehead was beyond me. I didn't care one bit. We were having a good time. I'm sure if I delivered her to her YaYa filthy dirty, a bath would ensue. There was only one thing about Riley that I knew for certain: she loved baths. She continued to play in the water long after it had gone cold.

She slapped her hand against her head. Her cherub face scrunched up as though she had sucked on a lemon. I chuckled. "Brain-freeze?"

She nodded. "Ouch."

I coughed into my hand as I tried to cover my laughter. She looked up at me with a twinkle in her eye. Then, as if on cue, she went into a fit of giggles. "I cwazy."

My abs constricted with discomfort from all the laughter. I couldn't have scripted a better moment with her. I cleaned her up the best that I could. YaYa would definitely have to give her a good soak.

We pulled in to the drive. I sat in the driver's seat for a couple of seconds longer, needing to prolong the inevitable.

"Get me out, pease." She wiggled excitedly.

I hung my head low, dreading the moment I had to let her out of the car. The moment I unbuckled Riley, she shot out of the car like a cannonball. She ran as fast as her little legs would carry her, right into her YaYa's arms. I grabbed her suitcase and headed up to the porch.

I extended my arm and shook their hands. "It's a pleasure to meet you, Mr. and Mrs. Russell."

Mr. Russell squinted and applied more pressure than necessary. I gave him the most sincere smile I could and let him squeeze my fingers. They felt as though they were being pinched into a vise.

Mrs. Russell smacked his hand playfully. "Cut it out."

An evil glow came over his features. "I trust that you have my daughter and granddaughter's best interest at heart." His tone took on an authoritative growl.

I understood his reaction to me. If I met one of Riley's boyfriends, I'm pretty sure that I wouldn't be as accommodating. "Yes, sir. You have my word."

He nodded with acceptance.

Mrs. Russell stood with Riley on her hip. They were both watching our exchange with mild curiosity. "Please call me Cindy. Would you like to come in, Forrest?"

I angled my body toward her and Riley. "No, thank you, ma'am." Riley stretched out her arms. I grabbed her and held her tightly against me. "You be good for your YaYa and Pappa. Have fun with my parents. Give them a kiss for me." My voice became gruff. I don't do well with good-byes. "I'll miss you, princess. I love you, sweet girl."

She squeezed me as tight as she could. "I wuv you too, Fowwest. I pwomise to be good." She placed a tiny kiss to my cheek. I handed her back to Mrs. Russell and turned to get into my car. They all waved as I backed out of the drive. I honked my horn and headed back to Candice.

***

With Riley gone, our alone time became subdued and riddled with anxiety. The both of us picked at our dinner, neither hungry nor excited about the circumstances of our kid-free night. Under normal conditions, I'd have already had Candice naked and panting, marking her before she left for work. We lounged on the couch until she went to get ready.

I had a difficult time letting Candice go into the VIP room tonight. This weekend would be long and arduous. I ground my teeth together, imagining other men touching what was mine. I itched to tell her to quit and find something else. As much as I despised her job at the moment, I couldn't ask her to do that. She needed her independence. If and when she wanted to, I wouldn't jump up and down in front of her. Oh, no, I would fist pump the air in my mind.

She put her hands on my thighs. She bent at the waist and gave me a very vanilla kiss. "You can do better than that." I gleamed at her wickedly.

"That wasn't good enough for you?" She cocked her head to the side with a pout.

I shook my head. "Nope. You are going to be gone a long time tonight. I need a little bit more than a kiss that felt as though it came from my grandmother."

Her eyes widened and her mouth parted in mock surprise. "Grandma, huh?"

She climbed onto my lap. She cupped my cheeks and brought my face closer to hers. She licked her lips, driving my blood south. She looked down as my cock hardened beneath her. Grinning wickedly, she lowered her mouth to mine. I didn't waste any time thrusting my tongue between her moistened lips. She matched my intensity. Right when I began swiveling my hips against her heat, she pulled back. I threw my head against the back of the couch with a painful groan.

She climbed off my lap, swung her purse over her shoulder, and walked away. She had bested me at my own game——easily walking out and leaving me raging hard.

She spoke over her shoulder. "That felt good enough to me." Her laughter rang out and could be heard long after she shut the door. A slow, torturous seduction would play out much later. A grin spread across my teeth at the images that ran through my mind.

***

My connections in the security field still held clout. I made sure that I had left on good terms. In fact, a couple of those buddies owed me. It was time to collect a few.

"Hey, Mack, how you been? You back on home soil yet?"

"Forrest! Finally! I'm still finding sand in places that it shouldn't be. What a shit hole. I'm flying high, enjoying my free time before my next job. How the fuck are you? Heard you walked away after your last assignment."

"Fuck, I had to, man. I'd seen too much disturbing shit. It was getting too dark for my blood. It's all good, though. I'm going to start up my own security business. When you're ready, I want you on my team."

"Will do. As much as I'd love to reminisce with you, I'm sure this isn't a social call." He chuckled at his own joke.

"I need you to locate a Eugene Launer. Then, I need you to find all the information you can on him. I want habits, financial status, friends, etc. If you can find it, then I want it."

"Do I want to know why I am collecting this intel for you?"

"I'll tell you later." I smirked. Mack would get me what I needed regardless whether he ever knew the specifics.

"Am I going to get a call to help with removal?" There was an underlying seriousness to his voice. He liked to be informed of that beforehand.

"Maybe," I growled.

"Alright. I'll get you the info as soon as I have it."

"Thanks. Talk to you soon." I hung up relieved, that I would have some answers.

Mack was a wiz at finding information on people that even government officials couldn't get. He was a good man to have on your side. Disposing of a body wasn't new for us nor would it be an issue. It would be done swiftly but carefully and strictly between the two of us. For a job like this, I only trusted Mack. Not only would he have my back, but he wouldn't balk at a dirty job. Now it was a wait-and-see kind of game. In the meantime, I would bide my time and wait to see whether Eugene would show himself.

21 CANDICE

I may have left Forrest hard as a rock but he had me just as wet. Without realizing it, he had marked me for good. He had tattooed himself all over my body. Anyone could see that I was hooked. I had severe doubts about how tonight would go. *Could I handle rubbing myself all over my clients? Could I make my clients come with the same body that belonged to Forrest?* It was all an act and I received no pleasure from them but would my mind and heart separate enough to do my job? I huffed out an aggravated breath and walked into the bass thumping club. I smiled all the way to the dressing room even though on the inside I screamed at the unfairness of it all.

I caked the makeup on my face until I was barely recognizable. My reflection laughed hysterically back at me. I looked like a dried-up rodeo clown coming off a three-day bender. *What the fuck had I done to myself?* If I weren't on such an emotional roller coaster, I'd have laughed. I only had twenty minutes to get my shit together. I glared back at my reflection. I tipped my chin up, squared my shoulders, and wiped the hideous goop off my face.

I flung all of the used wipes into the garbage. Feeling

marginally better, I donned my stage attire and waited for Cinnamon to come through the doors. The stage music switched numbers. She normally came back to the dressing room between numbers. It wouldn't be long now. The doors flew open and Cinnamon sashayed over to her vanity. I watched her freshen up her makeup. It was now or never. I trudged over to her wondering whether I could give it all up.

My smile grew wider the closer I got. Yeah, I most definitely could. "Hey, girl."

"What's up Candy? You need to borrow something?" She barely gave me a passing glance.

"Nope. What would you say if I asked you to take over my clientele?" I smiled sincerely so she knew that I wasn't pulling her leg.

She turned her head slowly and gaped at me. "Are you serious?"

I couldn't stop my toothy grin from making an appearance. I was dead serious. The sense of relief that crashed through my body reinforced my decision.

"I'm hanging it all up. You want them or not? You're the best girl for the job. If you want them, then you better get ready because you only have ten minutes before you're scheduled to go in. I'm going to talk to Logan."

"Thanks, girl. I'll do you proud." She shot up and rushed around, pulling together her outfit.

I changed into my street clothes, grabbed my bag, and headed directly to Logan's office. She would be pissed as shit. I couldn't care less. I should have done this a long time ago.

I rapped twice on the scuffed six-panel door. Her commanding voice drifted through the wood. I opened up the door and took a confident step into her office.

"Sit," she barked out.

I continued to stand, not caring one way or another whether I offended her. I was done, which gave me the courage to stand on my own two feet. "I'm fine standing, thank you." I inhaled a deep breath and exhaled slowly, "Logan, the only thing that I regret at this moment is that I didn't give you proper notice." I held up my hand. "Before you lay into me, I've got my clients covered. Cinnamon will do an excellent job. Honestly, I haven't been doing so hot lately. Irregardless——shit. Regardless, I'm out. I can't continue to work here." Another weight lifted off my shoulders. I felt my diaphragm balloon as I sucked in gulps of air.

Her steely gaze traveled along my skin. Goose bumps prickled along my arms. Her calculating stare had me biting the bottom of my lip. My stomach twisted in knots as I awaited her response.

A trace of a smile ghosted her mouth. "I figured tonight would be the night you'd cash it all in. That's why I had Cinnamon on standby."

My mouth hung open as my brain tried to play catch-up.

"Don't look at me like that. I don't operate a profitable business from only my looks. It is my business to know what goes on inside and outside of the club. It pays to stay a step ahead of your dancers. Surprises in this business cut into profits and I don't ever want to operate in the red." She waved her hand across her desk and motioned for me to sit.

I practically fell into the chair, glad to have something solid underneath me.

"I've been doing a lot of thinking. You are going to want to hear my proposition. I will give you the weekend to think about it. I want an answer by Monday morning." A real smile transformed her normally scowling persona into a more pleasant person.

I squirmed in my seat. Perspiration coated the pits of my shirt. My leg bounced up and down. Her eerie transformation loomed in the room. I could handle the scowling bitch that she normally presented. But this amused stranger before me scared the shit out of me. I did a piss-poor job of hiding my nervous reaction.

She grinned as though she had clutched her prey in her claws, her greedy leer ready to sink her canines into soft flesh. "I'd like to make you partner."

My screech echoed off the room. "Excuse me?"

She tossed her head back and let out a husky cackle. "You heard me. Look, I love running the club and I'm a damn good owner. However, I want some free time too. I have a life outside of here and I want to enjoy it. If you agreed to be partner, then we would split our time within these walls. We can iron out the details later. I don't want an answer now. I want you to go home to that fine piece of ass you have waiting for you." Her eyes shone with excitement. "Mull it over with your man."

I slowly pushed myself out of the chair as though I were nine months pregnant. My limbs were shaky and my mind flew through so many scenarios that I couldn't concentrate on one passing thought.

I scarcely mumbled, "Thank you."

She shooed her hand at me, back to all business. "Scram, before I change my mind."

My muscles finally engaged my bones into moving toward the door. I swiveled back around. "I don't know what I did to deserve your loyalty. I will have your answer by Monday. Thank you again, for putting up with all of my shit."

I wouldn't get an answer from her so I turned on my heel and left her office. Once I stepped outside the door, I bent over with my hands on my knees and sucked in huge amounts of oxygen. My mind went into scramble mode. Logan was unpredictable. She had thrown me for a loop more than once. *Would it be the same once I became partner?* The excitement churning in my gut told me that she would be completely different. With my mind made up, I slowly stood up as my heart rate came back into normal range. I held my head high as I greeted Ben. He escorted me to my car. I said a quick bye, eager to get home.

I didn't remember any part of the drive but here I sat, stunned stupid, in my driveway. I should go inside before Forrest noticed me sitting in my car when I should still be at work. I caught the flicker of the porch light turn on out of the corner of my eye. I opened up the car door, slid my weary body out and up to the front stoop.

My eyes roamed over the chiseled body that held open the door. The testosterone emitting from his body had my girl parts pulsating. He easily worked the part of a warrior taking no prisoners. Worry etched the lines around his face. His stance screamed battle ready. A toothy grin spread as I raced into his arms.

I wrapped myself around his body, using him as my lifeline. He backed into the house as though I were weightless He shifted his body and kicked his foot out to slam the door shut. "Not that I'm complaining, but you are home early." A lopsided grin transformed his stoic features. "Miss me that much?"

"Shut up and take me to bed." I wiggled my ass to make my point.

"Take-charge kind of gal. I like that." He hoisted me higher and took us up the stairs.

I nuzzled his neck and grazed my teeth upward, underneath his earlobe. I licked his most sensitive spot. He growled. Then missed a step. He righted us before we crashed into the railing. My tongue continued its lavish assault. He closed his eyes, lost in the pleasure. My hip clipped the corner of the doorframe as we moved into the bedroom. I was too charged to give a shit. I would worry about the bruise tomorrow. Tonight, my carnal need for him won against the irritating sting of my hip.

He sat on the edge of the bed with me still straddling his lap. He bunched up the cotton of my shirt. His rough knuckles scraped along my bared skin, sending delicious zings of pleasure over my ribs. The sensation of coarseness over my sensitive ribs had my hips grinding into his erection. His mouth captured mine and I swallowed his moan. He pulled away from me only long enough to wrench my shirt off. His impatience fed the flames that boiled my passion into a combustible heat. His sinful lips slammed back onto mine. Our tongues danced and dueled as they mated.

His deft fingers trailed a scorching path down my spine. He skillfully unclasped my bra. My back arched forward and poked my breasts into his chest. My nipples hardened into diamond peaks when they scraped over his chest. He lowered his head and sucked one nipple into his mouth. I tossed my head back to enjoy the pulling sensation. Moisture pooled into my panties as he slipped his hand over my covered pussy. I rose up onto my knees; my fingernails racked over his taut abs as they made their way down to the button of his jeans.

In one swift move, he had me on my back, caged within his large frame. I panted and thrashed my head from side to side as my body burned from the inside. He dipped his head between the valley of my breasts, licking and nibbling his way down to where I needed him the most. He hooked his fingers into my belt loops and slowly slid them down my legs.

He stood and shoved his pants down. His chest heaved as his gaze roamed my nakedness. Sparks of lust ignited the gold specks within his amber eyes. They glowed with a possessiveness that had me clenching my sex.

He crawled between my thighs. His massive hand cupped my glistening mound. My hips bucked and I rubbed myself into his hand. "This pussy is mine. I want to hear you say it."

A throaty moan escaped. "It's yours."

"Say it again."

He slipped a finger inside my heated channel. "Oh, God, Forrest. It's your pussy. Only yours."

He replaced his finger with the tip of his cock teasing my entrance. I wrapped my legs around his hips and crossed my ankles together, purposely pulling him closer.

"No more games. Fuck me now," I commanded gruffly. I couldn't wait anymore. I needed him inside me now.

My legs squeezed him tightly. I used my calves and

heels to push his hips closer. *Damn him*. He had barely moved an inch. I breathed heavily from exertion and neediness. The raging storm had me twisting and bucking, begging him to enter me.

His deep, throaty chuckle vibrated over my body. He skimmed his hands over my breasts and tweaked each nipple. The pain quickly turned into liquid hot desire. With no warning, he slammed into me, thrusting harder each time. His name escaped my lips through my moans the deeper he went.

My inner walls tightened around his cock to coax him closer to his own sweet oblivion. He reached between our rocking bodies, circling his thumb over my clit. My hips sprung upward at the onslaught of pleasure, which drove him even deeper. One rotation of his skilled thumb and I crumbled apart. I screamed his name as my muscles contracted. White sparks of light sprung behind my closed lids as my orgasm punched its way through me.

Forrest rolled to the side, tucking me into the crook of his arm. We lay there catching our breaths, relishing in the afterglow. He feathered a kiss along my hairline and then pulled the covers over our sweaty bodies. It wasn't long before I fell into a deep, satiated sleep with a grin affixed upon my swollen, well-ravished lips.

22 FORREST

My favorite thing to do in the morning was watch my angel sleep. Was it a bit stalkerish? Hell yes, it was, but I didn't really give a flying fuck. As crazy as it seemed, she became my center of gravity. Unbeknownst to her, she kept me grounded when the urge to fly surged through my veins. I was by no means shackled to her or Riley. I could leave at any time. I didn't want to; that's what made all the difference in the world. They would survive without me if I did but I wouldn't survive without them. In a fraction of a moment, they had become my world.

I swept her golden locks away from her shoulder so I could get a better view. She stirred and mumbled in her sleep. I brushed a butterfly of a kiss onto her shoulder and pulled the blanket farther up, covering her in the coolness of the morning.

Before I left the house, I checked the perimeter. I saw nothing out of the ordinary. I felt confident slipping out before she woke up. I left a note on the counter beside the coffee pot I had to meet up with Sal and Enzo.

I pulled up alongside the curb. Being the first one

here, I took the opportunity to make a call to Mr. and Mrs. Russell. "Hello, Cindy. How are you this morning?"

She smiled into the phone. "We are doing well. Riley is eating her breakfast and in about thirty minutes we will head out to the airport. Nothing out of the ordinary and no phone calls." She didn't need to elaborate. I understood exactly what she said.

"Excellent. Thank you for the update. Can I talk to Riley for a minute?" I asked, uncertain if I had any right.

"Of course you can. You don't have to ask permission, Forrest," she scolded.

I chuckled, feeling a little silly, but I didn't want to overstep my boundaries. I wasn't her daddy, even if I really believed that she was my little girl.

"Hi, Fowwest. We go on an airpwane today." Her excitement bubbled through the phone.

"Yes, you do, baby. You have a good time on your big trip, okay?"

"I be good. Pwomise. Bye. Wuv You."

"Love you too, princess."

I didn't even get a chance to connect back with Cindy because Riley had already disconnected the call. What a smart little girl. She probably understood how to work my cell phone better than I did.

My chest throbbed with pain, missing her. I stared at my phone and sighed. Mack had better get back in touch and soon. It would be a waste of time to call him. He would contact me as soon as he had what I asked him for.

I checked my watch and figured I had enough time to call my parents before we started to work. The phone went straight to voicemail. They were probably still asleep. I forgot about the time difference.

Their cheery voices played in my ear. Another ache crushed the air out of my lungs. Damn, I missed them. Once I heard the beep, I left them a message. "Please keep your clothes on in front of the Russells——more importantly, Riley. I love you guys but not everyone is as accepting as Phoenix and I are. Try to keep the other families equally dressed as much as possible. Let me explain it to them about how you all live. Now is not the time for them to be ambushed. Call me when you pick them up from the airport so that I know they got there. Love you and miss you."

With a few minutes to spare, I got out of the car and dashed up the temporary steps into the house, eager to start. At least these steps wouldn't give out. My mental checklist continued to grow daily. However, there were some scratches made. The roof had been replaced: check. Okay, that was it as of right now. Hell, that was hardly a small job.

The guys had already torn out the wrap-around porch and were halfway finished with the outside paint job. A multitude of projects were going on at once, but it wouldn't take long. All the outside projects would be done before winter hit. My job involved sanding all of the hardwood. Enzo would work his magic and bring it back to its original glory. Essentially I became the grunt man, which was fine by me.

I stood in the foyer, surrounded by silence. Soon it would be filled with laughter and Riley's pitter-patter. An image of Candice pregnant flittered through my mind. Riley and maybe a dog would be running around her feet.

Just as quickly as the picture formed, it shattered.

Enzo and Sal clamored through the door, bickering about some football game and whose team would decimate the other. Sal complained that the refs called too many penalties that weren't warranted. Enzo laughed in his face and told him to get over it. The refs didn't have it out for his team and that he was a paranoid fuck.

I chuckled quietly to myself. There was no way in hell I wanted to be a part of that conversation. I knew enough about football to shoot the shit with the guys but didn't really give a hoot about the game one way or another. I enjoyed a good fight.

Enzo noticed me first. "Hey, what's up? You ready to get to work?"

"Yep. I should be done with the floors today. I'll start on the staircase next."

"Sounds good. We should have the outside of the house painted today. Then tomorrow we'll start building the porch. Due to its odd shape and how big it is, it will take some time and money." Sal looked at me inquisitively.

"Understood. Whatever it takes. I'm good for it." I mentally sighed as the dollars flew out of my bank account.

It didn't matter in the long run because it was all for Candice and Riley. They deserved it and more. I had a ton of contacts for the business so jobs should come in quickly. We wouldn't hurt for money.

I felt the vibration of my phone before I heard the shrill ring. I hastily pulled it out of my pocket in hopes that it was Mack. A quick check told me it was only Phoenix.

I clicked the Answer button. "Yeah."

"Well, somebody is in a mood today. Did you get your period?" He openly laughed at me.

"Hardy har har. In the middle of sanding and kinda busy. What do you want?" I huffed out. Sometimes he was a royal pain in my ass.

"Want to get some dinner with Lucy and me tonight?"

"Yeah, that sounds great. What time and where?"

"My house around six. Bring Candice if she isn't working."

"You got it. See ya," I ended the call before I even heard his reply.

I didn't have time to talk to him. I needed to put my ass in gear and get to work. The floors wouldn't sand themselves.

The three of us quit for lunch. We planned to order some pies from Dispenza's Pizzeria. I've been told it's the best pizza place in town. I'd never tried the place before. Sal and Enzo looked at each other with raised eyebrows. They turned back toward me, each wearing a secretive grin.

"I'll call it in if you go get it. I forgot to measure a portion of the deck. Sal, I'll need your help." Sal and Enzo went out the door. Their cackling echoed off the walls.

I shook my head, not having a clue what the inside joke was. How hard was it to pick up pizza? I sent Candice a quick text.

You hungry? The guys and I are getting pizza. Want to join us? I'll come pick you up in five.

Before I could set the phone back in my pocket, the bubbles lit up to let me know that she responded.

Starving. Dispenza's?

Yep.

Then come pick me up and I'll ride with you.

On my way.

She must have been watching for me. As soon as I pulled in to the drive, she was halfway to the car. She either missed me or she really loved pizza. I assumed it was more the pizza.

Once she got in the car, she leaned over the center console and gave me a scorching kiss.

She pulled away too soon for my liking. "Let's roll."

I licked my lips and tasted her vanilla lip-gloss. *Yum!* I wished we had more time so I could explore her tasty mouth. Instead, I adjusted my jeans and headed to pick up the pizza.

I kept my eyes on the road. "Did you get a chance to talk to Riley today?"

Out of the corner of my eye, I saw a sweet smile spread across her plump lips. "Yes. She's so excited to fly on the plane. She practically screamed into my ear the whole conversation. My parents were having a good time with her too. They seem excited to visit with your parents." She turned her head toward me. "They have never traveled far from Indiana, so this is a first for them too. Thank you for thinking of it. I know it's not ideal conditions but it will do them good." She threaded her fingers through mine.

I couldn't reassure her with words so I squeezed her hand to let her know I understood and worried right along with her. She wasn't alone. My small gesture seemed enough for her. Her tense muscles around her jawline relaxed as she exhaled a breath that she had been holding. Every minute that Eugene kept hidden would ultimately be his demise.

23 CANDICE

I had known Sal and Enzo long enough to realize that they were sending Forrest into the lion's den. Momma Rose would smell fresh meat a mile away. Forrest was in for a real treat. I couldn't wait to see what she would come up with this time. Momma Rose could be compared to a loose cannon. You never knew what would fly out of her mouth. The old gal had no filter whatsoever.

The bell above the door jangled when Forrest opened it, alerting the staff that customers had walked in. Most importantly, it alerted Momma Rose. She had hearing as sharp as a dog; she heard a cheese wrapper crinkle in a dead sleep. She whipped her head up so fast she should have had whiplash. She peered through the cut out in the kitchen and zeroed in on Forrest and me.

I waved in greeting. She disappeared from the window just as quickly as she had spied us. She busted through the swinging red double doors as though the kitchen was on fire. She moved with lightning speed, which, given her body proportions, should have looked more waddled than it was.

She wore all-black, thick-soled loafers. Probably the same ones she wore the first time I met her years ago. Her stockings lay scrunched around her thick ankles. Her apron tied around her bulging waist. The long strings disappeared between her belly and the waistband of her gaucho pants. She marched right up to me and pulled me into a tight hug that had my ribs aching from the pressure.

She held me at arm's length and pinched my arms into my sides. "Candice. It's good to see you. Where is your little spitfire? I miss her help in the kitchen. Nothing but a bunch of bums in there now. At least she worked." She winked at me.

"She is with my mom and dad for the weekend. I'll bring her by when she gets home." I flinched as the pain increased.

She finally released her iron grip and focused her gaze on Forrest She twisted her body toward Forrest. "And who is this strapping young man? Is he yours or is he up for grabs? It's been a long time since I've had a good romp." She tossed her head back and laughed deeply at her own joke. Her belly bounced up and down the harder she laughed.

Forrest didn't even bat an eye. He laughed right along with her. He wrapped his thick-corded arms around Momma Rose and squished her to his chest.

"I think I'm in love." He tilted his head up with a big grin plastered upon his face. His eyes twinkled. "I'd say you have some competition, Candice. If she bakes half as good as she hugs, you might just be replaced."

Momma Rose pushed at his large chest. He released her instantly allowing her the upper hand. She smacked his chest hard enough to make a thumping sound.

"Madonna mia! My God, you are a big tease. All those muscles." She fanned herself and lumbered back into the kitchen.

Forrest looked at me with his eyebrows raised in question.

I laughed and shook my head. "You passed. You're such an ass kisser."

He chuckled, unfazed by the whole confrontation.

We walked up to the register and paid for the pizza. Tracy, the head waitress, brought out our pies.

Momma Rose pushed her head through the cutout, "Don't be a stranger, young man! Bring Riley around more often, you hear."

I nodded my head. "Yes, ma'am." We grabbed our pizza and walked out of the restaurant, giggling like teenagers.

As soon as the door opened and we walked into the house, we could hear Enzo and Sal laugh. We strolled into the kitchen.

I put the pizzas down on the counter and grabbed some napkins. "What are you two bellyaching about?"

"You see our momma?" they shouted over each other.

Without a hint of joking, Forrest looked at me, "Was she the hottie who gave me a kiss I will never be able to forget?"

I tried to follow his lead without laughing but it was damn hard. I coughed to cover up my giggle. "Yep."

"What do you mean she kissed you? Hell, she already has a damn boyfriend. She doesn't need another one. My goodness, flirting at her age, seriously?" Sal sounded disgusted.

Enzo caught on much quicker than his brother. He slapped his hand on the counter as he laughed. "Sal. Come on, you know Momma. She would never kiss anyone like that——well, maybe Lyle." He laughed.

"That's just gross. I hoped she'd have thrown her boob at him or something. Flirting at her age is just wrong." He shook his head and grabbed a slice.

Obviously the mental picture he had of his mom did nothing to deter his appetite. I smiled to myself. Boys!

"She throws her boob at people?" Forrest asked, appalled at the idea.

The three of us couldn't contain our amusement.

"Don't ask. You'll witness it soon enough." I grabbed my own slice.

Forrest shook his head and mumbled to himself. "Impossible."

I stayed in the kitchen and cleaned up lunch as the guys went back to work. I didn't want to get in the way, so I grabbed some paper towels and some generic cleaner and went to work shining up the kitchen. When I was done with the kitchen, I continued my work, going from room to room.

I grinned with satisfaction for all I had accomplished. It was hardly the best cleaning job I had ever done but it was enough to knock down the dust from the sander. It felt good to feel useful. I headed downstairs as Sal and

Enzo were cleaning up their tools.

They waved good-bye and headed out. Forrest and I picked up any remaining items.

"I forgot to tell you that Phoenix and Lucy invited us over for dinner tonight. Do you have to work tonight? You came home early last night so I wasn't sure what was going on."

"Oh my gosh. I forgot all about that. You had distracted me."

"I can provide another distraction if you want." He winked at me and moved closer to me.

He pulled me into his chest and kissed down the length of my neck. I couldn't help but moan at the exquisite torture. He pulled back slightly to gaze intently into my eyes. "So you going to tell me what's up with work?"

"You're cruel. You got me turned on then want to stop and ask me questions." I huffed, a second away from throwing a tantrum.

He grinned wickedly. "I could torture you some more if you like. But the end result will still be the same."

I groaned. Then I leaned in and bit his lip hard enough to make him lose his mind. Give him a taste of his own medicine. I sucked on his bottom lip until he ground his pelvis into me. I giggled.

"I couldn't stand to go into that room. I felt as though I was cheapening what we have. I only wanted you to touch and taste me. So I marched into Logan's office and quit."

He interrupted my story with jubilation. "Thank fucking God."

"Wait. What? You wanted me to quit?" My mouth hung open in shock.

"To be honest, yes, I wanted you to quit but I would never ask you to do that, especially if you didn't want to. It's always your choice, Candice. I would never demand something of you."

I kissed him long and hard. "Right answer." I rained tiny kisses along his jaw. "Long story short, Logan offered me a partnership. She gave me until Monday to give her my answer. I'm going to take her up on it."

He smiled as though it was the best thing that he had heard all day. Maybe it was. "I think it's a smart move. Especially for you and Riley. If you still want to dance, I'm sure that you could still do that."

I bit his earlobe. "You are not paying attention. I have no interest in dancing for strange men anymore. The only one I want to dance for is you."

He took my cue and ran with it. He lifted me up onto the counter, bunching my skirt up around my waist as he set me down. He scooted my ass to the edge and roughly pulled my panties out of his way. I banged my head against the cupboard and moaned at his dominance.

He pushed two fingers into my wet pussy. "So ready for me."

I opened my legs wider in answer. He unzipped his pants and let them fall to the ground. He thrust his thick cock into my entrance with so much force I banged into the cupboard. The harder he drove into me the louder the doors clanged into their casing. Our moans mixed in with the sounds of the cupboards being slammed.

I placed two fingers over my clit.

"Watching you pleasure yourself while I am fucking you has got to be the sexiest thing I've ever seen."

He hammered into me harder and picked up his speed as my muscles milked him. "Shit, Forrest. I'm going to come. Feels so good," I panted out as my body convulsed from the explosion of my orgasm.

He closed his eyes as he grunted his own release. With his cock still twitching inside me, he placed his forehead against mine. "You're going to be the death of me."

I placed a gentle kiss on the tip of his nose. "Death by orgasm. No better way to go."

My body jerked as he slid out of me. He grabbed a couple of clean towels and cleaned us both up.

***

We banged on the door as loud as we could. We punched air as Lucy pulled open the door. We laughed as though we were about to ditch and run.

"You better not be hiding a flaming pile of dog shit."

We both bent over grasping our sides as they ached from our giggle fit. Once I caught my breath, I bear hugged Lucy. I hadn't seen her much and it felt great to be in her presence again.

"Get a room. On second thought, let me go get Phoenix. Stay right there." Still chuckling, Forrest swept past us and into the house.

We pulled apart and walked inside. I loved every inch of their home. The large scale of it could make you feel intimidated but Lucy and Phoenix made you feel comfortable in it. I could go right to the fridge and grab anything I wanted and not feel as though I had to sneak it. They were down-to-earth people and I loved them for it. I was so happy for Lucy for obtaining the life she deserved. Not only was Phoenix burn-your-eyes hot, he worshiped the ground Lucy walked on. In the back of my mind, I thought that he didn't even hold a candle next to Forrest.

I gave Phoenix a quick hug. "How you been?"

He gave me a friendly peck on the cheek. "Nothing shy of incredible." He winked at Lucy. She had the audacity to blush. I chuckled and grabbed a pop from the fridge.

I looked over my shoulder, with the door open. "You want anything, Forrest?"

He came up behind me and pinched my ass as he bent over me and reached in for a beer. He whispered close to my ear, "Just your sweet, drenched, and swollen pussy later."

Hot tingles shot right to my core. How the hell was I supposed to concentrate on our friends when he got me worked up this quickly? I half moaned and sighed. I stood in the fridge for a second, trying to cool off my heated body.

"You have enough time to cool off?" Lucy laughed behind me.

"Shut up. You are no help." I grinned back at her and shut the fridge door.

She rolled her eyes at me in a classic Lucy move.

"Please. I have used that same technique so many times that I'm surprised we haven't had to replace it yet." She grabbed her beer. "Come on, let's go. No use hiding——he will come and find you."

Their backyard looked as though it crawled off the pages of a home and garden magazine. White vinyl fencing created a private, secluded oasis. Slate flooring covered the entire patio floor. Tucked into a private nook were four thick cushioned lounge chairs that surrounded a rock walled fireplace. A cutout over the top boasted a flat screen. The roof extended out with built-in surround sound. Phoenix had music softly crooning through the speakers.

Off to the other side, an outdoor kitchen fit for kings stood encased in the same rock as the fireplace. Phoenix stood behind the largest stainless-steel grill I'd ever seen. He was so relaxed and in his element. His cooking skills were mostly inherent. He didn't go to a fancy culinary school. His talents lie within his passion for cooking. His dishes wreaked havoc on your palate. Every bite ensured a mini orgasm.

"What's on the menu for tonight?"

"Plain old steaks and a basket of peppers, zucchini, and onions."

My mouth salivated. "I'm sure it'll taste horrible but I will choke it down so I don't hurt your feelings. Do you need any help?"

He laughed at me. "Nope. I've got it covered but thanks. Why don't you go join Lucy and Forrest before she drags information out of him that you would normally want kept a secret?"

I groaned. She would interrogate him too. "Oh,

God."

All conversation ceased when I plopped down next to Forrest. He pulled my legs over the top of his lap and ran his fingers up and down my shins. *Oh, sweet Jesus, that felt incredible.*

Lucy interrupted my moment of ecstasy by speaking. "You not working tonight?"

I hadn't realized that I had closed my eyes. "What? Oh, no. I quit."

"'Bout damn time."

"I mean I quit and then Logan offered me partner." I smiled, happy about my decision. "And I'm going to take her up on it."

Lucy's face lit up in excitement. "That's awesome, Candice. I am so proud of you. You must have done something good because we all know what a hard ass she can be."

I laughed because it was true. "I have to give her my answer by Monday. She offered me the weekend off to mull it over."

"Good for you. You deserve the break. It will be good for Riley, too. More days off and you'll be less stressed. Speaking of the princess, where is she? Does your mom have her?"

I looked over at Forrest, unsure of how much I should say. I didn't want Lucy or Phoenix in the middle of this. Lucy had been tangled up in my shit storm for a while now. *What if he came over here and threatened them?* The less they knew, the better off they were.

Forrest answered for me. "Yeah. I wanted Candice all to myself for the weekend so we kept her there."

He picked up my hand and placed a gentle kiss to the inside of my palm. Then he added a little more heat by darting his tongue out. I'm pretty sure I swooned. Thankfully Phoenix announced that dinner was ready. Otherwise, I would've embarrassed myself by straddling him right then and there.

"Phoenix, you have outdone yourself once again. The steak melted right in my mouth. And those vegetables were to die for." I looked over at Lucy. "How do you get through a meal without jumping his bones?"

They looked at each other and busted out laughing. "It's usually cold by the time we finish eating."

"You ready for dessert?" Phoenix looked between Forrest and me.

"I don't know about him." I pointed next to me. "But I couldn't eat another bite. Can we take some home?"

Phoenix winked at me. "Sure, no problem. I'll go get it ready."

We said our good-byes and made it home in record time.

24 FORREST

All I could think about was getting Candice naked and beneath me. Even in this frame of mind, I noticed that something felt off. Goose bumps raced along my arms and they weren't from Candice nibbling my neck.

I stopped midstride. I whispered, "I need you to stop for a minute and be as quiet as you can."

I gently set her back on her feet and strained to hear. The only sounds that stood out were Candice's heavy breathing and the chirping crickets. My eyes had adjusted to the darkness long before. Nothing seemed to be out of the ordinary. I placed my finger over my lips, reminding Candice to remain silent and to stay behind me.

I crept up the small walkway and up the concrete step that led to the tiny rectangular porch. The house remained silent. It didn't offer up any of its secrets. I slowly reached out and covered the doorknob with my hand. I deliberately twisted the knob, testing whether it had remained locked. I met no resistance and upon further inspection, part of the doorframe had been tampered with.

I reached around to the back of my waistband to pull my piece and my fingers wrapped around empty space. *Fuck!* I hadn't been carrying because I didn't want Riley to accidently find it. Now was not the time to go all superhero right now. I let go of the handle and stealthily walked toward Candice. I pulled her back into the car while I dialed 911. She would be an easy target, standing outside in the open.

I hated feeling inept at protecting Candice. I hadn't taken the threats from Eugene seriously and had let my guard down. Of course, I didn't know what kind of threat loomed before us but I assumed that the house had been tossed and the culprit was long gone. I couldn't officially link it to Eugene but I was pretty sure it had to have been him. On the outside, I looked calm but below the surface, anger simmered as hot as volcanic lava flowing beneath its mountainous peak.

Blue and red lights flashed in the night sky. The sirens screeched eerily through the thick silence of night. Three cop cars skidded to a stop in front of the house.

Two young officers and one seasoned officer got out of their vehicles and walked up to me. "Are you the one who called?" the seasoned cop asked.

"Yes. I went to unlock the door and noticed that it had been tampered with. We didn't go inside. We walked back to the car and I called you guys. I don't know if they are still in there or not," I stated matter-of-fact.

"Alright, sir. You guys stay out here while we take a look around."

I didn't answer him nor did he expect me to. We had eyed each other up as we spoke. He was confident that I would stay put. I couldn't go in guns blazing, especially if I wanted my plan for Eugene to go off without any glitches. I had to stay off of everyone's radar.

One of the cops took the front, one went out back, and the other took his place behind the older cop. With their guns drawn, they entered the house, shouting "Police!" Lights flickered on throughout the house, lighting it up room by room as though they were on a delayed timer.

Less than twenty minutes had passed and the three officers exited the house through the front door. The elder cop came over to me as the other two got into their cruisers. He took my statement.

He stopped taking notes and looked up from his flip pad. "There was no one inside but I have to warn you the house has been tossed. Make a list of any items that have been stolen. Call this number once you have that done." He handed me the piece of paper.

I slid it into my pocket and crumbled it with my fist before I slid my hand out.

"I'll file the incident report so that they will be able to link the two together. If you can think of anything else, don't hesitate to call. It's safe for you to go into the home."

"Thanks."

I knew that there wouldn't be anything stolen. Eugene did this to hurt Candice. He wanted to make her feel violated in her own home. He wanted a reaction from her. She never showed one iota of fear in public from the slashed tire or the threatening note. She never deviated from her routine and it pissed him off. He had to take it to the next level. I wouldn't be surprised if he was out there lurking in the shadows, watching to see whether she would break. I wouldn't allow her to do that. She was tough and a lot stronger than he gave her credit for.

I opened up the car door for her. I reached my hand down for her to take. Gracefully, she stepped out of the car. I hugged her to me. I tipped her chin up with my finger and placed my mouth against hers. I wanted to reassure her that she wasn't alone. If Eugene played hide-and-seek in the darkness, he'd get the message that she was mine, and I protect what was mine.

She moved her lips against mine. I pulled back and studied her face. Her cheeks were flushed with color and her nostrils flared with desire. Her eyes swirled with emotion. The blue hues lazily lapped me up the way the ocean caresses the sand on the beach. I smiled and committed her precious features to my memory. Once we walked into the house, it would fade.

We strode soundlessly into the house. She gasped when she saw all of the destruction. The furniture was tipped over. Dishes lay broken on the floor. Lamps were turned over, with the bulbs busted out. We walked through each room, never uttering a word. The vast amount of damage surprised the hell out of me. The only room that hadn't been tossed was Riley's. That told me it was definitely Eugene. He at least cared enough about his daughter that he didn't want her things harmed.

We saved her bedroom for last. I had a feeling that it would be the worst one. Candice walked through first. Her hands flew to her mouth and covered the whimper that escaped. My heart broke for her. The pillows and bedding were torn to shreds. The mattresses were tossed off the frame. On each mattress, a long, serrated gash cut through the middle. We stepped over clothing thrown around the floor and walked into the bathroom.

Her perfume bottle lay shattered into tiny pieces of glass. The shower curtain had the same slashes as the mattresses. I turned around and written in bright red lipstick on the mirror was the word whore. *That motherfucker would burn for this.*

She tucked her chin into her collarbone and leaned her delicate frame in to my chest. I wrapped my arms around her as tiny rivers slid down her face. I tenderly lowered us to the floor. With my back up against the tub, I held her in my lap and rocked her until her tears of anguish subsided.

She looked up at me with red puffy eyes and sniffed. "Why would he do this?"

I wanted to tell her because he was a sick, twisted, and cowardly fuck. "I don't know, baby. I just don't know." I rubbed her back. "I kept the apartment. Let's pack a bag and we will go there for the night. We can come back tomorrow and get the place cleaned up and put back together."

She nodded her head and stood. With her head hung low and her shoulders hunched, she sifted through the mess to find her bag. She tossed in whatever she could find. We shut off all the lights, locked up the house, and headed toward my place.

The thick atmosphere weighed heavily on my shoulders. Candice didn't move or speak. She stared vacantly out the side window as the scenery blurred past. The reality of what happened had finally sunk in. He hit too close to home this time. I looked over at her, willing her to gather her strength and keep fighting. A heavy breath left her body as her chest descended.

I parked the car and grabbed her bag. We headed into

the depressing apartment. This wasn't a home. No personal pictures hung on the wall and the furniture looked sterile and stiff. I rented it for its functionality, not its warmth. I didn't want Candice here. She deserved better but it served as a safe place for now. We would only be here, at most, a night or two. Eugene didn't know about this place.

I didn't have cable, so we laid in bed and talked about our plans for the new house. My mom had called on our way home from Phoenix and Lucy's place, so we got our Riley fix in. Her excitement bubbled through the phone. She decided to call my parents Grandma and Grandpa. They were planning a trip to the zoo tomorrow morning. My parents and Candice's seemed to be getting along well. They were kept fairly busy chasing after Riley. At least Riley was miles away, oblivious of this cluster fuck.

***

We sat at the scratched-up table and drank our coffee.

"I guess we can't stall any longer." Candice sighed heavily and pushed away from the table.

"Actually, I was thinking about going to pick up some of your clothes and we can stay here until we figure some things out."

She paused. "What about cleaning up the house? I can't leave it like that. What about when Riley comes home? I'm not going to let her stay much longer. I agreed to a week. I want her home after that." Hysteria bubbled underneath the surface.

I rubbed my hands over my face, trying to wipe away my frustration. I understood that. I wanted her home, too, but not until this situation was resolved. "I know. I will call a cleaning crew and have them put the house back together. I don't want you being in there any longer than you have to." I pulled her in to me. I gently cupped her cheeks. "We will figure it out. I promise."

She nodded her head. She twisted on her heel and left my embrace. I let my arms hang loose at my sides as the weight of emptiness lied brutally on my chest. If Mack didn't ring me today, I would put a call into him, and force him to come up with some kind of information. If he couldn't deliver, then I would go hunting.

25 CANDICE

The pounding in my head increased the closer we got to the house. Little elves tinkering on a drum set had taken up residence. The aspirin that I had popped earlier had done nothing to alleviate the pain. I pivoted my head so that I could soak in Forrest.

He alone had become the glue that held my sanity together. I didn't fear Eugene anymore. I realized that I would either die by his hands or he would die by mine. I prayed that it wasn't me. I would go down fighting. What I did fear sat right next to me. I feared for his safety. He didn't belong in this mess. He could handle himself but it wasn't fair that he had been dragged into it.

His long, muscle-clad body encompassed half of the car. His iron-tight fists gripped the steering wheel. His focus was so intense he hadn't even realized that I was ogling him. His eyes squinted and his mouth thinned in anger. He flinched as I placed my hand on his shoulder and squeezed the tense muscle underneath.

I kneaded his tight muscle until I heard him sigh and

sink into my hand. He cocked his head to the side. His right eyebrow rose a fraction.

I couldn't control my burst of laughter. "It's way too tense in here. Look, Eugene is going to keep doing petty shit. It's who he is. He liked it when I was underneath his fist. He no longer controls me and it's pissed him off."

He interrupted me vehemently. "I will not let him touch you again."

I shrugged in mock resignation. "What will be will be. I don't know how to find him. I'll have to wait for him to come to me."

His eyes hardened as he threw the gear in park. "You will not go anywhere near him. Ever!" He pinched the bridge of his nose. "I'm sorry, I didn't mean to shout at you. Don't you see, I'm trying to protect you? I wouldn't know what to do if I lost you."

I leaned over the console and used my finger to push his chin toward me. I placed my lips upon his mouth and used my tongue to open him up. His hands fisted into my hair, holding me hostage to his mouth.

I pulled away, slightly dizzy. "I don't want to lose you either. I've waited my whole life for you."

His wicked grin breathed hope into my complacent thoughts. "You won't."

"Good. Let's do this then."

We stomped into the house on a mission. I stood, partly frozen in the doorway. My eyebrows arched in surprise. The damage looked worse as I looked at it through clear eyes. I would not let this tamper with my mood. They were just things and could all be replaced.

Hell, this house would be sold soon. I tried to look at it as a fresh start. Less I had to move when the Victorian was finished. Screw this house and the shit in it. Hell, if Eugene wanted to burn the fucker down, he could.

I packed a small suitcase in less than five minutes. I ran down the steps to let Forrest know that I was ready. I rounded the corner, prepared to speak, when I noticed he was on the phone. I quietly sat on the bottom step and waited for him to finish.

He shoved the phone in his pocket and then turned around. His face was a scowling mask of rage. A sudden thin chill hung in the air. I rubbed my arms to try to dispel the goose bumps that had arisen along my skin.

In two quick strides, he stood before me. He lowered his hands in front of me as though I was a frightened animal. I softly placed mine in them and he pulled me up from the step.

"Let's go. I'll take you back to the apartment if you want, or I can take you to Lucy's for the night. I'm going to the house to get some work in." His voice held no room for argument.

"Are you sure you don't want my help? It would help me take my mind off all of this." I swung my arms out, demonstrating my point.

His lip curled up in the corner. "Nah. I need to do something with my hands for a while. Get rid of some of this anger."

I grinned wickedly at him. "I know what you can do with those hands."

"Mmm. As tempting as that is, can I take a rain check? Or how about I drop you off at Lucy's and then come back and pick you up later? Then I will explore and taste your body until you are begging for release."

"Then drop me off already so that you can do wicked things to me later." He swatted my ass as I turned and sauntered back to the car. I texted Lucy to get the rum ready.

***

Phoenix had kitchen duty tonight, so it would be just us girls. As I sat in the lounge chair out back, sipping rum and pineapple juice, I thought this was exactly what I needed to relax and forget about everything. The alcohol had a nice dulling effect.

"Have you heard from Gage lately?" I asked, needing some kind of normalcy.

"Yep, that cocksucker texts me every day. Telling me about all the sweet tail he is getting. He won one fucking fight and he thinks he is a rock star." She rolled her eyes but the love that shone through had the reverse effect.

I laughed at her pretended indifference. "You know he has a big ego. Why do you continue to stroke it?" I busted out laughing. "Stroke it."

"Oh, you got jokes tonight, sister. I don't stroke anything of Gage's. At one point in time, I may have wanted to but have you looked at Phoenix? Why would I waste my time on puny game?"

"Come on, Lucy. You know I'm playing with you." It was my turn to roll my eyes at her. She could get worked up quickly when it came to Gage and their past. Like she had to defend her feelings for Phoenix. "Girl, you don't have to explain yourself to me. I know you adore Phoenix and would never lay a hand on any other man."

"You're damn right." She stood. "Need a refill?"

I tipped my cup to her. "Yep. Why don't you just bring that shit out here and set it between us? I plan on finishing the bottle."

She tossed her head back, full of cackling laughter. "Fuck yeah. Then maybe you'll tell me the truth about what's going on." She narrowed her eyes at me before she turned and walked back into the kitchen.

Damn that saucy bitch. I couldn't hide anything from her!

She slipped through the sliding glass doors, each hand full, and a bag of chips tucked under her arm. I smiled at her thoughtfulness. She knew that when I got shit faced, I loved to gorge on honey barbeque chips. They were our staple for comfort food. Then I'd run home to Rico! Didn't have to this time. Hopefully, Forrest would be primed and ready when he picked me up.

I mixed a heavy dose of rum in with a splash of juice. I tipped the cup to my lips and took a healthy swig. The great thing about rum was that you could never put too much into your drink. Its sweet taste flows smoothly down your throat. There was no burning, body convulsing, and no bitter aftertaste. Well, as long as you didn't drink it straight. Otherwise, it tastes like straight up diesel fuel. Good if you want hair to grow on your chest.

Lucy crinkled the chip bag as she opened it. She tilted it in my direction. My greedy fingers snatched the bag from her and dug in. I reached in the bag and grabbed a handful and then gave it back to her. I placed the sweet and salty chip into my mouth. My eyelids closed in bliss as I munched on the crunchy goodness.

"Alright, girl, spill it," she mumbled with a mouth full

of potato chips.

I slowly opened up my eyes, not wanting to dish, but I knew that Lucy wouldn't let it go until I did. I lazily rolled on my side and faced her. I reached for my glass and took a healthy gulp to steel my nerves. As the sweet burn slid down my throat, my courage increased. "Eugene has been threatening me again."

"What?" She shot up into a sitting position and crossed her legs underneath her. "I'll kill that motherfucker."

My laughter held a bit of hysteria. "Get in line." I mimicked her body and put my drink between my thighs. The cold sweat of the glass sent an icy shiver straight through every disk of my spine. "It started out subtle and has gotten worse. He slashed my tire one night while I was at work. A note was left on my windshield a couple of days later." I scrubbed my hands through my hair. "Then, the night we left your place, my house had been broken into. We called the cops but there is nothing that they can do. They put in an incident report but you know that they can't link it to Eugene. I didn't even mention it to them. It would have been pointless."

"Shit on a brick in the hot sun. That is fucked up. What's Forrest say about all of this? What are you going to do? Do you want to stay here? Where is Riley?"

Typical Lucy, firing off questions so fast that I could hardly keep up. "Forrest is angry, of course, and promises me that he will take care of it. Whatever that means. Honestly, I don't want to know what he will do if he finds him." I took a deep breath in. "Thanks for the offer but I don't want to drag you or Phoenix into this. I don't want you guys hurt. We will deal with it. Riley, my sweet baby, is with my parents and Forrest's parents. They flew out yesterday to California. Thank God, she is oblivious of the whole thing. She thinks that she is on vacation and having the time of her life. She comes home on Sunday. I'm not sure what I'm going to do if this isn't resolved before then."

Lucy moved from her seat and nudged me over so that she could sit with me. "He is such a sorry waste of space. He doesn't deserve to breathe the same air as we do." She pulled me into a warm embrace.

Her anger fueled mine. "You know what the kicker is? He didn't touch a damn thing in Riley's room. Tore the house to shreds but left her stuff alone."

She rubbed her strong fingers through my hair as though she were a mother comforting her child. I lay in her embrace and allowed her to soothe my worries away with each stroke of her hand.

"You'd make a great mom. When are you going to have a baby?"

Her hand stilled and then resumed its combing. "I'm not sure. Right now I am enjoying our time together. I think later on down the road, we might try. He hasn't voiced an opinion one way or another." She giggled. "I don't think I want to share him just yet. I'm selfish and love all of the attention that he lavishes on me."

I looked up into her dazed face. "I understand but you know when I look at Forrest and Riley together, it only intensifies my love for him. I don't feel slighted in any way."

She tilted her head down to look at me. She placed a smacking kiss on my forehead. "Ditto."

I smiled up at her. "Love you, too, girl."

She pushed me off her and chuckled as I slammed into the back of the lounge. I laughed until tears shimmered down my cheeks. "You're such a brat."

"You love me anyway. We got more drinking and gossiping to do." She wobbled over to her lounge and refilled our cups.

By the time Forrest came to collect me, we were both three sheets to the wind. Giggling like schoolgirls at a sleepover. I looked up into Forrest's towering frame and I smiled seductively at my brutish knight. At least, I think I did but then again he chuckled deeply at my inebriated state. He slipped one thick arm underneath my legs and the other slid under my neck. He picked me up with ease.

He nodded and winked at Lucy. "See ya later, Luce."

She grinned smugly at him. "Forrest."

I shouted a drunken garbled good-bye over Forrest's shoulder as he carried me through the house.

26 FORREST

My girl lay in my arms, giggling and drunk as a skunk. She whispered all of the dirty things that she wanted to do to me in my ear. My dick sprang to life as her words caressed my body. *Holy fuck.* I loved this playful side of her. I carefully set her in the passenger side, made sure all of her limbs were tucked inside the car and buckled her in. Then I slammed the door and ran to the other side. I jerked open my door in haste and it slammed back into me; the corner of the door clipped into my shoulder. *Fuck!* I seethed out a painful breath. I slid in my seat, roared the car to life and fishtailed it out of the drive.

On the way back to the apartment, Candice softly snored next to me. She wasn't getting out of her wifely duties just because she passed out on me. *Did I just say wifely duties?* I mentally groaned, in a good way. It made me all tingly thinking about her as my wife with my ring around her finger. I was a goner. I'd keep that little nugget of information to myself. If my brother found out, he'd bust my balls about being pussy-whipped. I totally was but that's beside the point. I wouldn't give him the bragging rights.

I cradled my sleeping angel in my arms once more. Her limp body felt as though I carried dead weight, yet still was light enough for me to carry without breaking a sweat. One arm was tucked snuggly into my chest and her side. Her other arm stood straight out and her head lolled to the side. If only I could get to my phone. I'd have taken a picture just to see the fire in her eyes once she saw how drunk she had gotten.

I gently laid her down upon the bed and removed her clothes, in a complete nonsexual way. Don't get me wrong—I still gazed upon her glorious body. I left her panties and bra on and sighed at a loss of a good opportunity for her to make good on what she whispered earlier. *Oh, well.* Mack had flown in earlier with the info I needed. I had to go over the shit he downloaded onto a flash drive. I told him to camp out at the Victorian and if anybody asked, he came in to help finish up the house.

It was a good cover. Mack was as talented as Enzo and could help me kill two birds with one stone. Pun most definitely intended. He had quite a bit of lag time before his next job, so he had the free time. *What the hell else would he do besides drink beer?* He could do that here.

I walked out into the small kitchen and fired up my laptop. I inserted the drive. A file marked Restoration popped up. *What a clever bastard.* Not like anyone would find this anyway. Once I memorized the important details, I would destroy the drive. I scooted my wireless mouse, driving the arrow over the document. My pointer finger a hairpin away from double-clicking, I heard Candice murmur my name. I shut the computer down, put the drive on the highest shelf of the empty cupboard, and went to check on Sleeping Beauty.

She had rolled onto her side. The blanket barely covered her exposed skin. I groaned inwardly. A saint would have trouble maintaining their composure. I looked up toward the ceiling and breathed in slowly through my nose and exhaled through my mouth. I undressed and slid between the blankets. I snuggled into her back and inhaled her soft vanilla scent. She moaned in her sleep and ground her luscious ass into my already hard cock. I closed my eyes to eradicate the lust that drove my entire blood south. I'm being punished——I just know it.

She pushed her ass into me again and purred my name. "Shh, baby. I'm right here. Go back to sleep." I wasn't thinking that at all. I wanted her to wake up.

She angled her head toward me, her eyes at half-mast and still masked with sleep. "I've been dreaming that you were making love to me."

Being the gentleman that I was, I would make her dream-like state a reality. I ran my fingertips over her knee and up her thigh. She tipped her head into my shoulder and moaned. Shit, she had me hard as a jackhammer, ready to plow into her. Her perfect round ass slid up and down on my dick. My hand traced an imaginary line over her hip, down her mound, and along the seam of her swollen pink lips.

Her hips moved back and forth, in time with my finger. I pushed my finger into her warm center, swirling it around and around the wetness. She moaned and more of her essence pooled around my finger.

"Oh, fuck, Forrest. I've been waiting all day for this." She opened her legs.

I pulled my finger out and pushed my cock into her. Her hips sprang forward as I drilled into her. I moved my finger from her pulsating nub and reached up and tweaked her pebbled nipple. I bit down on her shoulder hard enough to elicit a bit of pain and then licked the marks, soothing the sting of my bite.

Her back arched at the delicious sensations. She was exquisitely wet. I skimmed my fingers down her stomach until I reached her clit. I circled the sensitive bud. She called out my name as her inner muscles contracted around my cock. She milked me, as a newborn calf would suckle its momma's teat. I followed right behind her.

I gradually slid out of her warm center. I cradled her in my arms. I kissed along her salty shoulder. "Love you."

"Love you more."

I got up as dawn broke through the darkness. I placed a glass of water and two aspirin for when Candice woke up. I left her a note nestled underneath the glass of water to let her know that I'd be at the Victorian and that her car was in the parking lot. I set the keys right next to the water. She had to go into work today to talk to Logan, so I had Mack drive her car back to my apartment. I dropped him off at the house before I picked Candice up.

The house sat quiet in the early morning hours. It wouldn't be long before the sound of the shrill whining of the sander would echo through the house. The pop, pop sound of the nail gun driving the nails into the wood boards to create the new porch would reverberate around the neighborhood. It was music to my ears. Before I got lost in the relaxing melody, I had to touch base with Mack.

I walked into the house, expecting Mack to be up and around. Instead, loud bear-like growling vibrated the walls of the house. I shook my head and chuckled. My boots traveled stealthily across the wood floors. Not a creak or groan, only deadly silence as I moved toward the sleeping bear. I grinned wickedly at the prospect of sneaking up on my longtime friend. Anticipation coursed through my veins. Adrenaline had my heart pumping furiously.

I stood within an inch of his slumbering body. His eyes were open, which created the illusion of him being awake. The snores arose from deep within his chest. It was eerie the way he slept. I'd been on multiple jobs with him and I never got used to the sight. We were equals when it came to hand-to-hand combat. Our builds were similar. Where we differed were our job philosophies.

He could be a stone-cold killer. I had to weigh all of my options before I extinguished a life. Sometimes you didn't have time to do that and harsh decisions needed to be made on the spur of the moment. Luckily, in our line of work, we dealt with mostly the bottom-feeders of our vast world.

I reached my hand, palm facing down, ready to cover his mouth and nose. His hand moved lightning fast. I didn't have a chance to pull back. He bent my hand back and applied pressure to the point that my knees buckled. Then he lifted his leg up and around my waist, throwing me to the floor on my back. I laughed so hard I got a cramp in my side.

"You idiot. I could've killed you." He laughed back at me while never letting go of his hold.

My hand felt as though it would split in two but I kept on laughing until he released his hold. "No, you wouldn't, you big pussy." I rubbed my sore wrist and sat up.

"Please. I'm the pussy who had you in a pretty tight hold, ready to snap your wrist like a twig. So who is the pussy now?" He rubbed the sleep off his face, now acutely aware of his surroundings.

"You know I love pussy. Come here and give me some love." I wrestled him backward and slapped a big wet kiss on his forehead.

"You know you are one twisted fuck." He smacked me upside the head.

We both laughed as I climbed off him. We wandered into the kitchen. I grabbed a beer for us and we got down to business. We had a couple of hours yet before the rest of the crew sauntered in. I wanted to formulate a game plan and have it sealed airtight before I put it into motion.

"What's your girl say about what you are doing?"

With my head still bent, I peered over the computer with my eyes. I didn't need to say a word.

"Ah, she doesn't know." He whistled nonchalantly. "Probably better in the long run anyway."

"I bet my last dollar that she would be happy that he wouldn't bother her ever again. Just not thrilled about how it's going to go down. Something that she doesn't need to know about."

"Am I going to get to meet the infamous woman who managed to capture you?"

"Sure, why not? Not like you have a chance in hell of stealing her from me."

He squinted. "Challenge accepted, bro."

I laughed, firmly secure in the knowledge that Candice had eyes only for me. "Alright, fucker, let's hash this out. I want this done in the next couple of days before he makes another move or runs."

"He won't. He is holed up in one of the abandoned houses on the edge of town. I paid the place a visit. He was high as a kite. Couldn't tell his head from his ass."

I looked up at him with deep frown lines. "What the fuck, man? You trying to blow it?"

His brows drew together and his mouth thinned out. "Seriously? You gonna ask me that?"

"Sorry, man. I want to get this guy so bad that I'm not thinking straight."

"Exactly my point. You better check that caveman shit at the door if we are going to pull this off."

My phone buzzed in my pocket. I took it out. I couldn't help but smile at the text my girl sent me.

Going to see Logan. Thanks for delivering my car. Meet you at the house for lunch. I'll bring everyone pizza. Love you.

Thanks, babe. See you soon.

"Speak of the devil. That must be your favorite tail."

My hands fisted at my sides. "Don't you ever speak about her like that ever again!" I ground out between my teeth.

"Stand down. I'm just playing." He chuckled to himself.

The plan started to take shape in my mind. Getting to him wouldn't be that difficult. The house where he squatted was vacant and rundown. It sat in the middle of nowhere, imbedded around overgrown fields. The aerial shot that Mack captured showed enough detail that getting in and out would be a piece of cake.

"Forgot to mention that I put a tracker on him. Our phones will ping when he is on the move. No more surprises for Candice. Between the two of us, we should be able to intercept him before he gets anywhere near Candice."

The smile that lit my face would be enough to scare children. "Good job. That's a nice little token. I'm hoping that we will move in long before we have to rely on it."

We would have everything we needed and ready to roll out the next night. I felt giddy with anticipation. I may be going to hell in a handbasket for feeling this way but I would do anything to keep Candice and Riley safe. We finished up as the guys came barreling through the house. I make introductions. Mack seamlessly fit into the mix. It felt good to have him around and watching my back. I hoped he'd seriously consider my previous offer.

27 CANDICE

I lifted my heavy eyelids. My head screamed with pain. I groaned as the honey barbeque chips from last night tried to claw their way back up my throat. I managed to grab the aspirin off the nightstand. I popped them into my mouth and took a heaping gulp of water to chase them down. I hoped to hell I could keep those down long enough to let them work their way into my bloodstream.

I read the sweet note that Forrest left. My blood boiled just thinking of him. Sparks of heat shot right to my core. I shook the memory of last night from my mind. I shot him a quick text and then got my aching body into the shower. I felt marginally human once I stepped out. My head no longer felt as though it had entertained a death metal band all night.

I called Logan on my way in so that she would expect me. I parked in the club's lot. The only cars parked were Logan's and now mine. For the first time, I knocked on the club doors and waved into the camera to be let in. Logan buzzed me in and I headed for her office.

Her door stood wide open, which caught me off

guard. For as long as I had worked here, the door always remained closed.

"Are you going to stand around gawking or you going to bring your ass in here?" Logan offered as a hello.

"Good morning to you too," I commented cheerily.

Her lips twitched into an almost smile. "So what's the verdict?" She lounged back in her chair with her arms crossed over her ample bosom. She appeared to be aloof but I could tell that she hung onto the silence, awaiting my decision.

I wanted to drag this out but thought that it was unfair to her. As much as I'd like to tease her, I also wanted the job. I feared her more than I wanted to taunt her at the moment. I reached my hand out to her. "Partner?"

A genuine smile blossomed along her tight face, making her look younger. She should smile more often. "Partners!" With a strong grip, she shook my hand. She sat back down and pulled open her desk drawer. A healthy stack of papers flopped onto her desk. "This is all of the paperwork. I want you to go over these in depth. If everything is agreeable, then sign it and bring it all back to me tomorrow morning. Training will start right after. Is this acceptable?"

I nodded my head greedily. "Yes. What hours will training occur and for how long? I need to know so that I can make arrangements for Riley." I hated to sound demanding but Riley always came first.

"Quite understandable. Training should only encompass a month. It will be during daylight hours for the first two days; the remaining will be at the highest peak hours. Once training is done, I will have you working days at first. Once I feel like you have a hold on the place, then we will switch until you are comfortable with both aspects. Then we will rotate so that we alternate weekends and we can also trade day shifts as well."

My legs bounced with nervous anticipation of my new role. To be honest, I was terrified that I would let her down. This would be a huge transition for me. Dancing and part ownership of a club are totally different. Not that I wasn't up for the challenge though.

"Alright, kid. This is your last free day. I suggest you use it wisely." She wiggled her eyebrows suggestively.

A nervous giggle erupted. I quickly reached out again to shake her hand. "Thanks, Logan. I am looking forward to working alongside you."

"Me too." She handed me the paperwork and then twisted her chair back toward her computer, signaling to me that it was time to go.

I got up and swiveled on my heels and practically skipped out of the club like a curfew-free young girl. I pulled out my phone and placed my pizza order. I tossed my purse and paperwork onto the passenger seat and pointed the car toward Dispenza's. It took me all of ten minutes to get there, so I grabbed the stack of papers and headed inside to read while I waited.

I was so engrossed in the lawyer mumbo jumbo I didn't realize that Momma Rose had sat down next to me. I should have become conscious of her when the booth dipped slightly.

I looked up and over at her radiant smile. Her whole face lit up like a mosquito latching onto skin and draining its liquid gold. I had to laugh because the crazy woman was up to something. "Hello, Momma Rose. I'm sorry I didn't acknowledge you sooner."

"I haven't been sitting here that long." She patted my arm lovingly. "Only long enough to know that you got yourself part of a club."

"Momma Rose!" I chastised her for being nosey.

She shrugged definitely not sorry. "What? I know that lawyer lingo anywhere. I've been in the business so long those contracts are easy to read once you wade through the jargon bullshit and get to the meat."

With an open mouth and wide eyes. I asked, "Do you think you could help me understand this stuff? My eyes are watering from the dry lingo."

"Sure. Your pies will take another thirty minutes or so. Should be plenty of time to get the gist of it." She snatched the packet of papers.

"Thank you."

"Hush, child. I'm trying to read."

I wanted to chuckle so bad but thought better of it, not sure whether she would continue to help me or not, so I coughed instead to hide my shaking shoulders. True to her word, she riffled through all of that jargon in about ten minutes.

"It's pretty straightforward. Fifty/fifty on everything——your boss isn't a bit stingy. She must really want you as a partner because these are the best terms I've ever seen. If I were you, I'd sign on the dotted line." She handed over the paperwork.

"You got a pen?"

"Nope. I didn't mean sign them right now. Madonna mia! Child, take this to your sexy man and have him go through it too. Then decide with him to sign. Make him feel a part of this too."

I wrapped my arms around her squishy waist and planted a kiss on her plump cheek. "I love you. Thanks!"

Her round cheeks took on a rosy hue. She scooted from the booth. "I'll go get your pies."

I checked out with Tracy and hefted the boxes to the trunk of my car. I didn't want them to slide around the backseat while I drove. All of the gooey cheese topping would stick to the cardboard box and ruin the pizza.

I pounded on the large oak door with my foot. I was careful not to leave any scuffmarks from my shoes. The door opened and I stood momentarily transfixed with the sight before me. A broad-chested and muscled specimen blocked the doorway. My eyes roamed over his body. His corded arms held onto the doorframe. His soft black shirt strained tightly against his chiseled muscles.

The gray color of his eyes looked haunted and yet they made you want to beg him to do naughty things to you. Three-day-old hair cropped out over his square chin. A long, jagged scar ran from the corner of his sculpted eyebrow down along his cheek and stopped at his defined jawline. His almost perfectly handsome features contradicted the ruggedness of his candor.

"Do you like what you see?" His voice was chock full of lust.

I openly laughed at him. Oh, I did like what I saw but I loved what I had more. I slapped him on the chest.

"Move, you big 'ol tease. I got hot pizza to deliver." I

pushed past him and into the kitchen. Oh, he was nice to drool over but he couldn't set my body ablaze like Forrest could.

From the doorway, I spotted Forrest's powerful set of shoulders. His long, sturdy and powerfully built legs carried a commanding air of self-confidence. He moved gracefully toward me. My mouth hung open as my body vibrated with eagerness. He grabbed the pizza boxes from me and twisted his torso to the side as he planted a toe-curling kiss upon my mouth.

I licked my lips. "To be continued."

He laughed. "Promises, promises."

I pulled out a roll of paper towels to place the slices on. I had forgotten that there were no plates in the house. The new guy took some and loaded it with a stack of warm slices.

"Candice, this ugly brute is Mack. He is a good friend of mine." Forrest took a big bite.

I shook Mack's thick hand. "Nice to officially meet you. Thanks for helping me bring in the pizza," I taunted him sarcastically.

A huge laughed escaped his gorgeous frame. "It was my pleasure. I think I like you, Candice."

"At least you're not hard on the eyes. Makes your personality easier to tolerate."

"Fuck, if you weren't Forrest's, I'd make you mine."

I playfully slapped his cheek. "Only in your dreams."

With the introductions formally out of the way, we all

got down to business. Every last slice was gone. Holy shit, those boys could eat. I gave Forrest a sultry kiss good-bye and headed back to the apartment. I attempted to read over the paperwork again but my eyelids became heavy with every paragraph. I slid them off to the side until Forrest came home. I picked up the phone and called my parents.

Riley's sweet voice answered. "Hewwo, Mommy."

"Hi, baby girl. I miss you so much." I fought hard to stay upbeat. A lone tear escaped.

"I miss you too. When I come home?"

"Soon. I promise, just a bit longer. Are you having a good time?" I suddenly worried that she was homesick.

"Yes. We go to the zoo and see giwaffes, wions, and monkeys. Then Grandma and Grandpa took YaYa, Pappa, and me to the ocean. Thewe no shawks, though. I wanted to see one but none came out." She huffed out an agitated breath. "I wanted to swim with them in my bathing suit."

My heart squeezed at the thought of not being there with them. I was jealous. They got to spend all that time with her and I didn't. "That sounds like a lot of fun. Sharks maybe not so much. They kind of scare me."

"Not me. They awe awesome. You wanna tawk to YaYa?"

"Sure, sweetheart. I love and miss you very much."

"Hewe you go. Wuv you too. Bye."

My mom got on the line. "Hey, sweetheart. How are you?"

"Good but I miss you guys so much." I sniffled.

"We miss you too and can't wait to get home. As soon as you get the time, you should really visit. Daisy and River are wonderful people." She took a deep breath. "Has anything else transpired since we left?"

"No. Nothing lately. I'm hoping that you guys will be able to come back home by Sunday at the latest." I didn't mention the break-in. No point in making her worry any more than she already was. "I do have some good news, though. Logan offered me half ownership in the club. I met with her today and accepted."

"Wow. I am so proud of you. That is incredible. You have worked hard for this type of opportunity. I am excited for you. Are you happy about this?"

"Yeah. I really am, Mom. I can't be a dancer forever. My body won't allow it. I'm glad that she has given me this opportunity. It's a big step for her as well. To my knowledge, she has never entertained an idea like this. I'm really shocked that she even offered it up."

"Well, don't assume the worst. Look over everything and you always have the choice of backing out before you sign anything. All right, honey, we are heading to the beach again before dinner. I love you and miss you."

"Love and miss you too. Give Riley a kiss for me."

"You betcha. Take care and we will talk soon."

I hung up the phone, slightly depressed. I should be there with them, making the same memories. Eugene was a son of a bitch. He always managed to ruin everything. He hadn't done anything lately. I hoped it stayed that way. I wouldn't count on it, though. He was like a bad case of herpes. He'd disappear for a while and then flare back at any given point. Mostly when you'd gotten comfortable without a flare-up. In my entire life, I could say that I never hated anyone. Sure, I disliked many people but Eugene I fucking loathed to the point of wanting to strangle his scrawny ass myself.

To distract myself, I turned on some music and cleaned the tiny apartment. I barely worked up a sweat but I showered anyway. I decided to rummage through the fridge to see what I could make for dinner. Hopefully there was something in there that I could put together so that Forrest had a hot meal ready and on the table for when he got home.

The light came on when I opened up the door, illuminating the empty shelves. *Guess that means I have to run to the store.* On second thought, I'd just run to the house. The house had been stocked before everything went down. If I didn't get it now, it would spoil soon. I grabbed my keys. I wouldn't be long. There was no need to take my purse or cell phone.

28 FORREST

The house came alive with the plethora of music. We had a docking station belting out eighties rock. Vying for the spotlight were the saws, sander, nail gun, and other electric tools that joined in. My ears were covered by a set of safety earmuffs that dimmed all of the background tools.

My body and mind tuned in with the motion of the sander. I had maintained that Zen-like trance since Candice left. A herd of elephants could stomp through here and I wouldn't know the difference. My headphones were knocked off my head. The whirling sounds assaulted my ears. I turned quickly to see who the hell was fucking with me. I slammed into Mack's concrete chest.

I staggered backward before I righted myself. "What the fuck?"

"I got a ping. We need to leave right fucking now." His separate brows furrowed into one. His normally smooth forehead creased in anger.

"Where is he headed?" I already knew the answer but wanted to be wrong.

"Toward Candice's house."

I whipped out my phone. I saw the ping as well but didn't hear or feel the vibration of the warning. *Shit!* I dialed Candice but it rang and then went to voicemail. I didn't have time for a message. I kept ringing her phone as we raced to the car. I peeled out as though I were a professional NASCAR driver and raced toward her house praying that she wasn't there.

My hands gripped the wheel tightly, to the point of pain. "She isn't answering. I'm hoping that she's at the apartment. Let's assume that she isn't and be ready for anything."

Mack lifted up his jeans. On the left inside of his ankle nestled a Ruger. "I won't use it unless I have to. We will stick to the plan."

I seconded that motion by nodding my head in agreement.

I rammed into the drive behind Candice's car. I killed the engine. We simultaneously shut our doors as quietly as we could. If Eugene happened to be in there, then I did not want to draw his attention to our presence. Better to have surprise on our side. I motioned for Mack to take the front and right rear of the house. I would take the left and we would meet in the back before we entered the house.

I turned around and moved silently to the rear of the house. My ears twitched, straining to hear voices. Nothing until I came upon the kitchen window. I heard whimpering along with a deep, guttural voice. *Fuck.* I didn't have to look to know that Eugene had her cornered. I lifted myself onto the tips of my steel toes and peeked inside.

That motherfucker had her pinned up against the fridge. His boney arms encased each of her shoulders as she shrank her body as small as it would go. Her body vibrated with a combination of anger and fear. Her eyes were clear and focused. She looked as though she was biding her time, waiting for the right moment to attack. I smiled. *That's my girl; claw his eyes out.*

Mack moved beside me. I moved out of the way so that he could get a look at what we faced.

He whispered, "You think we should interrupt them?"

"I think we give her a minute to decide if she is going to fight him."

I didn't want her to get hurt but I would love for her to get some good punches in first before we called the cops. She has a no-contact restraining order out on him.

Mack grinned sadistically. About that time, Eugene slammed his hands back against the fridge. Candice flinched and then she raised her chin defiantly. She leaned into the fridge and used it as leverage as she rammed her knee into his groin. The ear-piercing scream jostled us into action.

We barged into the back door and ran into the kitchen. Candice held the phone in her hand, talking to the 911 operator. I crossed over to her and raised my eyebrows. I silently asked her whether she was okay. She nodded a quick yes. Mack and I went over to Eugene. We picked him up off the floor by his armpits. We pushed him into the kitchen chair and stood guard so he wouldn't make a move. A banging on the door told us that the cops were here.

Candice let them in and they barreled in to the kitchen as though they were cow wranglers. He sat, painfully subdued. We graciously moved out of the cops' way. They forcefully wrenched his arms behind him and slapped on the handcuffs. They read him his rights as they hauled him up and out to their cruiser. Mack and I took a seat in the kitchen and waited for them to come back inside and ask us a bunch of questions. Our shoulders shook with silent laughter, like two kids in the principal's office, waiting for detention.

Candice stormed over to me, madder than a wet hornet.

I grinned up at her as she towered over me. "You are kick ass, woman. I've never been so turned on in my entire life. I couldn't be more proud of you for taking him down."

Her anger dissipated at my compliment. "He deserved worse. Thank you for coming to my rescue. How did you even know I was here?"

I chanced a glance at Mack. "You didn't need to be rescued. You took care of business all by yourself. I tried calling you. When you didn't pick up, I got worried. I came straight here."

She tilted her head toward Mack. "And why are you here?"

He chuckled. "For backup. Looks like we got here a little too late. Although, I do have to agree with Forrest—that was fucking hot."

She laughed at him. "You better watch it. I have more where that came from. It might just have your name written all over it."

He lifted his hands in the air in surrender. "I like my women feisty."

I leaned over and smacked the back of his head.

One of the cops came back in and took our statements. He looked over at Candice. "My partner is taking him to the precinct. He will be arrested for violating the protective order. I can't say for sure if he will be charged or serve jail time."

She whipped her head around. "What? I showed you the restraining order. He clearly violated its no contact terms as well as threatened me." She threw her hands up in the air. "Does he have to physically hurt me or terminate my life before ya'll start taking this shit seriously?"

I wrapped my arms around her before the cop told her to calm down. She didn't need to make the situation worse. The quicker we got the cop out of here, the better. Mack knew one of the detectives at the precinct. We would monitor him that way. We would sit back and wait for him to be released.

I told Mack to go ahead and take my car back to the Victorian and I would meet up with him later. I led Candice to the living room. I sat on the couch and pulled her into my lap.

She leaned up against my chest and huffed out a heated breath. "I'm so sick of this. I am the one being imprisoned by him. Jail time is not going to stop him. It would serve as a reprieve for me and that's it. Then the shit would start all over again once he served his time." She let her stress go and sagged farther into me. "Next time, it will be worse. Riley will be home too." She looked into my eyes as the tears fell down her cheek. "What am I going to do, Forrest? I can't continue to live like this and I sure as hell will not put Riley in danger."

I stroked her hair, hoping to infuse some of my

strength. "I won't allow anything to happen to you." I tilted her chin up to me. "Trust me?"

Her lip quivered. "Yes. I trust you."

We sat there until the room became nothing but shadows as the sun had set long ago. I stopped through the chicken place and grabbed us some dinner. After she was settled into the apartment and seemed to be holding up, I texted Mack.

Any info?

Yeah. I'll pick you up in the morning.

That's all I needed to hear. I let the breath that I had been holding out and never gave it another thought. If Mack decided to pick me up in the morning, then that meant Eugene was still at the station. We had a worry-free night and I was going to pamper my girl.

I went into the bathroom and drew Candice a bath. *A bath needed bubbles, right?* Shit——what to use? I looked around until my eyes landed on my shampoo bottle. I tipped it over the water and squirted out a healthy amount. I set it back on the shelf. I reached my hand into the warm water and jostled it around. Bubbles lined the top of the water all the way around the tub, like a thick layer of micro foam on a cappuccino. I rubbed my hands together, pretty damn pleased with myself.

I called for her. She trudged stiffly into the bathroom. I stood up from kneeling on the floor and faced her. I gently placed my lips upon her sullen mouth. It didn't take long for me to coax her tongue to dance with mine. She lifted her arms in the air. I leisurely bunched the shirt up and over her tossing it to the floor. I licked my way down her neck and to her breast. I licked the hardened peak. She arched her back and shoved her breast into my face. I grinned and grazed my teeth along her nipple. I switched to her other breast to pay it equal attention. I used my fingers to slip in the waistband of her pants. I pushed them down her legs. She stepped out of them and stood naked before me.

Her pert breasts stood as beacons. They heaved up and down as she took deep breaths. I ran my fingers up and down her tiny waist. Her stomach quivered in excitement.

"Step into the bath," I commanded.

Without a word, she put one leg into the water, and then the other, sexily sliding into the water. She laid her head back against the hand towel I had placed there earlier. I grabbed a washcloth and undressed in record time.

"Lean forward."

I stepped in behind her. As I lowered myself down, I spread my legs as she drew herself into me. I lathered up the washcloth. I started along her neck and worked my way down her back. I moved the rag over her hips and up her stomach. Then I swirled it under and then over each breast, making sure that I tickled her nipples as I moved up her neck. She moaned as I left her breasts.

The washcloth hid the feeling of her silky skin. I tossed it over the faucet. I took the bar of soap and lathered my hands. I ran them along each of her arms. She lifted each leg as I lathered more soap. I ran my hands up the inside of her thighs. She opened her legs wider the closer I came to her pussy. I cupped her shaved mound with my palm. Then I slipped a finger inside her channel. She squeezed tightly around my finger. I inserted another finger. I pushed in and out of her as my thumb circled her clit.

She laid her head back on my shoulder and moaned my name. Her inner walls contracted as her orgasm built. I eased off her clit but maintained the rhythm of my fingers. Her hips pushed up, beckoning my fingers deeper. Water sloshed all around us. I nibbled along her neck as I fucked her with my fingers. My thumb found her little nub again. I circled the pulsating bundle of nerves achingly slow.

A breathy sigh escaped. "Forrest. Please. I can't take anymore. I'm burning up from the inside."

I pinched her clit hard enough to elicit a tsunami of pleasure to her core. She screamed out my name as she came all over my fingers. I eased my pressure but continued my onslaught over her clit and inside her channel. She moaned softly and tried to reach around to stroke me. I blocked her easily enough. She had another orgasm beckoning. I continued a barrage of kisses along her neck and shoulder.

As her orgasm subsided, I increased my pressure once again. I added a third finger and my thumb circled faster and faster.

"Oh, shit, Forrest. It's too much. It's too intense."

I growled into her ear. "Come for me. Now."

She opened up her mouth but no sound came out. Her body vibrated and shuddered as her orgasm rippled through her. Tiny spasms seized my fingers and held them captive within her channel. I gently eased my fingers out of her moist heat.

I leaned her hourglass-shaped body forward. I gripped the sides of the tub and stepped out onto the bath mat. I hastily dried myself off. She stood, glistening, before me. Droplets of water cascaded off her body. Desire rippled like mini tide pools within the depths of her beautiful eyes. A magnetic pull held me prisoner to her. I could neither move nor look away.

Her porcelain skin erupted in tiny bumps. The hair on her arms stood at attention. She shivered as I raked my heated gaze from head to toe. I covered her delectable body with my towel. I picked her up and cradled her to my chest as I walked us into the bedroom.

I laid her gently down on the bed as though she were a fine piece of china. Her head slightly angled to the side so she could see me better. I took my time exploring her body as though I were a teenage boy learning how to please a woman for the first time. Her soft exhalations spurred my traveling mouth and fingers. Her body splayed open and invited me to strum each of her pleasure chords.

My cock twitched with each moan and husky exhale. I painstakingly inched my way into her wet heat. I threw my head back as her walls stretched to accommodate me. This was home. I could hardly draw a breath at the way love and adoration for her coursed through my blood.

I made love to Candice as though this would be my first and last time. I worshiped her body as though it were an extension of my own. I memorized every curve and moan. I seared them into my brain. She cupped my cheeks and gazed into my eyes as we rode out our release.

29 FORREST

Morning came too soon. My arms tightened around her waist as she snuggled deeper into me. My cock jerked to life. *Down, boy!* As much as I wanted to sink into her, I didn't want her scent on me. My mind and body needed to be free of her so that I could finish this job. It wouldn't be pleasant but I would do what I had to do to ensure Riley and Candice's future.

I placed a kiss on her sleepy mouth and told her to call me before she went into work. I strode out the door, whistling "Twisted Nerve" by Bernard Herrmann. It had a calming and yet sinister effect on me. I climbed into the car next to Mack.

"Whistling that twisted song again?" Mack dryly commented.

"You know what kind of day it is then," I grinned.

"Sure do."

We rolled up to the Victorian, hashed out our plan

one more time and then got to work on the house. We needed to maintain our presence here all day. We would make sure that we didn't need an alibi but in case shit went wrong, then it was good to have potential witnesses.

As I covered my ears with my hearing protection, my phone buzzed in my pocket.

"Hey, baby." I cooed like a love-struck buffoon.

"You snuck out on me this morning. I was hoping for some more action." A pout was clearly noted in her tone.

I chuckled. "How 'bout a rain check to be cashed in as soon as I get home."

"It will be cashed in. I will be late tonight. I won't be home until after midnight or later."

"Not a problem. I will be home waiting for you. Naked and in bed."

She giggled. "You'll make someone a great wife one day."

I busted out laughing. "Yep. Aren't you glad that I'm yours?"

"Yep. See you tonight, wife. Love you."

"Love you too. Later." I shook my head as I hit the End button.

An eerie calmness over took me. With my conscience settled, my body relaxed into my work. While the guys took an extra-long lunch, Mack and I rehashed our plan one more time to make sure that all angles were covered.

By the end of tonight, the wrap-around porch would

be finished. All of the woodwork inside would be sanded and ready for Enzo to bring to life the original carvings. With all of the overtime and extra guys coming and going, the house would be finished in less than a month. I don't know how the hell Sal and Enzo managed to pull it off but they would. Best crew around.

Darkness settled around us. The crew headed to parts unknown. Mack and I loaded up our bag and pitched it in the trunk of the car and headed to the bar; a couple of hours of listening to bad karaoke and drinking ice-cold draft beer to fuel the body and to generate another possible alibi.

We snuck out of the tavern and headed out to the middle of nowhere drug house. We parked the car on a deserted, overgrown tractor entrance surrounded by thick cornstalks. We fitted ourselves in black long-sleeved shirts, black cargo pants, and thin leather gloves.

I hitched the long shoulder strap over my shoulder and neck. We grabbed our night-vision goggles and set out through the field. We stealthily made our way through the maze of corn; not a sound could be heard. We were sheathed within the evening's cloak. We both bent at the knee about a hundred yards from the rundown house. We took off our night-vision goggles and allowed our eyes to adjust to the blackness.

Candles flickered inside and illuminated the place in an eerie glow. Shadows danced along the tattered sheers. We counted possibly of five people in the dilapidated house. We waited until the house grew quiet and the candles burned out.

Mack and I nodded to each other. We replaced our goggles. I took off the bag and snatched only what we needed. When we returned to the fields, I would grab the bag. With our pockets full, we crept to the house. The second story had a sagging porch attached. The room located beyond those doors was where Mack had found Eugene the last time.

Mack bent at one knee. I used the raised knee and stepped onto his thigh for added height. It was enough for my hands to latch onto the bottom flooring of the porch. Luckily for me, the railing had been missing. It made my climb that much easier. I turned around, lay on my stomach, and reached my hand over the porch and down toward Mack.

I felt his hand close over mine. Inch by slow inch, I pulled him up next to me. We pushed into a sitting position and listened for any kind of footfalls or voices. Hearing absolutely nothing, we slowly slunk toward the door. I twisted the handle of the door. It gave without much force. The door swayed open without so much as a creak. *Thank God for small miracles.*

The room was void of any homey furnishings. The only thing in the room was a stained mattress in the opposite corner. A ripe, pungent stench permeated the room. A naked torso lay sprawled upon the bed. We slunk along the wall and crept closer.

Eugene lay passed out in all of his scrawny, emaciated glory. Track marks decorated his body. Dark shadows perched along his lifeless skin. I swiftly positioned my body on top of his. I held his arms and legs securely, incapacitating him with my body. Eugene had lapsed into some drug-induced high because he barely flinched when I used my weight to hold him down.

Mack grabbed the needle full of heroin. I grabbed the needle with my gloves and jammed it into his neck. I pushed the plunger of the syringe and emptied the contents straight into his jugular vein. I continued to hold him down until his lips turned a cold blue. I pushed my body off and stood next to Mack as Eugene's body convulsed with muscle spasms. His body tensed and seized. We watched as the last breath of life passed through him. Then it grew still. I placed a hand to his neck to check for a pulse. No pulse. I laid my hand upon his chest to feel for a small rise. No rise.

I backed up a step and nodded to Mack. Our job was done. I lay the needle by the tips of his lifeless fingers, making it an obvious assumption of overdose. Not even the occupants of the house would realize what happened until it was too late. We retraced our steps out of the house and back to the bag at the edge of the field.

We drove the speed limit back to the Victorian. I placed all of our items into another bag for Mack to dispose of. We popped the tops to our beers, clinked them together, and chugged them down.

I squeezed Mack's shoulder as a thank-you for putting his life on the line for me. "See you in the morning."

"Yep. I'm sleeping in, so don't come calling bright and early."

"Well deserved, my friend."

I hated to leave Mack stranded without a vehicle but he could defend himself. He housed a small arsenal strapped to various parts of his body. I didn't foresee any problems. Without being able to predict the future, being prepared for anything became a necessity.

The radio played Johnny Cash. My fingers tapped against the steering wheel as I drove back to the apartment. I belted out the lyrics as though I was one of his backup singers. My chest felt light as the promise of our future beckoned.

Thankfully, I beat Candice home. I quickly got in the shower and scrubbed away the images that floated in my mind. I couldn't completely cleanse my soul. It was something that I'd learn to live with.

I pulled back the covers and climbed in. The adrenaline that had pumped through my veins earlier had long since drained away and had left me sluggish. I folded my arms behind my head and drifted off to sleep.

30 CANDICE

I inserted my key into the lock and dragged myself through the door. Exhausted wasn't even strong enough to describe how tired I felt. My vision blurred from looking at the computer screen and security feed all night. Logan ran a tightly disciplined ship. It was all in black and white. At least the paperwork was.

Dealing with the issues of the dancers and other personnel would inadvertently drive me bonkers. I hated to have to deal with drama but it came with the territory. People had lives outside of the business and well, life happens. Not everyone scheduled would make it and or they had to run home for their sick kids, or their babysitters had to leave. The list was endless.

You name it, it happened. It was a totally different beast when you were the boss. You couldn't openly sympathize with them. You had to maintain a backbone or they would zero in on you and descend like a wake of turkey vultures honing in on a dead carcass.

I chugged down a glass of water, wetting my dry

mouth. I stripped all of my clothing before I hit the bedroom door. I tossed them in the hamper. I cleaned my face, brushed my teeth, and walked naked to the bed. Forrest lay asleep. Only half of his body was covered with the blanket. His defined chest was uncovered for my viewing pleasure. I took the opportunity to adoringly admire the strong man who held claim to my heart, body, and soul. He embodied the definition of sexy.

I climbed in next to him and laid my head over his chest. He immediately wrapped his arm around my shoulders and pinned me to his body. I smiled as the rhythmic beating of his heart lulled me to sleep.

For once, I woke up before Forrest. He must have stayed late working on the Victorian because he normally took off long before I got up in the morning. I stretched, feeling rested and invigorated. I had another long night at the club. This time, I was excited to go. I enjoyed dancing most of the time, but being the boss of my own club felt ten times better. The girls seemed to be handling the transition pretty well. At least to my face, no one grumbled about it. They were mainly shocked when they found out. I received a warm welcome. Usually, transitioning from one side of the fence to the other doesn't go that smoothly.

I never got the chance to raid my own cupboards so the kitchen cupboards lay barren. The only thing we had on hand was some fruit and instant oatmeal. I made a bowl and cut up some banana to put in it. I would have made two but I wanted to let Forrest sleep. Lately, he only caught a few winks here and there.

I finished up the oatmeal and gave Riley a call. I never knew what they were going to get into that day, so it seemed best to call early if I wanted to catch them home.

"Morning, Mom. How are you?" I smiled when I heard her cheery voice.

"Morning, love. We are well. How are you and Forrest doing?" Her tone tensed.

"Good. Eugene had come into the house and threatened me but I kicked him in the balls. Forrest and his friend Mack came in as he fell to the floor screaming like a little girl." I laughed so hard that I started to cough.

"Seriously? Oh my goodness. Did you get hurt? What happened?" Shock and awe were clearly evident in her voice.

"I'm fine, really. I called the cops because he violated the restraining order. They hauled him away and as far as I know, he has been arrested. Otherwise, I'm sure that he would have already come after me again," I sighed, hoping that what I had said held some of the truth.

"Well, thank goodness you weren't hurt."

"So, what has my baby been up to? Is she being good for you? Only a couple of more days and you come back home. I miss you guys so much."

"I know, baby. We miss you too. Riley misses you terribly. She is behaving like she always does. You don't have to worry about her. She is homesick but plays it off. Smart little girl you are raising."

I smiled through the phone at her compliment. "Thanks."

"I think your father is ready to come home too. This is the longest he has ever been away. River and he have gone golfing, hiking, and fishing. He won't admit it, but he is enjoying himself."

"I'm really glad in spite of the way you had to leave. You deserve to get away and do something for yourselves once in a while."

"We will. Daisy and River have already invited us to come out again. Did you know that they live in a commune?" she stated, a bit shocked.

"I didn't know that. Really, like a hippie commune?"

"Yep. They told your father and me that this is the longest that they have worn clothes in their life." She laughed so hard that she snorted.

I chimed in, "Seriously? They will probably be glad when ya'll leave!"

"I know, right! Oh, well——to each his own. Well, honey I'm going to let you go. I would let you talk to Riley but she was up late and is still sleeping. I love you and give me a buzz later."

"Love you too. Tell Dad and Riley that I love them. Give River and Daisy our love as well."

"You got it. Talk to you later."

From behind, Forrest began to squeeze the tension from my shoulders.

"That feels incredible," I hummed.

"Good. Did you talk to Riley?"

"No. She was still sleeping. She is ready to come home but not admitting that to my parents." I chuckled and bent my head back so I looked up at Forrest. "How come you never told me that your parents were nudists? I had forgotten Lucy's comment at the wedding until my mom mentioned it on the phone."

"Ah, fuck. Are they wearing their clothes around Riley?"

I laughed even harder. "Yes. According to my mom, it's the longest that they have gone dressed in a long time."

He slapped a hand over his face. "I love them but shit, really? There are no words to excuse them. I never understood it. I just deal with it. Phoenix feels the same way as I do. We turned out completely different than what they expected us to, especially with all of the free love bullshit floating around."

"You poor baby." I puckered my mouth.

He bent down and claimed my pouty lips. "I was thinking that maybe we can take our belongings back to the house and I can let this apartment go. What do you think?"

I paused for a brief second. "Do you think it's safe?"

"More safe with Eugene behind bars."

"You are probably right. I'd like to go back home."

He kissed my mouth one more time. "Alright then. I'll gather our stuff and take care of the apartment on my way to the Victorian. I'm going to head out. I told Mack we'd start as soon as I got there. The other guys have probably started showing up by now." He pecked my cheek. "I'll meet you at the house tonight. You working late again?"

"Yep. See you later on. Love you."

"Love you more."

I watched his tightly sculpted ass walk out the door. I couldn't wait for the Victorian to be done and his business to be set up. I wanted him to feel settled here and a part of us. I bounced my way to the shower, excited for Riley to come back home. I enjoyed my time alone with Forrest, but I was more than ready for my girl to be in the mix too.

After I had showered and dressed, I picked up our shaving kits and any other miscellaneous items and stuffed them into my bag. There wasn't much. I shut the door behind me, thankful that I was on my way back home.

I walked through my door and breathed in the familiarity. It seemed as though I had been gone for a lot longer than a couple of days. I set my bag down and walked through every room in the house. The cleaning crew that Forrest had hired had done a thorough job. Anything that had been broken had been replaced or repaired. All of the writing in the bathroom had been scrubbed clean. The mattresses and shower curtain were brand new. Evidence of Eugene's terror had been wiped clean.

It might take me awhile to fully feel comfortable being back here but it beat living in a tiny apartment. Here, I was surrounded by everything that I loved. I heard banging on the door. I paused, unsure whether I should answer it or not. Curiosity got the better of me. I went downstairs and peered through the peephole. Two uniformed police officers stood on the other side. *What the fuck happened now?*

It was now or later. I opened the door. "Can I help you?"

The cop who arrested Eugene stood in front of me. "Ma'am, can we come in for a minute?"

I opened the door wider and waved them through. "Would you like a cup of coffee or anything else to drink?"

They followed me to the kitchen. "No, thank you."

I looked over my shoulder. "Do you mind if I make myself a cup?"

"Not at all." They took a seat at the table.

"Are you sure you don't want a cup too?"

I raised my glass to my lips and let the hot coffee burn my tongue and throat. I pulled out a chair opposite the two of them. I pushed my chair in close to the table and rested my hands around the steaming cup's warmth. I didn't want them to see my shaking hands. My thoughts scrambled my brain and my nerves felt fried.

The arresting officer——I couldn't remember his name for the life of me——spoke while the other one sat there in perfect statuesque form. "This morning, we got a call to check out an abandoned house. The only thing that we were told was that a possible body was inside. To give it to you straight, we found your ex-husband inside."

My hand flew to my mouth in shock. My hands shook as I waited for them to confirm that he was dead. I wanted him to be dead. I had no love for this man, not after what he had done to me. I couldn't show my elation, so I masked my giddiness with shock. Years of playing a character for men had taught me well.

The cop cleared his throat. "As I was saying, Eugene was found dead upon arrival. Seemingly from an overdose. I can't confirm that until the autopsy comes back but that's what it strongly points to. If I had to guess, one of the other people who squatted in the house freaked out and called it in."

I nodded as the information flowed to my brain. I nodded but didn't say a word, too afraid that hysterical cackling would slip out. Better for them to think that I was in shock. I'm sure that they wouldn't find my laughter very comical.

The female officer looked at me. "Is there any one you want us to call for you?"

I shook my head. "No. Thank you for letting me know."

They stood to go. "We will call you when the coroner releases the body."

I walked them to the door and thanked them again. I carefully shut the door and slid down the back of it to the floor. I put my knees into my chest and cried tears of joy. I'm not sure how long I sat there, but it had been long enough for my ass to go numb. I stood up gingerly and let the blood flow back into my butt and legs.

I made a quick call to Logan and told her what was going on. She told me to take a few days off but I declined. Work was exactly where I wanted to be. I wanted to call my mom and tell her that it was finally over but I didn't want to ruin the trip for Riley. I would tell her after Eugene's body was released and I had the funeral arrangements made.

I left for work a couple of hours early and drove straight to the Victorian. I hopped out of my car. I waved hello to Sal and Enzo on my way inside and ran straight into Mack.

He braced my arms with his large hands. "Where's the fire, little lady?"

I laughed like a lunatic. "Move, you big lug. Where is

my man?"

He let me go and stepped to the side and pointed upstairs.

I climbed the stairs two at a time. I was out of breath before I reached the third floor. I walked through the double doors of the room and stopped in my tracks. Forrest was bent over, staining the wood trim. He was bare-chested. I watched the muscles ripple along his back and down his arms as he moved the brush back and forth, lovingly caressing the wood. I clenched my legs together as moisture soaked my panties.

Some would probably call me a coldhearted bitch for not being an ounce sad over Eugene. I couldn't mourn a person as despicable as he was. The tears that I had shed throughout the years I was married and many after were the only ones that he would ever get from me.

Forrest must have heard my panting because the next thing I knew, he stood before me, tilting my chin up and searching my face.

"What happened, baby? Is Riley okay?" The concern in his eyes was my undoing.

I slammed my lips against his. I thrust my tongue into his mouth and elicited a groan from him that I greedily swallowed.

He pulled back slowly. "Not that I'm complaining but what brought that on?"

"The cops paid me a visit this morning."

His eyebrows drew together and his lips thinned. "For what?"

I laughed as though I should be hauled away in a straightjacket. "I guess they got a call from someone stating that there was a body in some house. Come to find out, the body belonged to Eugene. They said that he had probably overdosed. They are going to do an autopsy to determine the cause of death and will let me know when his body will be released."

He touched his forehead to mine. "I'm so sorry. Are you okay?"

"I'm fucking ecstatic. I couldn't be more happy than if you asked me to marry you." I slapped hand over my mouth. *Shit! Sometimes stupid stuff just pops out.*

He picked me up and twirled me around. "Did you just propose to me?"

I smacked his shoulder. "No. That's your job."

EPILOGUE

Eugene was laid in his final resting place shortly after the coroner released his body. The coroner officially ruled it as an accidental overdose of heroin. I arranged a small funeral. The only ones in attendance were Riley, Forrest, and me. The minister read a passage from the Bible. Riley walked over to the burial plot before they lowered the casket into the ground. She threw a red rose onto the casket as it descended into the earth. With her head tucked into her chest, she walked back to Forrest and me. She wedged her tiny body between us and grabbed for our hands. We bowed our heads in final prayer. The sun shone brightly as we stood near his casket. The day reminded me of a fresh, clean start. It was time to bury the past as well.

We shielded Riley as much as we could. She was too young to truly understand. We had told her that he had become sick and never recovered. Which was partly true. I wasn't surprised. Time would have not been kind to him in the long run. I didn't care how it happened. There was no love lost for me. However, I would never deny her the right to keep his memory alive. I grieved for Riley and the loss of her daddy.

***

Riley and I stood on the sidewalk in front of the Victorian. She held my hand. We both wore blindfolds. The sun shone brightly. Even though the blindfolds denied the sun access, the heat of the sun warmed my skin. I could feel Forrest walk in front of me by the way the air heated around me. He reached his hands behind my head and gently untied my blindfold. I blinked to adjust to the brightness that assaulted my eyes. I watched him squat down and untie the little scarf around the back of Riley's head. I hadn't looked at the house because I didn't want to miss Riley's reaction to it.

Her eyes turned as wide as saucers and her mouth hung open. She jumped up and down excitedly. "It's so pwetty. Can we go in? Can we?"

Forrest picked up her vibrating body. "What do you think, love?"

Tears pooled and overflowed down my cheeks. "It's beautiful. I can't believe how stunning the place looks."

He bent over and kissed my cheek. He reached his hand out and I threaded my fingers through his. We walked hand in hand up the wide steps and onto the stark white painted porch. Off to the right corner, a wide-benched swing with colorful thick cushions hung underneath a gazebo that attached to the rounded corner of the front porch. Forrest set Riley down and she ran straight for it.

She tried hard to get it to rock as I walked around the porch and admired the columns. Another gazebo sat along the opposite side of the porch. Underneath the intimate enclosure sat a picnic table. I could imagine eating our dinners out here on warm summer nights. The opening had a mosquito net draped around the outside of it so that no bugs would dare interrupt us.

What I loved the most were the hanging baskets. They were hung evenly along the porch. Each basket hung below eye level. I appreciated the beauty of the ornamental kale planted in each basket.

I finally turned back around and followed Riley and Forrest into the rest of the house. Once we crossed the threshold, all of our friends greeted us. I couldn't believe that they had all taken the time to celebrate with us. I didn't have the time to take a tour and see everything but that could wait. I had the rest of my life to explore. Right now I wanted to be surrounded by my family and friends.

Even Mack had decided to stay in town. He stayed in the house until it had been completed. He rented an apartment in the same complex that Forrest had when he first arrived. Mack and Forrest teamed up and started Global Securities. The two of them made a formidable team. They had no trouble obtaining a generous customer following. They were the best of the best. Every now and then, one of them would fly out of town to do a job for their customers, but they took turns so that neither of them was gone at the same time. Mack had also weaseled his way into mine and Riley's hearts.

Mack strolled over to me and pulled me into a meaty hug. I think he did it to piss Forrest off. Forrest would growl at him every time he did it. I chuckled because it was hilarious to watch Forrest become enraged with jealousy.

Forrest pulled me out of Mack's tree-trunk arms. He slowly lowered himself to one knee. He clutched one of my hands. The other shot over my mouth. "Candice, you saved my life. Before I had met you, I was running around the world, lost. You brought me home. Please do me the honor of becoming my wife?"

Tears of joy flowed freely down my cheeks. I choked out a yes and nodded fervently. He placed a stunning antique princess cut diamond set in platinum around my ring finger. He stood and I wrapped my arms around his neck, clinging to him for dear life. I whispered into his ear, "You weren't the one who needed saving."

Our friends hooted and hollered. Riley bounced through the throngs of our friends and jumped into Forrest's arms. "If you mawwy Mommy, then you get to be my weal daddy." She placed a tiny kiss onto his cheek. "Wuv you."

This was the first time Riley had called him Daddy. His eyes shone with unshed tears. He squeezed her tightly. "Yes, princess. I'm your daddy. Forever."

"Pwomise?"

"Pinkie promise."

Everyone took turns congratulating us.

Lucy came up beside me. "So when do I get to plan the wedding?"

I laughed. "As soon as it all sinks in."

Gage came out of nowhere and gave me a hug. "Are you sure you want to do this? I'm still unattached."

I slapped him upside the head. "Absolutely. I wouldn't touch you with a ten-foot pole. God only knows where you've been."

He grabbed his heart and stepped backward. "Ouch. Candice, that was way harsh."

I smacked his shoulder. What can I say? He brought out the violent side of me.

I laughed harder as he stumbled backward into Rachel. She squealed in pain as his mammoth foot stepped on her much smaller and more delicate foot. He almost knocked her down. His reflexes kicked in and he grabbed her before she fell.

I caught Lucy's eye and we busted out laughing harder.

ABOUT THE AUTHOR

Jenni Bradley lives in Indiana, with her husband, three daughters, four dogs, two cats, and four horses: pretty much a small, funny farm where there is never a dull day. She enjoys riding most days. The other days are usually met with hard dirt and a happy horse.

You can find Jenni online at jennibradley.com to find out more, plus news on upcoming books.

You can also find Jenni on Facebook at https://www.facebook.com/Jenni-Bradley-1453178658324928/

Other books:

Release Me